TONY ACREE'S ABSOLUTION

RACHAEL RAWLINGS
MARY ELLEN QUIRE

Hydra
Publications

ISBN: 978-1-948374-31-6

Hydra Publications

Goshen, Kentucky 40026

www.hydrapublications.com

To all those fighting COVID 19, those who have lost the battle, those still fighting, and to to those who have yet to begin the fight.

FOREWORD

With the release of Vengeance: A Samantha Tyler Thriller, the world of Victor McCain and the Hand of God expanded. I asked Rachael Rawlings, a fabulous writer in her own right, to co-write the book with me and thus a new series was born.

When it came time to write book two, I invited Mary Ellen Quire to join Team Samantha. Mary Ellen, author of the Price MacCann Assassin series, has a no holds bar writing style perfect for the world of Samantha Tyler and Victor McCain.

Absolution is a fast paced, seat of your pants thriller and I was blown away by the novel turned in by Rachael and Mary Ellen. I know you will be too.

Turn the page and then hold on tight.

Tony Acree

ALSO BY TONY ACREE

Victor McCain Thrillers

The Hand of God

The Watchers

The Speaker

Revenge

Victor McCain Short Stories

Nightmare

Back to Hell

Lonnie, Me and the Hand of God (written with Marian Allen)

Samantha Tyler Thrillers

Vengeance

ALSO BY RACHAEL RAWLINGS

Grave Reminder Series

Dearly Departed: Grave Reminders

Dearly Remembered: Grave Reminders

Dearly Beloved: Grave Reminders

Another Fine Feathered Mystery

The Parrot Told Me: Another Fine-Feathered Mystery

The Cockatoo Called: Another Fine-Feathered Mystery

The Macaw Muttered: Another Fine-Feathered Mystery

The Cockatiel Cautioned: Another Fine-Feathered Mystery

Talitha: A Haunting

Speak to Me

A Raven Mystery

Midnight Dreary: A Raven Mystery

Some Late Visitor: A Raven Mystery

Bleak December: A Raven Mystery

Spirit Passing: Animal Assisted Paranormal Investigation

Spirit Taken: Animal Assisted Paranormal Investigation

ALSO BY MARY ELLEN QUIRE

Defined Volume 1

Sheldon's Diary

Dark Deliverance

Penned under Mary E. Rose:

Link Detonator

Detonator, Time's Up

CHAPTER ONE

Lightning streaked across the midnight sky, its raw electric tendrils reaching out through the thick dark clouds and branching off into jagged lines with the intention of striking ground, Mother Earth, terra firma. A deep roll of thunder rumbled through the air, gained momentum, and then clapped so hard the ground vibrated underfoot. Declan shuddered. No one knew what he really was, what he was capable of, or what he was doing. No one that is except for probably God, definitely Satan, and a few unmentionables the majority of the human world refused to believe existed.

He bent forward, his hands on his knees, trying to catch his breath. He could feel his heart pounding, pushing the blood through his veins in the flesh's effort to compensate for his exertion. Another flash of lightning tore through the darkness and with it came a gale so strong it threatened to push him face forward to the hard-packed ground. The oaks, maples, locusts, and countless other trees felt the force as limbs and the leaves they bore bent and swung, whipping around in supplication to the wind, scattering their silhouettes over the flora beneath them. Okay, so God definitely knew what he was doing and by the looks of the storm overhead, he could assume God was not all that happy about it. The ominous clouds above let go. Raindrops large enough to make an audible splat onto everything below, including him, began soaking his dark brown hair and straightening the wavy strands until they lay plastered over his naked shoulders. Rivulets of water streamed down his bare back. He straightened and turned his dark brown eyes up towards the sky. The rain beat against the front of his body, on his face, down his neck, over his pectorals and the age-tarnished pentacle which rested heavily between the dead center of his chest. Nope. God wasn't happy at all.

The amulet, however, didn't seem to mind the rain, didn't protest the wind, and didn't even have anything to say about being stolen from the Abbey of Saint Aelis in France. In fact, the amulet didn't do a damn thing but hang from the old metal chain on his neck. It had failed. He had failed. Declan leaned back onto the wooden timbers of the cabin's outer wall and watched the downpour wash over everything it could reach, cleansing off the layers of dust and grime caked on by the dry August heat. There hadn't been rain here for nearly a month and the grass and leaves had given up their vibrant greens for the brittle brown color brought on by drought, but now they would be revived, rejuvenated. They would flourish, wouldn't they? Just add a little water and boom there you go, a second chance at life. God was good at giving second chances, at least to His favorites; humans mostly and sometimes the beasts of the fields, but creatures such as himself? Not so much. He ran his fingers over the pentacle, gripped it tight enough he felt the sharp edges cut into his flesh, and gave it a yank. The chain broke and slid out of the amulet to the ground. Declan's square jaw clenched as he eased his fingers away. Blood mixed with the rain and trailed down his arm to the elbow where it ran off in dripping spurts to meet the same fate as the broken chain. He stared at the amulet for a time before stepping forward, reeling his arm back to chuck the piece of useless shit as far as it would go, and then froze.

A slow steady clap sounded from the group of trees to his right like the obligatory applause of a bored audience. With it came the shadow. Human shaped, it walked towards him with confident purpose, hands coming together in time like the monotonous tick of a metronome. Declan made out the smell before his eyes could separate dark from light. Brimstone. His upper lip curled at the rotten-egg stench. He lowered his hand, his gaze hardening as the form stopped mere feet from him. Clean cut and sporting what looked to be a dark-colored Armani suit, the man ceased clapping, his lips stretching back in an amused smile. It was a smile that did not reach the man's icy blue eyes.

"Well, well, quite the show," he said. "I must offer you my heartfelt congratulations."

Declan could feel the rain soaking over the waistband of his faded jeans now, through the thick denim material and onto the lower half of his body where it trickled over his crotch and ass, down each of his long legs to the leather work boots covering his feet and the absorbent socks he was wearing. The man in front of him, however, didn't appear to be feeling the effects of the storm at all. Dry as a bone. His golden blonde hair in its Ivy League style never wavered, not even a single strand shifted in the blowing wind. The dark material of his suit coat, trousers, the red silk tie; none of it moved, not even a flutter. It was as if the man was encased in some sort of glass box, shielded from the tempest like just another innocent golden boy sitting up in his high tower.

Declan set his jaw. Appearances are deceptive more than

naught and the man before him was no exception. In fact, this man was the very root of the tired old saying which in turn had spiraled off others like warnings to beware the sharp-dressed man, the wolf in sheep's clothing, the monster hidden beneath a fancy suit. No, before him stood the being for which Hell was truly created, not some Ivy League jerk off flashing his pearly whites and his thousand-dollar suits. Oh, the o de la brimstone had been a nice hint of course, but the smell only tipped him off to the place where the man called home plate. It was the look in those icy blue eyes which really confirmed any suspicions he may have had if there had been a doubt, which for Declan there had not. He was well acquainted with the man before him, and to be honest, he liked him about as much as everyone else did, which was not at all.

"What did you say?" Declan asked, bristled.

"Congratulations," he said. "You do know the meaning of the word?"

There was a hint of cruelty easing into the amusement of the man's smile now.

"Of course you do," he continued without waiting for a response. "By taking on the epitome of such a fine British chap, I would have expected no less. English is your native tongue after all."

Declan glared at him. "What do you want?"

The man raised a brow, the smile which revealed his showroom pearly whites still locked into place, and replied, "To offer my—"

"*Congratulations*," Declan snapped. "Yeah, I got that. What the fuck are you congratulating me for is what I'm asking."

The icy blue color of the man's eyes swirled a little as if the iris were more alive than is typical for the eyes of any living thing. Declan noted the shadows which flickered in and out of the swirling blue and knew them for exactly what they were; the souls of the damned. He'd seen his eyes do this very thing before, but just not while staring at him. Declan blinked and the swirl and shadows were gone, leaving those icy blues looking just as they had before.

"On your complete and utter fuck up of course," Lucifer replied. "Had you come to me first, I could have offered my advice, told you it wouldn't work, let you in on the fact you— what is it you blokes call it again? Ah, yes. I could have let you know with all bloody good certainty that you nipped the wrong artifact, you fucking wanker."

Declan flinched as the amulet he'd been holding vanished and then reappeared in Lucifer's hand. The old devil turned it slowly one way, then the other, studying it for a moment before tossing it to the ground at his feet. The weight of the pentacle was enough to sink it in the muddy puddle and Declan watched it disappear, noting the fact that the soles of Satan's designer shoes never even seemed to touch the surface of the dirty water. When he lifted his eyes, Lucifer was right in front of him, barely a hair's breadth away and the smell of brimstone came along for the ride. Declan felt his nose and eyes burn.

"No, my friend, should you have come to me, I would have told you there really isn't a way out, not in the way you are thinking. What was it Lady GaGa said? Ah yes, I do believe it was, baby I was born this way."

He laughed lightly and moved in closer where he was nearly cheek to cheek with Declan. The reek was almost overwhelming now and it took everything Declan had not to pull away. Lucifer leaned into Declan's ear and the hissing whispers sent chills up his spine.

"She lied," Lucifer told him. "They'll do that you know, the righteous, they will lie to protect their own. Do not believe their words. Believe mine. Wrong artifact."

Lucifer paused for a moment and Declan could feel the demon smiling, like bugs crawling on his skin. He opened his mouth to try and say something, anything, but the action only made him want to gag.

"Since you seem to enjoy treasure hunting," Lucifer continued to whisper, "you will do a little favor for me. There is an artifact that also rests in Aelis. I want you to obtain it and return it to me, its rightful owner. Once you have it in your possession, make certain it stays there. Do not allow another of our kind to lay so much as a finger on it. And most importantly, do not use it. Should you do so, the power within it will destroy you. It will make your existence up until now seem like a stroll through the park. Do you understand?"

Declan forced himself to nod, wincing as the last couple of words penetrated his ear with a much stronger hiss like the sound of a punctured tire releasing air. The smell was unbearable now and if he didn't put some space between himself and the Devil he was either going to throw up or pass out or both. If Lucifer noticed his discomfort, he never let on, just continued his whisperings describing the real artifact and where it lay hidden in the abbey. Declan listened as best as he could, feeling a draining sensation overtake him and a light spinning in his head.

"Ah now," Lucifer murmured in the same hissing low tone, "treasure hunting is a bit draining, isn't it?"

The Devil leaned back and gave Declan a sly smile.

"Sustenance will strengthen you, Incubus. I suggest you feed before you board the plane."

Declan closed his eyes and just tried to breathe for a moment. When he opened them Lucifer was gone, the smell of brimstone thinning. The storm still raged and now a tempest was brewing inside of him. He laid a hand on the timbers of the cabin's wall to steady himself as the rain beat down in stinging torrents. *So hungry*, he thought, *just so damned hungry.*

When he made it to the door, he shoved it hard enough to fling it off the hinges and into the front room. It slammed into an overstuffed gray couch where it bounced off and hit the carpet with a muffled thump. Inside he could hear the steady prayer and an overlay of whimpering cries. He had been forced to take the other one. The nun had been walking with a village girl near the abbey and there was just something so tempting about the two of them together, like a pair of ripe plums ready for plucking. He shoved the door open and regarded the two. The young sister had her head down, her chin resting on her chest as she prayed in a steady voice.

The village girl was much more satisfying to watch, with her glassy panicked eyes and sniffling. Declan had already decided to feed on her first and so she laid tied spread eagle and on her back in the bed. Plastic zip ties held her wrists to the headboard posts and the same secured her ankles to the rungs of the footboard. The nun was very tempting, not in the sexually attractive sense but more so a punch in the eye of the high and mighty. His intense hunger, however, was driving his lust more so than any immediate need for vengeance. He would feed from the village girl, but he needed to let out a little of his pent up frustration first lest he drain the girl too quickly to enjoy.

Pluck up an artifact for Satan? He thought as he stepped closer. *How fucking ridiculous. But what was he going to do? Refuse? Yeah, right. That was definitely not going to happen.*

Smiling grimly, Declan strolled around to the back of the wooden chair where he'd bound the nun. He used a pocket knife and sliced through her binding. Even as she eased her hands around to the front, he grabbed a handful of her veil and yanked it off her head.

She was silent, and when he circled around her, he saw her eyes were dark and dry. Still staring at him, the nun began to pray again, this time in Latin, the words unfamiliar but pricking at his skin with a supernatural pain. Declan pushed the pain aside, he was no stranger to its sting and backhanded the nun across the face. It was enough to cause her to pause and the pain lifted as if it had never been there. He shoved her in the chest with the intention of reeling her backward ass over tea kettle, but he wasn't up to his full strength and although the nun did fall back with the chair, she managed to roll with the pull of gravity; her legs swinging up, her palms to the floor pushing her swiftly into a brief handstand and then onto her feet. The black material of the habit moved with her in ebbs and flows as if it too had been trained to protect itself rather than getting caught up and tangled about the woman's body.

"Very suave," he said with a laugh. "Did they teach you that at the convent?"

The nun stayed silent, positioned her body in a ready stance for a fight, and glared at him.

"Guess that's a yes," he replied. Declan gave her a wry smile and a wink. "Let's dance then. I'll lead."

With that, he closed the distance between them and threw the next punch at her face southpaw style to throw her off guard. It connected and he drove his fist into her right jaw. The nun's head jerked back with the blow but she recovered, readjusted her stance, and then side kicked him in the ribs. He felt a slight snap on his left side as one of the bones gave way and Declan grunted from the pain but stood firm, blocking a right fist coming his way. Blood oozed from the nun's mouth and her cheek and jaw were already beginning to swell, turning a nice shade of reddish-purple. He sent another blow from the opposite hand, this one meeting the other side of her other jaw, and she spun slightly from the force towards the downed chair behind her. The nun picked it up as she stood and swung it at him. Declan ducked just in time and then leaned out of the chair's reach when it came back around for another cut through the air. The chair hit one of the foot posts on the bed and broke, sending pieces of it sailing over the village girl who uttered a startled cry. The nun, with her lips swelling and bloody, began her tireless chanting prayers in Latin again and Declan felt their sting as she took another swipe at him with one of the broken wooden rungs. He retreated a step to move out of the way of her newly acquired stake and then threw a roundhouse kick, connecting with her wrist when she'd thrust it towards him. Her wrist snapped and the rung hit the floor with a clatter. She backed up, holding her broken wrist against her chest, but he stepped ahead of her in a blur of movement. It took the nun off guard and with a back foot sweep Declan took out the leg which held most of her weight. Her chanting ceased abruptly as the bones cracked, replaced by a quick cry of pain as she hit the floor hard and skidded back on the polished wood, colliding with the wall and scattering bits of bluish robin egg paint and drywall pieces on the bedroom floor with the force of her impact. Stunned, the nun attempted to rise on her uninjured leg but wavered and landed back on her ass.

Declan looked at her with contempt. "You lied to me."

The nun said nothing.

"You told me the artifact was real when in fact it was just a piece of junk."

She looked up at him with her pained dark eyes. "You shall have your reward in the end, demon. No artifact will protect you from God's wrath. For, in the end, we all get our just rewards."

He struck hard and fast, plucking the woman up one-handed

by the front of her neck, squeezing her windpipe as he yanked her upright to face him. Her dark eyes widened from the intense pressure and her face first reddened and then took on a blueish-gray hue. She did not look away from him, even as her life drained. Declan paused, inclined his head in a nod of acknowledgment, and replied, "And now you shall have yours."

Quickly shifting her up higher, he lifted his leg and then slammed her onto his knee with back-breaking force. There was a loud crunching sound and a high pitched scream from the girl bound to the bed, but barely a grunt from the suffocating nun. He tossed her broken body onto the floor at his feet and with one booted foot raised, came down hard on her face, stomping the last bit of life out of her. Declan shifted his eyes to the girl and smiled. Her scream was silenced, morphed into her own prayers in French.

It won't do you any good now, he thought as he yanked off his boots and socks, tossing them to the floor. *You would be better off just screaming.*

Declan peeled off his rain-soaked jeans, revealing the toned lower half of his body, his erection from the fight with the nun was evident and the lust-filled feed to come caused his blood to surge, coursing hard throughout him and numbing the pain from the injury to his ribs. He crossed the room and climbed onto the bed, positioning himself between her spread knees as he tore away the girl's sensible underpants and bra; the days of any modesty she might have had were over for her now. She tensed, pinching her tear-filled eyes closed and continued praying until he lay over her, entered her, and then took every bit of life she had for himself.

———

I tossed the dice for a final roll, watching them tumble along the green felt, not caring what the numbers were but rather what was going on to my left. My best friend and confidant, Alex, was decked out in a skintight sequined dress, the slit going up her thigh showing a lot of skin but not the .22 she had strapped to her opposite leg. Part-time doctor, part-time secret agent, I thought wryly.

To her left, a stout man was leaning over the table, slurping a drink that smelled strongly of whiskey. Banner was a small-town, small game drug dealer, but he had some ties that were definitely not the best. I got wind of some of his less than sterling companions, and when the human trafficking ring was connected with his lucrative drug business, well, I just couldn't step away.

Banner's hands, beefy with too many rings to match the gold chain around his neck, darted out as he took his turn. My hand itched to grab for the dagger tucked into the sheath cleverly disguised as my decorative belt. To plunge the blade into that big belly would be satisfying.

I laid my hands flat on the felt. No, being this bloodthirsty was not normal for me. And it wasn't good. I had been hired to find someone, and now that I knew where she was, I needed to finish the job.

"We're good over here." The hissing voice came through the earpiece. I smiled and put my hand on Alex's shoulder.

"I think we're about out of chips," I told her in an undertone.

She graced me with a grin, her blue eyes bright under heavily darkened lashes.

"Do you want to get out of here?" she asked.

I gave a little nod. My wardrobe for the evening was a little more freeing than hers, tight black pants that shimmered in the flashing lights and a form-fitting silk shirt. My boots were nice too, nice for holding a few weapons and an assortment of tools I might need for a little late-night breaking and entering.

"Hey, where are you ladies off to?" Banner's voice was too loud, and his speech was slurred with a little too much alcohol.

"We have somewhere to be," I replied, satisfied that this overblown, overfed figurehead had done his job. He gave up where the girls were being kept. Even now, some of Alex's friends from Atlanta were ripping the place apart.

I stepped back, jerking my head. Alex gave a quick nod. We began to stroll toward the door, and I was sure to keep the man at the table in my sights. I wouldn't turn my back on this guy. We stepped out on the sidewalk when I caught a movement in my periphery. Not our nasty Mr. Banner, but someone was tailing us.

We almost made it to Alex's car, a sporty little red Mazda Miata, when I felt a hand drop to my shoulder. I spun, my hand going instinctively to my belt, hovering over the blade.

The man at my back wore a poor-fitting suit. He was half a foot taller than me, remarkable since I am a tall woman and my heels made me three inches taller.

"Hey, whoa," the man said, taking a quick step back and raising both hands as a conciliatory gesture. "My boss just wanted one more word with your friend there." He gave a gesture in Alex's direction. "Just a minute."

"We're busy," I said, my body stiff.

"Just next door," the ogre went on. "We are getting a drink next door, and you, my lady, are invited."

My stomach rolled at his smile. Someone must have told him to try to be charming, but he was failing tremendously.

"Not interested," Alex replied, eyes narrowed.

"I must insist." I didn't see him draw, but now the handgun was tucked in his massive paw, like a lethal toy.

I stifled a sigh. If Banner was going to insist, I figured I would comply. If he wanted us so much, I would grant him his wish. I was pretty sure he didn't know what he was dealing with.

"Fine," I said tightly.

He gestured with the gun and we proceeded him back across the street. I didn't kick up a fuss. I wasn't about to try to get any attention from innocent bystanders. I wasn't sure how far these guys would go to cover their tracks, and really, we could take care of ourselves.

The storefront next door to the small gambling dive used to be a restaurant, but it wasn't in business now. The smell of spices and tomato sauce lingered in the air. Hmmm. Maybe I was getting hungry.

Banner was seated at one of the back booths, his girth tucked in behind a wooden slab table.

"Ah, good. So glad you decided to join me. Take a seat, will you?"

I glared at Banner, but slid into the leatherette cushioned bench seat. Alex followed, sitting close enough to me that I could feel the tension in her body. I darted a glance in her direction. Surely she wasn't enjoying this?

"You seem to be in a hurry to leave," Banner stated, his expression bland.

"We have somewhere to be," I replied.

"I'm feeling used," Banner answered, his red lips in his doughy round face set in a petulant pout.

"I don't know what you mean." Alex's voice was velvety smooth, her Georgia accent strong. She was playing this better than me.

"You asked me a lot of questions," Banner answered. "Too many, I think."

I just looked at him blank-faced.

"I still don't have any idea where you're going with this," Alex replied.

"I find it particularly interesting that you ladies needed to find that address," Banner said. "Think I'm stupid, do you?" He shifted his considerable girth in the seat making the cushion beneath him squeal in protest.

"Maybe." It slipped out before I could catch myself.

Banner's eyes darted to me. "Think you're tough, do you? Any idea how much a feisty redhead gets on the open market." He gave me a smirk. "Quite a bit."

I tilted my head. Interestingly he wasn't keeping anything back. He had a plan. He was sure he was going to win this one, which made me wonder how many of his goons he might have in the back. Or was he so sure of his monstrous companion that he figured they could take two women?

"I have some friends coming by soon. I think they will be delighted to meet you," Banner continued. He held his cell phone up, reading the glass face. "Another few minutes, maybe."

I huffed out a sigh. He might be an idiot, but I wasn't sure how many reinforcements he had called in. Better to cut our losses than wait to see what bigger battle he had prepared.

"Look, I'm sorry about your friends, but I can't wait." I nudged Alex and she moved a couple of inches.

"Stop." The goon pointed the gun in our direction, and despite the dull appearance, I figured he was close enough to hit one of us if he fired.

"I don't understand," Alex replied, standing up anyway. "I don't want to join any party. I'm ready to go home." It would have been funny to hear her play the dumb blond if I hadn't been worried the big guy might accidentally fire on her.

"Stand still now."

I took his moment of distraction to reach beneath the table

into my boot. The short blade felt nice in my hand, balanced, well crafted. When I threw it, the aim was true, hitting the goon in the throat with a solid strike.

He immediately grabbed for the hilt, and when he pulled the blade out, a red fountain of blood gushed to the floor. The gun followed and hit the floor unfired.

"Should have left that," I said, shaking my head.

Banner appeared to be mesmerized by the slow toppling of his companion. As soon as the man hit the ground, Banner started to scramble out of his seat. I wasn't surprised when he pulled the gun. I was, however, a little astonished that he managed to get one shot off before Alex's bullet hit him dead center in his chest. He was thrown back, making his own discharge go wide. When he hit the floor, his gun hand smacked the wood, and the gun skittered away, hitting the near wall with a muffled thud.

I moved toward the first man down, determined to get my blade from where it fell from his limp hand. I used a cloth napkin from the table to wrap the blade and tucked it back in my boot.

Banner was moaning and rolling on the floor, his hands coming away scarlet from his chest. I could see air bubbles coming out with a spray of blood and figured he wasn't long for this world.

"Guess we need to head out," I stated, watching Banner's eyes glass over.

"Okay," Alex answered. "You want me to text Brother Joshua?"

I nodded. The holy man had his connections, and besides being the leash holder for Victor McCain, the official Hand of God, God's bounty hunter, he also had an efficient cleanup business. They would turn this place upside down and inside out, cleaning away anything that pointed to the killing, including the victims.

My cell phone started to vibrate and I frowned. There weren't many people who had my number, and when I saw the screen, my concern increased.

I hit the green button.

"It's Sam," I said.

"Samantha," the voice was not what I expected. Sister Evangeline was on the other line, and rather than having one of the younger nuns call me, she was contacting me directly.

"Sister."

"You need to come here now," she said. "Something has happened."

I glanced toward Alex and nodded to myself.

"I'll be there as soon as I can."

CHAPTER TWO

Declan caught a redeye to Chicago and spent a couple of hours in O'Hare wiling away the layover time reading a novel by James Patterson. He wasn't a huge fan of the author but the feed from the village girl had been one hell of an energizing rush, much like someone who downed a huge cup of Death Wish coffee then chased it with five shots of espresso, and he knew sleep was not an option. And like any other severely stupid and quite overly caffeinated person, his mind was abuzz. The book would help focus him enough to make it through the wait at the airport and the flight to Heathrow in London without fidgeting so much as to draw attention to himself. By the time he boarded the plane home, he was nearly halfway through Maximum Ride. He'd picked up Patterson's first attempt at a sci-fi novel while at a discount bookstore in Louisville, Kentucky the week before. The cover caught his eye and he'd purchased it. The plane touched down at Heathrow and Declan closed the book feeling cheated. He thought since the front cover depicted winged human forms, the story would have been about angels; it turns out they were just mutants. He gave the book his final opinion of it by tossing it onto a chair in the terminal as he made his way out through airport security and to his car parked in the lot. The black Passat waited for him like a forlorn lover and he settled into the driver's seat feeling much the same. Good ol' Ernestine. If Declan had a favored possession, she was it. It wasn't a sports car although the sleek black and shiny body gave it those small touches in all the right places, making it seem that way to him. The Kentucky cabin where he'd taken the two women after smuggling them into the states through an acquaintance who paid him for turning a blind eye to the man's human trafficking business, the flat in London, even his leasehold in Paris could all go to blazes, but he would keep the Passat thank you very much.

He parked the car in the lot, gave Ernestine's dashboard a loving pat, and then got out. The building where he'd leased the flat was pretty nondescript, just a three-story concrete box with a sign out front displaying the name as Waldridge Court. There was no courtyard, not in the front of the edifice where the only thing separating the street from the entrance was the walk, nor in the rear where it butted up to another complex with just a narrow alley in between. But he hadn't leased it for the extravagant beauty. Aside from the location which made his commute to the New Scotland Yard building a bit less tedious with the city's growing population and packed streets, it added to the persona he'd adopted as just another detective constable in London. No, this place was his cover and it kept those who might be suspicious of him, that chosen handful of humans equipped to deal with creatures such as himself, from relieving him of all his earthly cares.

Declan made his way into the building and up the elevator to his second-story abode. A hot shower and fresh clothes sounded great right now. After, he could head over to the Victoria Embankment and check in with his superiors at the Yard. He'd been on leave for over a week, taking time away when he'd learned of the artifact and what it was supposed to do. Now he would have to extend his leave to visit the old righteous order again to collect the one Lucifer was so set on having. Whatever the blasted thing did, it couldn't be good.

Don't let another of our kind touch it. Don't use it.

He had no intention of doing either. At best, the bloody thing did nothing and at worst, uh, he really didn't want to even think about the worst. The last thing the prideful son of a bitch fallen angel needed was more power.

Shedding his clothes, Declan turned the tap for hot water as far as it would go and gave it a moment before stepping into the steaming shower. Next to feeding, it was the only time his flesh seemed to warm at all and he stood under the pulsing spray for a while before soaping up. Cold, so cold, his victims would say as he plunged himself deep into them before warming and thrusting them into their last bit of ecstasy. And he'd taken them hadn't he? He'd taken their warmth and fed until nothing was left but a corpse so dry and brittle it resembled the mummies from long ago.

He finished his shower and pulled on a pair of black jeans and a dark blue tee-shirt. Brushed his teeth, more from habit than need, and put on his shoes. There wasn't a need for deodorant or cologne. Incubi never had a need for them or showers really. Much like their beauty, they attracted their prey with a natural alluring scent. Declan smelled like a combination of lavender and amber. To anyone with a nose and within smelling radius, it was as if he'd stepped out of the shower every moment of every day. He ran his fingers through his wet hair and then left it to dry on its own, foregoing any study of his reflection in the bathroom mirror. His image never changed and if he walked the earth for another thousand years it would still remain the same.

When he arrived at the New Scotland Yard building it took a good twenty minutes to make it to his direct superior's office door. Declan was well-liked, another product of being an incubus, and because of this everyone wanted to chat him up. He considered it an occupational hazard and kept most of the contact with his coworkers as brief as possible. Too much time in his presence would lead to unwanted adoration on their part and that was just too risky as too much attention for an incubus was bad news. He sat down in one of the two chairs opposite Merick Samms's desk and considered what to tell the portly bald man. To be honest, it didn't really matter what he said to his boss, whether it be the truth of needing more time away to steal another artifact or a lie like Satan's stench gave me a bellyache and now I've got bloody tadpoles shooting out my arse. He would get what he wanted, he always did where humans were concerned, but getting what he wanted wasn't the issue. The problem was he had no power to make them forget. They would remember what was said just as easily as if it was a normal human request, which also meant they could tell someone who could tell someone else and so forth, making it one hell of a gossip wheel. Not a huge problem unless the wrong person heard it, such as one of the righteous with an ax to grind, so he decided to keep it simple and offer no real excuse.

"I just wanted to talk to you about extending my leave," Declan told him. "Maybe another week?"

Merick nodded. "I've been thinking about taking off on holiday myself. The job does make your head spin about sometimes."

Merick tapped on the keyboard of his laptop and studied the screen for a moment.

"Well, you've plenty of time saved up and we don't have any pressing cases at the moment so I see no problem approving your request."

"Thank you," Declan replied, getting up to go.

Merick regarded him and then asked, "Is everything alright? Personally, I mean."

Declan paused. "Yes sir."

"No women trouble? Family issues?"

Careful now, Declan thought, anything you say can and probably will be used against you.

He gave Merick a boyish grin. "No. Everything's roses."

"Jolly good," Merick replied. "I'll see you in a week."

Declan winced at the cliched expression, not because Merick was a living and breathing cliche, but because it reminded him of Lucifer's poke at him earlier which was something he'd rather forget. In fact, any time spent with Lucifer was best forgotten. The fallen angel had a way of getting into your head and messing about just for the fun of it. He gave Merick a perfunctory goodbye and left through the front entrance of the Yard, walking out to Ernestine with a sigh of relief. He started the engine and Ernestine purred under him. A clean getaway, he thought with a light chuckle.

"Ah Merick, you gullible fuck."

Now on to France.

———

I gritted my teeth as we took the final curve, the Abbey grounds appearing before us. The lavender fields spread out like a carpet of purple. It was lovely, magical, and it brought back so many memories.

"Samantha, you must not let yourself become distracted by

those dark thoughts," Sister Evangeline was seated across the table from me. Between us was a single bead, shiny black like a bird's eye. "I will always prevail."

I glanced up toward her and her glasses caught a glint of light from the lit candle. The air smelled of fresh flowers perfuming the draft coming from the window. It was like nothing I had ever experienced. The pain in my hip distracted me for a moment.

"Focus," the older nun admonished.

I looked at the bead, still on the rough-hewn table. Focus.

Then the bead was gone. I blinked and shook my head. I put my hand out to the table, my fingers sliding over the cool grain of the surface.

"Focus," Sister Eva said, and she pulled her hand from within the draped sleeve of her robe. In her palm was the bead. I hadn't seen her move. "No sleight of hand, this," she noted. "Just focus."

I pulled myself from my thoughts. Focus. Sister Mary Carmella was missing. Sweet, strong, devout Sister Mary Carmella went to the village with a friend, a layperson, and hadn't been seen in over twenty-four hours. And that wasn't all. Sister Eva was concerned. There was the stink of evil to it. And I shuddered to think of what might be starting.

"It's beautiful," Alex's voice was soft and reverent in my ear. I nodded but didn't respond. The Abbey of Sainte Aelis had stood in this field for centuries, tucked into the mountains of France, outwardly growing and harvesting their patent crops of lavender to maintain their existence as they had for so long.

Inside was a strict training ground for the holy order, a place of worship and righteousness, a tightly organized faction of women chosen and called to be defenders of the faith.

I took a deep breath. Alex was right. It was beautiful, and it was hard for me to remember this was her first visit; I didn't know if any of my little group of companions had. But no, that was wrong. Abe most certainly visited here. Not that I heard any details of his visit. Abe and I hadn't seen one another for almost a month, just after the terrible confrontation with Rowan, an Infernal Lord, one of Satan's minions, had gone for my loyalty, and when it couldn't be had, my throat.

Abe proved his worth, though. He was a good fighter, a good driver, and cool under pressure. There wasn't anyone else I believed was as quick on his feet as this guy, except maybe me.

"It is lovely," I agreed. "And you'll find pretty quickly that the amenities are pretty sparse. It is primarily a convent, and they eschew worldly goods."

Alex nodded. She knew all this. She had met several of the nuns from the order, even fought beside one, and was comfortable with them. Their way of life, however, was a blast from the past.

"I'll be fine." Alex looked at me pointedly. "We'll be fine. You just do what you need to."

I nodded and braced myself as the truck swung around a final curve. There were only a few vehicles that came to the abbey. The occasional delivery of goods the sisters couldn't produce themselves from their own land, some supplies for their business, and, of course, the various weapons, ammunition, and accessories needed to carry out their singular purpose, the battle with the dark one.

The gentleman from the town who agreed to take them on this leg of the journey was a frequent visitor to the sisters. One of his aunts had joined the order years ago, he explained but left shortly after her initial stint as a novice, transferring to a nearby convent. I suspected I knew what had happened. The local girl wanted to devote her life to the order, not realizing this particular group of women was less about ceaseless prayer and more about militant action.

As we climbed out of the truck, I stood on the hard-packed drive and surveyed the surrounding area. There were no yellow taped warnings, no police vehicles, no sign that anything disturbed the peace and serenity of the sacred space. But I felt something, some inkling which traced up my skin and drove the momentary comfort from my mind. There was something here, something evil, something which took a pure soul for its own greedy needs.

"Get the bags and let's go in," I said. "We need to start looking around before any trail of them is lost."

CHAPTER THREE

Crossing the English Channel was a breeze these days and Declan took the EuroTunnel. Leaning back in the seat after he'd driven the car onto the train and parked in line behind a blue Dodge Neon, he closed his eyes for a moment. Ernestine's navigational system told him the entire trip from London to the abbey would take him a little more than twelve hours. The passage under the channel in the comfy confines of the train would be around thirty-five minutes, giving him plenty of time to relax and think. The Abbey of Sainte Aelis was secure enough that he'd had to employ the help of the village girl whose life he'd taken. What was it she called herself? Slyvie? Yeah, that was it. He'd met her the first day he'd arrived at the village. Immediately taken by her beauty, he'd struck up a conversation with her which was more easily done these days as women and girls were free to move about without the accompaniment of chaperones who made it their business to protect both virginity and honor. There was also the fact this particular sex of humans were now more open to conversing with complete strangers. He 'd pulled out his old British charm, positioned himself downwind to where she stood, and allowed his scent of amber and lavender to work what magic his physical appearance and personality could not. She was immediately taken with him, chatting quickly in French until he told her he knew very little of her language. When she switched to a broken and thickly accented form of English he knew he had her. A simple touch of his hand to the nape of her neck was contact enough for him to keep her attention, the deep and passionate kiss he gave her in an alley behind one of the shops secured his hold. Slyvie would do his bidding for a short time, but one short time was all he needed. She shared more than just the kiss with him; a little nibble of her life force of course, but more importantly the girl had confessed to visiting the abbey to see one of her nun friends quite often. What's more, when Declan described the artifact to her she immediately began babbling in French at first, blushed, and then switched to the broken English again to confirm the rumors he had heard.

"Oui," Slyvie replied, her eyes glistening, "it is true. My friend, Mary Carmella told me there is healing in the artifact you seek."

He nuzzled her neck, kissing it lightly, and she shivered in response to his touch. As he pulled back to study her face, he could see her eyes changing from their normal brownish color to an unnatural lavender hue. Declan asked her a question and then planted another light kiss on the base of her neck.

"There is a secret way," she breathed, "into the tunnels under the abbey. Mary Carmella took me there once."

When she told him she would be happy to retrieve it for him, Declan promised her the world; a worthless and empty promise she took to the bank and cashed in for her life. He also gave her a ride in the Passat, taking the narrow winding dirt road to a wooded section which butted up against a field of lavender. Slyvie waded through the field in her trance with the true goal in mind, to enter below ground level, navigate the tunnels to where she could access the stairs and get the amulet from the third level of the abbey so she could bring it to the most beautiful man she had ever laid eyes on. She did not disappoint him. Declan felt a genuine smile pull at his lips as he remembered how she felt, how she smelled, and oh how she tasted. When he'd entered her at the Kentucky cabin, driving himself deep inside, and discovered she was a virgin, he almost lost control and took her life right then instead of savoring such a delicacy slowly.

No, Slyvie didn't disappoint him at all. The nun, however, this Mary Carmella had either lied to the girl about the amulet's power or misunderstood it herself. Either way, she too paid in full. Declan felt his smile go broader with the thought of snapping the spine of one of the righteous. The nun should have kept herself tucked away in her abbey. Isn't that what they were supposed to do? Ceaseless prayers and all that? He wiped his face with his hands awaiting the announcement over the intercom to debark. When it came and the train stopped, he followed the Dodge Neon out.

———

Sister Evangeline was in her office, a spartan room with a large desk, two wooden chairs, and the only phone that functioned within the abbey. She stood when we stepped in, her face pale but expression controlled.

"Where were they taken?" I didn't need the polite greetings. I needed to move, to act.

"They were walking back from town," Sister Eva began. Her

eyes looked heavy behind her glasses, but she wasn't going to break, I knew that for sure.

"We believe they were just a few kilometers from the abbey's property. There were marks left by some kind of vehicle, both tracks showing it coming from town, and a messy three-point turn."

"They never came into the abbey?" I felt a shadow of a doubt. There was something that didn't feel right. I had an inner sense something had been here, someone, some entity, I wasn't going to assume it was just another kidnapping.

"We have found no trace of an intruder," Sister Eva replied. Her gaze sharpened. "But you feel something, don't you?" Her blue eyes swept from my face to Abe's and I followed her gaze.

Could Abe feel it? I didn't know much about the enigmatic Abe Shepherd beyond his claim that he was in finances and had a long history with the Sisters in the Abbey.But he had been an invaluable asset to my past investigation, so I wasn't about to doubt him.

"I believe there is something," Abe answered. He looked in my direction and I met his gaze.

"Do you think they were in here?" I looked from him to the older nun.

"We must find out," Sister Eva said. "There are so few facts we know about Sister Mary Carmella's disappearance. There were no witnesses. Photographs and molds of the tire tracks have been taken and are being examined. We have no idea why anyone would have tried to take these women."

I nodded. "I'd like to speak to the girl's family," I began. "We need to make sure the disappearance isn't what the police are claiming." I was shaking my head, frustration leaking into my tone of voice. The local law made it clear they believed there was a possibility the two women chose to leave together, a last-minute wild hair which led them to a bigger city for a little fun and misbehavior. The police could not have understood how ridiculous their assumption was. They had no idea what the nuns did there in the closed walls of the abbey, the skills that Sister Mary Carmella honed while she was here, the goal of her training. Sister Mary Carmella would no more leave on a last-minute fling than the Queen of England would run away for a weekend in Vegas.

"We can touch base with the authorities," Abe added.

I glanced his way. Perhaps he would be better suited to deal with the political red tape.

"You and Alex can go to the station, and I'll try to talk to the girl's family."

"Slyvie Bartan," Sister Eva said.

I looked at her curiously.

"The village girl. Slyvie Bartan. That is her name." She closed her eyes slowly. "God rest her soul," she breathed.

———

I went alone into the village of Murshon, proceeding Alex and Abraham by only fifteen minutes. I wanted to get a feel for the place before they showed up. There was something in the air here, something different, changing, and I had to make sure my awareness of Abe wasn't tainting my perceptions.

I didn't explain that to him, however. Whatever Abraham was, or his talents might have been, we hadn't discussed it.

I decided to walk to the village down the same dirt-packed road the women traveled on the day of their disappearance. Sister Eva told me it was their habit to make the trek together, laughing and enjoying the vibrant scenery before they entered the comparative hustle and bustle of the town. Sister Mary Carmella spoke several languages fluently, and it was often her task to barter with both the locals and more exotic sources to obtain supplies they needed. These items ranged from the day to day cooking and cleaning needs to the fragrant oils, poisoned perfumes, and finely wrought weapons that were part of their arsenal.

I paused in front of the tidy produce market, looking over their wares saturated with color in the sunlight. What possible reason would someone have for taking both the women? Assuming it had something to do with the nun's mission and not just a traveling serial killer who had wandered their way, what was the worth of Sister Mary Carmella and Slyvie? No, I was sure the reason the women were missing was because of the association with the convent, and more importantly, the treasures and mission the convent represented.

The address for Slyvie's family was written on a slip of paper in my pocket. Sister Eva gave it to me along with a small silver metal she requested I give to the anxious parents. It was round, with a circle of wire meant to hang on a chain.

"Saint Anthony," Sister Eva noted. "He intercedes for us to find lost things."

I nodded. I didn't believe in the same doctrine the nuns held so dear, but I wasn't about to question her or scoff at the idea. I had seen too much supernatural to dismiss anyone's beliefs in the divine. My belief that God was dead, I still kept to myself and held in a very dark, very closed place in my heart.

Slyvie's house was a charming stone cottage much like the rest of the village. The cobblestoned streets bumped up to the neatly trimmed boxwoods which parted in a trail just wide enough for a single person to pass. Like the rest Murshon, the flowers in crumbling clay pots were tumbling down the steps in a wave of color, lush and lovely.

I didn't pause to admire the view but went directly to the

door and knocked briskly. The door was opened immediately by a fifty-some-year-old woman with tight black curls that were in wild disarray. Her frantic eyes met mine, and I saw her deflate as she realized I was not who she hoped for, who she prayed for. She wanted her daughter back and her pain was almost palpable.

"I'm sorry to disturb you. Mrs. Bartan?"

The woman nodded shortly.

"I am Samantha. I came here at the request of Sister Evangeline. She asked me to check on you and to give you this." I held out my hand, the small metal resting in my palm.

"Merci," she breathed.

"I also wanted to help with the search for your daughter and Sister Mary Carmella. Could I ask you a few questions?" As I spoke, a short wide-shouldered man came up behind Slyvie's mother.

"We have talked to the police. We have told them all that we know." His voice was brisk, but his eyes held fear.

"I know you have, but I am a private investigator and I was hoping to help the police track the women down." I had stretched the truth a little, but my real job, revenge taker perhaps, was a little too dramatic.

Slyvie's mother sighed. "Come in," she said, her heavily accented English still intelligible.

I followed her into the dim interior. As I looked around, I felt sure I was seeing the place as it never had been before. There were empty coffee cups on the table, a scatter of papers on a couch that faced the darkened fireplace, and a pair of shoes, bright red and shiny, abandoned next to the door. I suspected clutter was generally not acceptable to this woman, but with her child missing, all of the external concerns were wiped away.

I followed her gesture and sat on the wooden chair. It was probably the same place the police sat when they came for their interview. They settled on the couch, side by side and close, gaining strength from one another.

I asked them the standard questions: when had they last seen their daughter, how had she appeared, did they know what the women were doing that day? I learned nothing I hadn't already gleaned from my earlier conversations. The day in question was so ordinary, the track such a habit.

I looked between the two of them. "Did Slyvie say anything about any strangers in town? Or any new activities going on?"

"There was a man," Mrs. Bartan sent a quick glance in her husband's direction. "Slyvie didn't tell me who he was or anything about him. But she had this look on her face. And the way she talked about him…"

"Was he a local? From the village?"

"From the village, no. We know everyone here. But whether or not she knew him well, I don't know and she wouldn't say."

Slyvie's father's dark eyes grew stormy, his black brows drawn together as he looked at his wife.

"I didn't say anything to you. I know how protective you can be." Mrs. Bartan's eyes filled with tears and she ran a shaking hand through her curls. "I thought it was a little romance. And Slyvie was with Sister Mary. I knew she wouldn't let anything happen to my little girl." A tear rolled down the woman's face and fell in her lap, leaving a dark spot on her blue slacks. "Ma petite fille," she whispered.

"And you told the police this? Le policier?"

She nodded silently. Her husband dropped his head, his palm cradling his chin.

"Okay, then," I replied. "I'm going to continue to search. If you think of anything, anything at all, I will be staying with the sisters.

CHAPTER FOUR

I caught up with Abe and Alex as they roamed the cobbled streets of the village.

"This is amazing." Alex appeared to be enjoying the visit to Murshon just as much as the view from the Abbey.

Murshon was a medieval masterpiece reflected in the Abbey's architecture. It was undoubtedly constructed of the same stone, but while the Abbey was surrounded by lavender fields with much less decoration, the village was a riot of colors in their flowers and greenery, their shops, and striped awnings sheltering people from the bright sun.

I couldn't enjoy the peaceful beauty of it. There was something amiss here, and I wouldn't rest until I knew exactly what was going on.

"Are you going in to talk with the police?" I asked.

"Yes," Abe responded. "Did you get any information from the girl's family?"

"The only thing they said that was suspect was the fact she recently met a man. The family hadn't met him and they didn't think he was a local. But they didn't approve. You could tell it from their expressions."

"Then our girl might have been out to meet a lover when she was taken?" Abe's eyes narrowed.

"I don't know about that. If I were going on a first date, I doubt I'd bring a nun with me."

Alex grinned. "You are too stuffy," she exclaimed.

I gave a grunt.

"Perhaps you are looking at this from the wrong angle. The two young women were friends. As friends, wouldn't you introduce your newest, um, companion to one another."

I frowned. Then I nodded slowly. Just because the woman was a nun didn't mean she didn't have the kind of friendship Alex and I shared. And I would surely want to meet any man whom Alex was seriously dating. The fact that she hadn't met Victor wasn't lost on me. But had we had a relationship? Could you have a relationship with the Hand of God?

"You're right," I agreed. "I'm going to scout around and see who else might have known the girl and maybe seen her with her new man," I continued. "We can meet back here at four. Then we can compare notes and head back for the Abbey. There is still something I feel like I'm missing over there."

We separated and Alex and Abe strolled on towards the square where the government building stood behind stone columns. I headed out in the opposite direction, towards the market teeming with people, with possible witnesses.

———

Declan made it to the village towards the late afternoon. He tucked the car into the public lot he'd used last time on the outskirts and pulled a small leather sheath which held a silver dagger with a black pearl handle out of the glove box. The dagger was sharp, deadly, and quite beautiful with the dark image of a dragon etched just above the tang. He lifted the leg of his jeans and strapped the sheath just below his knee where its shape could be hidden beneath the bulky denim material; he killed the engine and got out of the car. Declan activated Ernestine's alarm system and walked the rest of the way into the village. The most important thing was to get inside the abbey, retrieve the artifact, and then get out. If he needed to pull out his credentials for the Yard and spin a tale about an investigation he could manage it. Oh, the local authorities would frown on him coming unannounced but the lie that he was on his way to introduce himself wouldn't be totally unbelievable. He was British after all and an old French joke came to mind: if God put them on an island, there must be a reason. Declan began his walk into the village with no doubt he could pull this off, whichever way the wind blew.

For a small community, this was one of the most attractive ones he'd been to. It was nestled in a rural area, of course, so the greenery surrounding the village would be expected. Those in charge of this place or possibly its residents seemed to take great pride in landscaping the hell out of it though. Vibrant hues of reds, purples, pinks, and yellows washed against the shades of greens from evergreens, ferns, and boxwoods. It was almost like strolling the ways of some sprawling French botanical garden. Unlike London or Paris, there was very little concrete here, and where roads and walkways were a necessity cobblestones were used instead, giving the community a homey feel.

He passed a few shops and small cafe type eateries and decided to stop at one of them when the pedestrian traffic started to thicken. There was little chance he would be able to slip in the Abbey undetected by himself during the daytime as he would have liked unless he used his credentials to nose around. But he thought that option would greatly limit his access to the lower levels, so biding his time until dark would be the better. He quickly dismissed the idea of hiding out in the wooded area near the old building quickly. If this were his first trip here maybe, but since that first chance was over and done with he'd just have to deal with it. Using another village girl for the task was also out of the question, not without risking a mob of pitchfork toting villagers coming after him. Do it once, you may get away with it if you're crafty enough. Do it twice, and you're just a bloody idiot with a hard-on for death.

Declan opted for one of the tables outside instead of the close confines of the cafe where his scent would attract unwanted attention. A warm August breeze tickled at his skin as he sipped a cup of hot black coffee set in front of him. In truth, caffeine did nothing for him but he liked the taste and would have a cup every now and then. He'd yet to find any tea he actually enjoyed but he drank it anyway when he was at the Yard just to keep up his English appearance. From his seat at the small round table, he could see quite a large section of the cobblestoned village square where a stone fountain stood dead center. The water cascaded out of four brass colored spigots on each side of the stone pillar in the middle, lazily splashing into the rectangular pool beneath. He couldn't help thinking how nice it would have been living in a place like this if he'd been created as a human, but as an incubus it would be all of impossible. Too small. Too friendly. And much too watchful.

A couple approached the village square from the far end alley, a man and woman walking side by side. Declan took a sip from his cup as he studied them. The man towered a good head and shoulders over the woman. A mass of short dark hair covered his head in a prep boy cut and he had a light five o'clock shadow, giving him an all American look. Even at a distance, Declan could see the flat expression on his face. He would be hard to read, that one. The long stride of the man shortened in a chivalrous gesture to allow the woman to keep up and they paused a couple of feet into the square, both scanning the buildings across the way. The man lifted a hand, pointing at the municipal building, and Declan watched him mouth the word commissariat (one of the few French words Declan actually knew) before straightening his black-rimmed glasses and leading the way. The woman followed, not appearing the least bit bothered by his move ahead of her, and as they came closer to where Declan sat, he couldn't help being captivated. She was absolutely beautiful with her short blond hair which fell just below the base of her neck. The cut was adorable; wavy and mussed, it framed her heart-shaped face perfectly. The man said something over his shoulder and the woman's cherub lips smiled and then parted when she laughed lightly. It was a musical sound, that laugh, and Declan felt his breath catch in his throat. Allowing his eyes to fall from her face, he took in her slim curvy figure. She was wearing a short-sleeved white blouse which came just below the waistband of her tight blue jeans and was form-fitting enough he could appreciate the sinuous rise and fall of her breasts as she breathed.

He felt himself harden when she was less than twenty feet away and the warm breeze brought her scent to him, a light citrus and viburnum perfume that seemed to only highlight the natural smell of her body rather than cover it. As they passed by, he got a whiff of the man with her; sandalwood and cypress cologne. And beneath that, absolutely nothing.

The coffee in front of him had grown cold and he lifted his hand at a passing server for a warmup. There had been enough time for both women he'd taken to have been missed and it wasn't unreasonable to assume these were not newlyweds or lovers he was watching but possibly friends or family of the missing. Just as he downed the last sip in his cup, the pair reemerged and crossed the square in the same direction as they had come, passing him by mere feet as before. He inhaled the pleasing smell of the woman again and considered the man's lack of scent which was extremely strange. Every living thing had a smell to it, that was the way of things. For this man not to have his own was beyond bizarre and Declan couldn't suppress his intrigue. Perhaps he might spare a bit of time to learn more but not at the expense of the amulet, of course. That was the most important thing. Get it and get the Devil off his back.

When the couple was out of sight, Declan got up and walked to the front entrance of the municipal building. Halfway through the courtyard he met up with the same trek as the couple and got an unsettling sense of familiarity. It happened sometimes; kind of like walking in someone else's boots if he were to describe it. He looked over his shoulder to ensure there wasn't anything out of the ordinary; a couple of coffee drinkers rested easily in metal chairs set at one of the small cafe tables, both occupied in their cups like he had been just moments before, and several pedestrians padded along behind, none of them seem to notice him. He faced-front and continued walking through the square. The feeling, rather than fading with movement, seemed to strengthen to near overwhelming as he grew closer to the municipal building.

When his hand settled onto the door handle it had magnified into a tangible sensation, starting at his fingertips, into his hand, and up his arm; not so harsh as a static shock but more like a slight throbbing ache traveling upward until he could feel the throb in his head where it died off immediately. He pulled open the door and the ache returned with a vengeance, bringing with it a memory swirling right before his eyes.

Stepping over the threshold and releasing the door to swing

closed, Declan watched the front lobby morph from the modern-day French police station to the shabby in comparison front room of Scotland Yard when it had been on Whitehall Place. Computers, printers, and other bits of technology were replaced with paper and oversized thick leather-bound books. Sharply dressed detectives disappeared and in their place constables suited in the uniforms fashioned in the eighteen hundreds moved busily around the cramped space. On the far wall, he spotted the old Punch cartoon drawing of Jack the Ripper freshly clipped out of the threepenny magazine and held up with a single metal drawing pin in the top center. Sir John Tenniel had given the serial killer the look of Nosferatu, although Tenniel would have had no idea who that was when the cartoon was sketched in 1888, but the resemblance was uncanny. The drawing produced a lot of chuckling and head-shaking when it was passed around the front room. Declan hadn't laughed and he'd found nothing amusing about the killings of a madman.

France, he thought. *This is France, not London. Focus.*

He paused in his stride, the vision, the memory, fading from whence it had come and left him a bit confused. Why now? Why on Earth was he thinking about this now? The lobby didn't answer his questions, simply morphed back to modern-day chaos. Declan gave his head a gentle shake to clear the fogginess and continued on, passing by several people in suits and a couple of members of the local police force to the front counter where a slim and severe-looking woman with her hair drawn up in a tight bun atop her head stared out at the hustle and bustle of the lobby area through a pair of horned-rimmed tortoiseshell librarian glasses. She lifted her gaze to him, her blue eyes magnified to almost bulging by the thick lenses, and forced a smile.

"Bonne apres-midi. Comment puis-je vous aider?"

Declan gave her an innocent smile. "Je ne parle pas francais."

The woman gave him a look of disgust, mostly in those huge magnified eyes, and tried again.

"How may I help you?" she asked, her severe and now quite annoyed facial expression lost its ability to even fake the smile now.

Declan relaxed his stance and leaned his elbows on the counter, intertwining his fingers to give him the appearance of a man in search of a simple answer to a simple question.

"I'm trying to find my friends," he said. "We were supposed to meet in the square and I was wondering if they had been here; tall, dark-headed bloke, looks like he swallowed a lemon? He would have come in with a very attractive young woman with blonde hair."

The woman smirked. "I'm afraid you just missed them, but perhaps you can meet up with them at the Abbey of Sainte Aelis."

"Did either of them give you a number where they can be reached? I seem to have misplaced the one I'd been given."

"And England does not teach her children to put those numbers in their cell phones?" the woman asked sarcastically.

Declan feigned a blush. "My apologies. I was in quite a hurry to get here."

"Am I to assume you are part of the search party to find the two missing women?"

He nodded.

The woman laughed, not a pleasant sound, more of a snort really, and placed a card in front of him on the counter.

"Such ado about nothing," she said. "You will probably find the two of them locked away together in amour lesbian. But since Americans and the British like yourself enjoy spinning your wheels, I say bonne chance a vous tous."

Declan ignored her comment mainly because he didn't

understand a word of the last part of it, grabbed a pen from a holder to his right, and a slip of paper from a stack for notes next to it and jotted down the name and number from the card. He left the card where she laid it on the counter and bid her adieu with a quick merci for good measure. The woman gave a shrug and mumbled something about the English in general and Americans in particular before turning away from him to attend to her business. Declan turned and left, grateful for her bigotry and rudeness. It was better than an overly friendly attitude with a very long nose up his arse and he'd take it and go on with no further thought about it. Outside the building, he glanced down at what he'd written on the paper. A phone number, cell phone most likely, and a name. Alexandria McHugh.

CHAPTER FIVE

W e spent most of the afternoon covering the convent, step by step. It took almost an hour for me to find where an intruder might have gained access to the main building. The abbey had been built with several possible escape routes. Cycles of distrust in the Roman Catholic Church made the sisters cautious about their safety. The tunnels beneath the abbey, however, predated even their habitation of the old building. I knew of two. I was sure there were several more only a few chosen women were aware of. But this, this was their fatal flaw.

"Sister Mary Carmella did so much of our shopping," Sister Anna murmured in a low voice. I cast her a sideways glance and nodded. No one would have dreamed this slight woman with her golden skin and gentle eyes was the best knife thrower in the order. Perhaps more surprising was the number of nuns that could wield a knife with ease.

"Did she use this tunnel often?" Alex was looking around wide-eyed. We descended into the cellar where the convent stored not only root vegetables and jars of canned goods but row upon row of lavender bunches hung upside down from racks specially made for the task. I spent long hours here after spending the afternoon reaping the matured lavender flowers and binding the bundles of stems with twine. Each bouquet had to be individually hung from the rack for the drying process, the abbey's basement a perfect cooled atmosphere for the job.

But it wasn't just the strong scent of lavender we were detecting now. There was an underlying scent, something earthy and warm, not sweet, and somehow familiar. This, as well as the odd sensory gift that allowed me to sense the presence of the paranormal, led me down the long shelves to the false cabinet doors hiding the entrance to the tunnel.

"Whoever it was came through here," I muttered. I was puzzled. I detected something, but I couldn't figure out what it might be. Any proximity to an Infernal Lord or any kind of demon had my senses on high alert. A regular human perpetrator wouldn't ping on my paranormal radar at all.

Abe tugged at the handles of the cabinet and it opened silently. Inside were stacks of boxes holding rolls of twine, long tubes of brown paper for wrapping the flowers, and a few other bits of additional equipment. Abe swiftly lifted these items out and bent forward to feel along the sealed edge of the cabinet's back. Like a trick piece from a movie, the back panels opened up into darkness.

"You've been down there before?" I asked Abe. He was full of surprises. I hadn't known how well he knew the abbey until we arrived and he was greeted like a long lost nephew by the women.

"I have." He didn't elaborate but bent almost double to pass through the opening. Once inside, he reached to one side and with a click of a switch, the tunnel was lit with a string of bare bulbs anchored to the stone ceiling. "Did you want to come in?"

I gave a short nod and climbed through the opening. Alex followed, her petite form an advantage in the tight space. Abe continued to duck as we proceeded down the tunnel. I paused every few feet to broaden my senses. Yes, something had been here but it wasn't a vamp and it wasn't an infernal lord. This was something different. I gestured for the others to proceed, and I continued by testing the vibrations and atmosphere as we shuffled towards the end of the tunnel. It opened into one of the low berms which bordered the fields where the lavender grew in lush waves of violet and amethyst. Here the elusive scent which I was tracking blended with fragrant lavender and was lost.

"This is where it came in," I said.

"You're sure then," Sister Anna's voice was soft, her accent a charming blend of London where she had grown up, and the French which she spoke as fluently as any native.

"This was not something that just happened on the side of the road," I assured her. "Sister Mary Carmella and perhaps Slyvie was taken for some reason related to this," I nodded toward the tunnel. "I don't know if their captor made them lead him or her through the tunnel, or just used them to get the information, but I think there is no doubt this was the goal."

"The evil has entered the abbey," Sister Anna murmured.

"Yes," I answered. "But we have yet to find out why."

"Let's go back through the tunnel and see if we can pick up the trail inside," Abe said. "There is something here," he paused, his words halting as his brow furrowed.

"You see something?" Alex regarded him curiously. She wasn't accustomed to the decidedly paranormal aspects of our little group. I didn't know what talents Abe might have.

We turned and traced our way back out through the tunnel,

pausing periodically for Abe to shine his stronger cell phone camera on the stone floors. After repeating this several times, he hesitated.

"I think whoever it was came alone. I don't think he or she brought the women back through here."

"Whoever it was may have gotten the location from Sister Mary Carmella and then come alone."

"Then the women?" Sister Anna's voice was tinged with fear and I was sure she was thinking the same thing. The women had served their purpose if all the perpetrator wanted was to enter the abbey. After that, they were expendable. And being expendable for a victim was the worst place to be.

"We need to figure out where he or she was going when they gained access to the abbey," I said, not willing to voice my thoughts on the women.

No one asked any further questions.

Now that I knew what I was feeling for, what part of my paranormal senses were triggered, it was easier to follow the source out of the cellar. I lost it a few times, but Abe, with his keen eyes, was able to pick up the trail. I felt my heart sink as we entered the long hall on the third floor. This was where we would often spar and practice our knife throwing. This was where many of the weapons were stored, but more importantly, this was where the artifacts which had been painstakingly collected over the centuries were hidden behind locked doors. There were no exterior windows. One way in and one way out of the locked room.

Sister Anna pulled a large keyring from under her robe, tucked away in a hidden pocket.

"How many people have keys?" I asked.

"Only three of us," she replied. "Sister Mary Carmella did not."

Abe bent and studied the lock. "It could be picked. It would take time, but for someone who knew what they were doing, it's a pretty simple affair."

He stepped away and Sister Mary Carmella applied the key to the antiquated lock. The click of the mechanism releasing sounded loud in the quiet. The door swung open on oiled hinges and we stepped into the room.

If someone was unaware of the Abbey of Sainte Aelis and its ultimate purpose, they would have assumed this place was a chapel. Indeed, there was a line of five pews that made up the central space. On the back wall was a small altar, a snow-white cloth covering the surface, a gold tray with a cloth embroidered in the same metallic sheen lying atop it.

Flanking the altar were carved wooden chairs meant for cele-brants of the mass. Directly behind the altar was a majestic piece of gold, the scrollwork so intricate it shone like cut stone. This was the monstrance, a ceremonial enclosure for the blessed sacrament. Generally, there would be a person in the room at all times performing eucharistic adoration.

Today the room was empty. I crossed behind the pews, going to the far wall where an inset of finely carved wood hid a small closet-like structure. Inside were two seats, between them a curtain of crimson velvet, a place where the faithful came to have their confessions heard. I never participated in the activity, but I knew within the cubical there was a hidden button. I ducked inside and knelt on the padded kneeler, my fingers searching for the switch. In the closer atmosphere of the confessional where the air was suddenly blocked off, I detected the scent again. Pleasant, almost seductive, but it was not supposed to be here.

I depressed the button and the door swung open. Together we walked into the scene of the initial crime.

The inner room was much more utilitarian than the chapel

before. The ancient stones were mostly bare, a single crucifix made of worn wood hanging on the far wall. The rest of the space was filled with cabinets, well-worn metal ones that most likely dated back to the 1950s or earlier. They each featured a latch and a lock. They were all closed. Except one.

I put out my hands instinctively, but no one moved anyway.

"Has anyone been here since the disappearance?" I looked toward Sister Anna.

"No," she replied. "We did not even think to come here."

I nodded. This should have been a scene for the police. There should have been investigative black lights and fingerprints and all sorts of microscopic examination. But that wouldn't happen. No one came into this room, and that included the local authorities.

"I realize we must search for evidence, but if you would give me a few moments." Abe stepped forward and I moved back to let him pass. He possessed an air of authority.

"Finance?" I muttered as he drew out his cell phone and began taking pictures.

He looked at me with one raised eyebrow. "I didn't explain exactly what I did with finance," he replied.

He was as good as his word, keeping us waiting only a few minutes while he went over the area carefully. He didn't take fingerprints. The kind of person who would come into a space so well hidden wouldn't be stupid. The only clues left behind would be those he or she deliberately set out.

And our enemy did leave a single item for our benefit. A red rose, the petals a splash of crimson against the grey gunmetal of the cabinet, lay on the shelf. It showed no wilting, not even a single curling petal, and its perfection was strange and somehow unnatural.

"Don't touch the flower," I said.

Abe eyed me with faint amusement.

"Okay, I know you probably weren't going to anyway, but there's something…" I couldn't finish the statement.

"Sister Anna," Alex interrupted. She stood so silently I almost forgot she was there. Now I could see her quick mind churning behind those azure eyes. "Do you know what is usually stored on that shelf?"

Sister Anna gave a quick shake of her head. "I need to talk to Sister Evangeline," she said.

"If you wouldn't mind," I agreed.

She left with the soft whisper of rubber-soled shoes on stone, and several minutes later, the sound was replaced with the hard tapping of Sister Eva's footsteps.

I drew in a deep breath as the older woman entered, immediately feeling the wave of calm she seemed to exude. As she stood in the doorway, I saw an expression flash across her face, confusion, recognition, sadness.

"Slyvie was here," she murmured.

"How do you know?" I looked at her closely.

"I know," she replied. "She came in, but I feel she was not under her own volition."

I watched as the older woman walked to the shelf. Her fingers hovered over the blossom, but she didn't touch it.

"This is tainted," her voice was gravelly. "This is wrong."

"Do you know what was taken?" Abe was standing back observing.

"Yes, of course," Sister Evangeline replied. "It was an amulet, a piece said to be handed down from King Solomon. The Pentangle represents the five wounds of Christ or the five senses."

"Why would someone be after that particular piece?" Abe

was leaning against the wall, his expression thoughtful and reserved as usual.

"I don't know," Sister Eva replied. "There are many pieces that are worth more monetarily."

"Does it have any other, um, qualities?"

Sister Evangeline looked toward me, and I could see the comprehension in her expression. "No," she said. "There is nothing we are aware of."

I nodded shortly. I was well aware that some of the ancient artifacts stored in the abbey were imbued with some mystical qualities. It would have made some sort of sense if someone had broken into the abbey to steal something of great value. While it was true that the sheer age and history of the Pentangle would make it significant, it would most likely not be enough to make it worth the risk.

"Why," I said.

"Why indeed," Abe agreed.

CHAPTER SIX

Declan reached a small garden the locals used as a community park. Play-yard equipment was scattered about the cleared section near the entrance. The jungle gym, swings, merry-go-round, and seesaws stood abandoned as the heat of the day had left the area unused. Perhaps if the powers that be had seen fit to put in a swimming pool, the park would be hopping with activity. As it was, he only passed one elderly gentleman on his way out with a fedora pulled tightly on his head as he strolled along slowly, tapping the end of his cane along the cobblestone walk as he went. The quiet suited Declan just fine as he ducked beneath the low branches of a group of trees where a lone wooden bench stood. He needed a moment to think, plan all of this out a little better. But it was the village girl who came to mind first, throwing him off. He used his influence to send her after the artifact and she'd willingly complied as he would have expected. Before she climbed out of Ernestine's passenger seat, he produced a single red rose in a sleight of hand movement, and Slyvie had beamed at him, simply astonished at what looked to her like a magician's trick.

"Listen well, my love," he said, placing the rose into her hand. "You are to leave this in place of what you take, understand?"

Slyvie sniffed the vibrant red petals and lifted her lavender-hued eyes to him; the color a telling sign of his influence over her. She nodded slightly, completely enraptured.

"Speak of this to no one, love, not friend, family, or foe. I will pay you for this favor unto me just as the rose will be payment for the artifact."

Again she nodded. "My heart is yours, mon amour."

When she returned to him, the amulet in hand, he kissed her deeply and suggested she meet him outside of the village the next day for something more than a kiss. He had no idea she would come with a friend and a nun at that. At first, he was appalled Slyvie brought the righteous woman along, but the hunger within him quickly snuffed this out. He shuddered with the lustful idea of overtaking such purity; molding and transforming the innocence into burning desire before consuming it all; the idea all the more appealing for the woman's ignorance of what he was. It was the failure of the amulet, the visit from the prince of bloody darkness, and his stupid demand, however, which had caused enough frustration to forgo any sexual feeding from the nun, and he really had no one to blame for losing the enticing chance but himself. He should have spent more time researching the piece of crap, but he hadn't and he'd lost an opportunity because of it. He was able to influence the nun though and that newfound ability would have to be enough.

Declan leaned back against the wooden slats of the bench enjoying the memory of the young religious woman's surprise at finding herself in the thrall of someone such as himself, but then they always believed themselves above such things, didn't they? The righteous, so bloody high and mighty, walking the paths of life arm in arm with the bloke upstairs, thinking just because they believe in heavenly things that they are immune to temptation. He felt a slight grin slide on his face, more from satisfied amusement than any real joy.

No, the truth was no one was; why even Jesus was tempted, but of course the demon in that particular instance failed miserably. And why not? Declan learned early on it was better to shoot low, aim for the weaker ones of the herd, and never ever try to take on anyone with that much power. The demon learned his place though, banished back from whence he'd come by just a few words from Jesus himself. But the nun? No, the nun wasn't as wise or as powerful as the one she believed in and definitely not immune to his touch. It was a simple brush of his hand against hers, innocent enough, but it was enough to change her way of thinking and that was all that was needed to throw her off her guard and come around to his way of thinking.

She was safe, she could trust him, there was no need to be wary, come with your friend, come with me. All will be well.

Both women had come with him, willingly enough, and both were kept in their thoughts of bliss across the sea to the land of the free and the home of the brave. It was inside the cabin, once both were securely bound for his own safety when their illusion faded; first from the nun for her brush with his influence was brief, and then Slyvie who came to herself in fear and a heavy burden of guilt for having lured her friend into this shared fate.

Her cries pulled at him, not his heart or soul like humans claim these things do, but some other part of him; was it primitive? He wasn't sure. He wasn't sure of anything really. There was a war and a cleansing of the place humans called heaven, he'd heard all the stories. But he had not played a part in it, wasn't even certain those rumors were true. He was just suddenly *there* drowning in a lake of fire and burning in such lust he thought surely he would go insane. And where was Lucifer while all this was going on? Right there, standing over them all, burning right along with them and laughing, laughing, laughing. Declan shuddered at the memory of that terrifying laughter; way past insanity and filled with the kind of sick and twisted evil that left a dark residue on anyone who heard it whether they be righteous or not.

The next real memory was of being pulled out of hell by Asmodeus who told him he would always suffer some level of punishment, and while he walked on the terrestrial plane, lust would be the chosen burden until he returned to his place deep in the fiery lake where once again he would be tortured by both; flesh to flame and the intense burning cold of the lust he was forced to bear. No matter where he existed he would burn.

Declan heaved a sigh. At least while he walked in human form he wouldn't be burdened by both simultaneously and if anything he had that to be thankful for. And it really could have been worse, he could have been assigned to a demon worse than Asmodeus, and there were many. There is a hierarchy in Hell if nothing else and the ranks and titles were almost endless. As one of the seven princes of hell, Asmodeus was indeed lust incarnate, but Declan could have been given to one of the others just as easily; greed, sloth, wrath, pride, envy, gluttony. He felt a little nauseated when he thought of the last deadly sin on the list. Beelzebub was not only a bastard, but he was also beyond cruel even for a demon. No, it could have definitely been worse.

Like all demons, Asmodeus possessed a long sordid history in heaven, hell, and on Earth. He was no stranger to mankind and if the legends were as true as they proclaimed, the demonic prince was quite the thorn in King Soloman's ass. According to one tale hushed to the utmost by members of the top level, Asmodeus was one of several within the circle rumored to be either tricked or forced to help erect the temple Soloman called home. But lies ran rampant in hell right along with half-truths and truths with no real point to them other than to provide temptation or injury in some way, and so it remained an intriguing whisper.

Declan sat forward with his elbows on his knees taking in the natural surroundings for a few moments before his thoughts drifted back to Slyvie. Had she landed in the hands of Asmodeus instead, things would have been very different for her. The demon was not known for a gentle touch and he had a habit of making certain every negative thought or emotion stayed with his prey as they were taken in order to make it as painful as possible. Declan didn't hold to that type of thinking, not when it came to feeding. No, he did not make the girl suffer, not in either fear or guilt. He'd helped her through; pulled those things out of her and into himself and given her only a desire for him. And then he'd killed her, but she had died one bloody hell of a happy young woman. There was nothing for him to feel guilty about, was there?

The sun began to sink slowly towards the horizon as Declan mused and when he finally managed to concentrate on how he planned to proceed with liberating the artifact from the abbey he was interrupted by the smell of Hell itself. The empty space next to him on the bench filled, first with shadow and then form.

"You think too much," Lucifer said. "It isn't healthy."

Declan sneered at him. "What would you know about it?"

"Quite a lot actually and overthinking anything can be a cause for failure. Sometimes you must just leap ahead and let what happens happen."

"Oh really?" Declan asked. "Is that the same pep talk you

gave all your chums when you were preparing for the war you lost; just leap on in and see what happens, hope it doesn't just go balls-up right before your eyes?"

If the comment stung home, Lucifer didn't show it. He simply smiled and waited.

"Worked out great for you blokes, didn't it?" Declan continued. "No, if it's all the same to you, I think I'll be keeping my own council but thanks for your concern. Speaking of which, why the hell are you here anyway? Shouldn't it be Asmodeus making certain I don't get a moment's peace?"

This time Lucifer did react, broadening his smile which met his black eyes with wicked glee. It was not a pleasant sight.

"Ah, my boy. Just like you to get right down to the meat of the matter." He paused for a moment, tapping his chin with his index finger. "Now how shall I break this to you gently?"

Declan stayed silent. He could feel his stomach begin to churn, not just from the overlaying stench beside him but from the smug look on the face of the dark prince.

"Let's just say I didn't agree with Asmodeus's executive decision to set you loose on Earth so soon. You were not ready; not in the right...mindset. He disagreed. As to why I am here in his stead, I can only say that he is otherwise occupied, *contemplating* his mistake."

Declan frowned. He held no love or allegiance to Asmodeus, but something deep inside of him hated Lucifer more. The thought of the Devil holding rein over anyone, including the demon who took great pleasure in his torture, literally pissed him off.

"You're punishing him then because he didn't agree with you?"

"Punishment is such a strong word, Incubus. No, consider it a coaching opportunity. Asmodeus, much like you, has a lot to learn about power; who has it, who can take it, and above all, who knows how to use it. Rest assured, your lustful prince shall endure his opportunity at betterment until he has it down pat. Regardless, I have had some time to think over your position here and believe it could be very advantageous to our cause."

"Our cause? You mean yours. I have no bloody dog in that fight."

Lucifer narrowed his black eyes at Declan and the incubus could sense some of the life energy he had taken from Slyvie seep away.

"Your cause is what I deem it to be, Incubus. I have generously allowed you to remain on this plane, a decision which has not been a benign one mind you, and I expect it to be reciprocated. Besides, do you believe for one moment the righteous would forgive such a wretched creature as yourself? Do you believe they'd take you in as if you were normal? No, my friend, they would not. And if you believe it could happen, then you have spent too much time in human form. As I said before, you were born this way, created in my image and given the chance to stand against those who would oppress us. And although you're not nearly as smashingly handsome as myself, one wouldn't necessarily dub you homely."

Declan got to his feet. He didn't really care what the old devil thought of his looks or the lack in them but he sure as fuck had endured enough of his prattle. Lucifer laid a hand on Declan's arm and the cold sensation coursing through the incubus faded, quickly replaced with an excruciating burn jolting from where the contact was made and radiating throughout his entire body. Declan cried out in agony, all of his muscles seizing up at once and then released just as quickly, causing him to collapse to his knees. When Lucifer retracted his hand Declan pitched forward, barely catching himself before his face slammed into the ground.

The coldness returned with a biting vengeance, drenching him in sweat and pain so intense he nearly passed out.

"You will retrieve the amulet, Incubus, and you will bring it to me. Do not tarry."

Declan lifted his pain-filled eyes to see Lucifer standing over him. There was a satisfied smile stretched across his face like that of some little bastardly kid who just discovered he could pull the wings off of flies and they still lived to crawl on the ground anxiously awaiting the sole of the kid's shoe. He knelt down, coming face to face with Declan. Had the incubus been able to breathe at that moment, he would have reeled at a stench much worse than brimstone. As it was, the pain suppressed any effort to inhale, or even exhale with or without a scream. The smell of rotting flesh was lost on him but Satan's words were not.

"I dearly hope this is the only coaching session you will need, but I won't hesitate to repeat it if necessary." Lucifer patted him on the head, much like one would give a good boy to a dog, and then stood. "You have a pleasant evening now."

Declan pinched his eyes closed, fighting against the pain; or just trying to draw in a breath was torture.

Focus, damn you, he thought. *You have to focus.*

When he opened his eyes again, Lucifer was gone, leaving Declan on his hands and knees, coughing and gasping for air. He crawled to the bench, pulling himself onto it and forced himself to gain control. He was breathing now, the pain easing to a more manageable level. Focusing on drowning it out helped, but Lucifer had done more than cause agony with a simple touch, he'd drained him; not completely, but noticeably enough he would have to feed much sooner than planned.

Declan got up and started walking, unsteady at first, and then a little more sure. The sun had finally set and darkness was beginning to cover everything in thick shadows. If he was going to retrieve the artifact, now was the time. He headed to the forested area which banked against the abbey as his thoughts twisted and turned, trying to form some formidable plan for breaking inside and getting out undetected. There was no doubt in his mind the ride on the easy train was over.

I got the call just after sunset and I was on a plane not five hours later. I went alone. I needed Abe and Alex to stay in my stead, but there was somewhere else I needed to be. Alex and Abe would stay with Sister Evangeline, interacting with the local authorities while trying to track down the motive behind the kidnapping and robbery.

My goal was simple. Bodies had been located. Brother Joshua pulled strings to keep the crime scene under wraps. Only a few of his most trusted companions were allowed in. They were waiting for me.

A blank-faced man in a sports coat and jeans picked me up at Louisville International Airport and took me directly to a nondescript cabin a few miles from Crestwood. I sat back, watching the scenery go by for a few minutes when we hit Curry Road, then turned onto an unnamed one-laner, paved for a couple of miles before morphing into a gravel road. Another turn, this one onto a three-mile rocky drive which led us to the cabin. There was a single car pulled up close to the front door of the little building and I hesitated in the passenger seat. My chauffeur wasn't the chatty type, and I was glad for it. I spent most of the ride on my cell phone, using Google Maps to try to survey the area, but the little cabin's roof was completely obscured by the lush trees overhead. I doubted anyone witnessed someone traveling down the drive. It was too remote.

I climbed out of the car, but my companion didn't move. I bent and looked at him through the open passenger door.

"Will you be here when I come out?"

"I will."

The quiet type, I guessed. I strolled the three short strides to the sagging wooden steps and climbed them, my eyes on the ground. If someone had been dragged in here, there was no sign. The door was closed, the panel intact. I pulled out a kleenex and used it to push the door open.

"Watch your step." The words were rough but they matched the speaker. The man wore rumpled tan pants and a polo that stretched a little tight across a rounded middle. His hair was two shades lighter than his dark brows arching above keen eyes. He was watching me closely, and I gave a sharp nod.

As soon as I stepped into the room, the horror of the scene completely overwhelmed me. I have seen some terrible things and I've seen brutal murders, but this was nothing like I had seen before.

There were two bodies, and the identity of the first was immediately recognizable. Sister Mary Carmella had not died easily. Her face was dark, the whites of her eyes shot with bloody lines betraying the strangulation even before I saw the bruising on her throat. She lay on the floor, body broken, still in death. But her body was intact wherein poor Slyvie was not.

If I hadn't known the girl was missing for a short time, I would have believed the figure on the bed was a spoil from some tomb raider's unlawful activity. Either that or I'd been transported via the twilight zone to a museum featuring a modern-day sadistic mummy exposition. Long and lifeless hair sprawled across the pillow which supported nothing more than a dry and blackened skull with empty round sockets where eyes had once been. Lips, black as coal, were drawn back from a grinning set of teeth in an eternal grimace. The skin, dark and leathery, stretched over the body of bones which lay in a supine position with arms stretched out against the headboard; wrists which were probably bound tight to the bedposts, now hung limply in the white zip ties which held them.

I stayed in the doorway, my breath caught in my chest. This was not what I anticipated, and I knew the bodies were here.

"What did this?" I didn't mean to speak aloud, but the man standing behind me took it as a question.

"Nothing in heaven or on earth," he replied.

I was silent for a long moment before I walked into the room further. It was mostly bare, not a comfortable place for a tryst. And why did Slyvie and Sister Mary come here? How did they travel so far without being tracked?

I eased closer to the body on the bed. Sister Mary's cause of death was easy to assume. She was beaten and strangled. Her clothes were not displaced. If there was any torture done, it wasn't drastic.

But Slyvie? I doubted even those who knew her best would recognize her now. She looked as though she had been dead for centuries, not days, sucked dry from time and a constant heat.

"We know it's her?" I didn't turn my head to ask the question but kept my gaze leveled on the corpse.

"Yes." The man behind me stepped forward until I could see his shape in my periphery.

"Dental records?"

"Yes."

I knew this man did not go through the proper channels for identification. I knew he had connections, however, and I wondered what poor pathologist was brought here to examine the body to help the identification.

"She has a very specific dental repair from a childhood accident on the left side of the upper mandible. There is no doubt at all this is our victim."

I stepped closer. The room was full of the sour stench of death, hours old, and a peculiar undertone of something. I stood very still, inhaling delicately. The scent was strongest closer to the bed, closer to Slyvie. An overlay of lavender, yes, no doubt the floral scent permeated both women's clothing, but there was another…

"Do you smell it?" I stood over the bed and tried to ignore the desiccated figure in front of me.

He stepped to my side, his shoes making the faintest sound against the wooden floorboards. He was very still for a moment.

"Like perfume," he said.

I cast him a sideglance.

"Floral," he continued. "And there's something, spicy perhaps. That's not the right description, though." He was silent.

I turned and looked at him. He was studiously normal, incredibly unremarkable. Most of Brother Joshua's crew were like that. Except, of course, Victor, the Hand of God himself. But just because this man didn't stand out didn't mean he wasn't smart, and there was something in the stillness of him which made my senses come alive.

"You know what did this, don't you?"

He looked toward me. "I pray for all our sakes that I am wrong," he answered.

———

Declan moved swiftly and quietly through the dark wooded area. The night cooled some of the heat of the day, yet did little for the humid air broken only by a slight breeze which didn't do much more than ruffle against the leaves of the trees. He could smell the rain in the air, but the sky before entering the forest was relatively clear, so if it was on the way he should have time to get in and out of here before the sky opened up.

Since the Abbey was off a distance from the road, traffic noise didn't pollute the air. An occasional cricket chirped but aside from that the area was nearly silent. The moon was the curve of a fingernail waxing towards full, enough of a muted glow for him to navigate through the trees and brush with human eyes. Were it full dark, the eyes he'd been created with would have been needed; eyes providing perfect vision but not useful when stealth was required as the lavender hue tended to become luminescent when there was no light. He slowed his pace, then halted, spotting the break in the line of foliage. Through spaces between branches and leaves, he could see scant bits of faded color illuminated from the lunar glow, revealing the lavender field beyond. He paused here and contemplated many possible outcomes once he broke through the cover of the forest.

Stepping forward, he eased one of the branches aside and scanned what space it allowed. Positioned on an incline, Declan found his view better than he could have hoped; were he on level ground with the structure he would need to exercise a bit more caution and walk further down the tree line to catch a different angle or two.

The field with its rows of blooming lavender went on for quite an expanse before butting up against a stone wall that ran the length of the side portion of the abbey. The entrance to the tunnel Slyvie used, thankfully, was barely a fourth of that distance so he wouldn't have to be without cover for long but it would be enough for anyone who might be watching his way to catch sight of him. Declan gazed at the huge stone building. Two of the windows on the lower section of this side were filled with light, the rest were darkened. He studied all of them, the dark ones the most, and then lifted his eyes upward to the roof. Confident this angle of the building was secure of prying eyes, he moved his sights to the stone-sided dorm-like structure connected to the right of the main building, almost like that of an arm hanging by the shoulder. It was two stories with a huge window consisting of many smaller ones on the ground level. Several other normal-sized apertures flanked on either side of it and above it on the second and third stories. None of the windows were lit up and it took him a few moments to check each one for shadowed witnesses. There weren't any.

Declan retreated back into the forest line and began moving to the right towards a small copse of trees nestled within the field. Slyvie told him the sisters didn't have the heart to plow over the little island of lush evergreens. Perhaps it was that evergreens weren't prominent in the area or they just loved them, or possibly it was the large boulder nestled in the center of the copse; an icon put there either by accident or design weathering season after season for as long as Slyvie knew. Whatever their reason for leaving the copse unplowed, Declan imagined the nuns used its shade to take a break and cool themselves whenever they were working in the hot sun. When the abbey was constructed Slyvie told Declan they included many tunnels beneath it, catacombs so numerous that when the old regime moved on to their just desserts the knowledge of several of these passageways died with them. The village girl entered into one of only a few the order knew about, and even fewer used. She exited the same way and with a coaxing nuzzle of his lips upon the tender skin of her neck, she told him how to find it. Satisfied with himself for thinking ahead, Declan eased his way back to the forest line and scanned the area once more before moving through the field a short distance to the copse.

CHAPTER SEVEN

I was close enough to my little Middletown home just on the outskirts of Louisville to stop there for the night. The familiar setting went a far way in comforting me. The sight of the two women, one an innocent victim, the other a warrior of God, made my stomach twist in anger. This wasn't the usual man's inhumanity to man which showed up on the evening news every night. This was something otherworldly, like nothing I'd experienced before.

It was late and I was tired, but there was a phone call I needed to make, no way I was going to get any rest unless I spoke to someone at the abbey. I glanced at the clock. The sisters would be awake. Prayer times were round the clock at the Abbey following the age-old cycle instituted by the church long ago. But it was a little late for Matins, a little too early for Lauds. Chances were, the sisters would be resting, if a restless sleep, at least in their rooms. I used the cell phone to call Abe.

The phone buzzed once and Abe's voice, while hushed, sounded in my ear, clear enough he could have been standing next to me in the room. I didn't know what cell phone carrier he used, but maybe it was pumped with a little supernatural juice to get the connection so clear.

"Abe," I said in greeting. "It's me. I'm back at my house. I've gone to the scene, and it's not," I hesitated, "it's not good."

"Then the bodies were…"

"Sister Mary and Slyvie," I finished for him, "a positive identification. Sister Mary was easy. She died of strangulation or a beating. The petechial hemorrhaging in her eyes was evident. But there were also multiple contusions. No autopsy yet, so there could be internal injuries."

I paused and Abe stayed silent, seemingly giving me the time I needed.

"She fought," I said, firming my voice. "She fought hard and well. Slyvie's body concerns me the most. It was," I paused again, searching for the correct term. "It was mummified."

"What?" His voice held all the disbelief I felt. And it wasn't as if I hadn't seen things die in strange ways before. The infernal lords I faced in the past were no more human than a squirming fly, and their death was spectacularly wrong, their bodies going from apparent flesh and blood to dark ash, disintegrating into nothing with the breath of a strong wind.

"I don't know what this is, and by the looks on the faces of the people I've contacted here, they are as baffled as I am. Whatever this is, it isn't one of Brother Joshua's boogie men they come across all the time." I took a deep breath and strolled across my living room floor. My overnight bag was at my feet, but I was unsettled. I strolled down the hallway and into my bedroom. My closet door was closed. I pushed it open and shoved the hanging clothes aside, most of them staging for my hidden doorway in the rear of the space. Behind the loose boards was a long slender case. I couldn't fly with my katana, and having it in my hand made me feel so much better. I pulled the case out and laid it across my bed.

"How are the sisters?"

I could hear Abe moving around, imagine him raising his hands high in the air, arching his back and stretching up and then out as far as his fingers would go before straightening his stance, lowering his arms down towards his sides slowly in a sunset motion. He was no doubt in his room. I heard him stifle a yawn.

"Everyone refused to try and sleep at first but they finally relented." I heard him move around the room as I settled on my bed and flipped open the weapon's case. "Alex insisted she stay awake to help guard the Abbey, and then the sisters joined in with the same argument." He sighed. "And they insist on the same schedule for prayer."

I nodded. I knew there would be no arguing over the prayer part; indeed if there was ever a time for prayer this was it. Whatever creature, man or beast, which set its sights onto Aelis was a cause for some intense prayer if there ever was one.

"I eventually reasoned with Alex, allaying her stubborn refusal with the very honest fact she would have to relieve me of my post as sentry so I could sleep." He was quiet for a second and I thought I heard a slow opening of the door. "I told her then she could be all the mighty guard she wanted to be. Argument finished. Case closed."

"She's stubborn," I agreed. "But she's capable."

"Yeah, well, she was not so bad compared to the sisters. The abbey is their home, I get it. But, unlike many orders who rely only on God and the Saints for protection, these women take the saying of God helps those who help themselves to heart. They are nearly impossible to reason with, and have every intention of standing their ground, protecting it, and overcoming whatever or whoever has the audacity to commit such heinous crimes."

I could hear the easy brush of his stride and knew he was walking the halls again. He kept his voice pitched low, and the reception of his cell phone impressed me again. Those were thick stone walls, and the signal shouldn't have been as clear. I wasn't complaining.

"They are tough women," I agreed.

"Oh, I have no doubt they would succeed, but everyone needs to rest sometime and since Alex and I are here to walk the halls and tunnels anyway, it would be a shame to waste the opportunity."

As for prayer, God would hear their petitions whether they were said while guarding the abbey or at their bedside, I was sure. And I knew Abe was right. Even if sleep was out of their reach, they'd get some much-needed rest all the same.

I looked into the open case, my free hand caressing the handle of the katana, the single-sided curved blade reflecting the ceiling light with a slice of brilliance.

"Where are you now?"

"I've climbed the stone stairway from the basement level," Abe replied. "I've already walked a few of the tunnels completely from end to end." I heard him take a deep breath. "My stent as the sentry is nearly at an end. Alex and Sister Anna will take over and give me a few hours of sleep."

I was silent for a moment, just listening through the phone at the sounds of his movements.

"Where are you now?" I asked again as I pulled out the soft cloth from the case and was gently running the fabric up and down the blade.

"Top of the steps," he replied. I was sure he was walking quietly. His voice was a mere breath in my ear. I could picture him drifting along the stone floor, his footsteps barely a whisper in the quiet as he checked out the ground floor of the building.

"It all looks secure here," he continued, "but I'm going to make one final check." I thought of him wandering through the halls, cracking open doors to rooms that were for general use and ensuring all was well. It made me feel better to know he was there, keeping watch over those I valued more than my own life.

"Well," his voice was pitched low.

"What? Where are you?"

"Third floor," he replied slowly. "It's just something…" his voice drifted. "I'm going to check all the doors again."

I sensed rather than heard his progress down the long corridor, checking the locked doors or glancing in the darkened rooms before moving on. The feeling intensified when he approached the hidden room the sisters believed to be secure.

"I'm at the far room," Abe began, and then let out a sharp inhalation. "When I touched the false cabinet with the palm of my hand, I felt something, a buzzing vibration which spiraled from the center of my palm like an etching along my fingers and thumb."

"Considering what is stored in there, it can't be a surprise you might sense some of the residual energy." I stopped polishing my blade.

"I agree," he responded, "but there is something else, a hint of underlying, I don't know, familiarity maybe?" He waited for a beat. "I'm going inside to make sure all is safe." I heard the almost inaudible click of the catch opening up the false cabinet entrance, and listened as he stepped inside the hidden room.

———

Declan found the entrance to the tunnel from Slyvie's directions at the foot of one of the evergreens next to the boulder. Lifting the trapdoor by the metal ring centered on one end, it opened soundlessly; a huge yawn revealing its cellar-like steps leading underground. Pulling it closed behind him, he descended the stairs which seemed more like cuts in the dry earth than rock and moved along in the darkness with ease. When he reached the stone wall indicating the dead-end Slyvie spoke of, Declan ran his fingers over the unnaturally smooth surface until he found a catch about halfway down. The wall gave and slid forward, leaving a crack from ceiling to floor to his right. He pulled it to him and it came with barely a sound, allowing him to step through.

The hidden door slid closed and latched immediately back into place, and Declan walked on, turning the corner to a stairway leading up. Here, the darkness was broken at marked intervals with small round lights embedded in the stone and putting out just enough illumination to navigate the stairs without having to resort to his inhuman sight. He banked around the first landing and then up another flight where a closed-door indicated the ground floor. Up two more to the second, and another two flights to the third. His tread made not a sound as he climbed with effortless grace up the stairs.

Third floor, he thought, *flannel nighties, women's lingerie, and questionable artifacts.*

The stairs were separated from the corridor by an outcropping stone wall where a wash of dim light gave him pause, not totally unexpected since the nuns most likely discovered the theft by now, but unnerving all the same. There was also a sense of familiarity which tickled at him. Ridiculous. He'd never been inside of Aelis before.

He could turn back now and leave the way he'd come with no one the wiser, but Lucifer would have a field day with him if he left without the amulet. Asmodeus was bad enough, but Lucifer? Best not to think about it.

Erring on the side of caution, he lifted the leg of his jeans and gently pulled the dagger out of its sheath before easing around the outcrop and forcing himself forward towards the room. He was less than a few steps in when the shadow of a person flicked across the rectangle of light on the floor. The darkened form moved back into the light and Declan ascertained it to be either a man or a freakishly tall woman, but shadows were nothing if not deceptive so he ceased his advance and shifted to one side of the door, flattening his back against the wall. With the dagger held tightly in his grip, he waited and he watched.

CHAPTER EIGHT

"Turn on your camera," I demanded. I was impatient, but my senses were sounding the alarm. Abe was not one to worry unnecessarily.

I saw my phone screen flicker to life and a quick flash of Abe's face, his smile lopsided and a little condescending.

"I'm just going to check the shelves," he explained. He turned the phone so I could watch him as he ran his hand over one of the shelves of artifacts. It was an almost absent-minded gesture like a shopper going through a fuzzy pillow and blanket display feeling the soft brush of the material while passing. Except, in this case, he and I both knew better than to touch the myriad of objects with a bare hand. There were some things which these pieces of metal, leather, and glass could carry with them, things which couldn't be washed off no matter how hard you scrubbed.

So much power. So much intensity. So much trouble waiting to happen.

The sisters appointed themselves to one huge undertaking in

keeping these things safely hidden out of the public eye, away from wicked hands which could possibly use them for less than holy pursuits. And now this; the breach of such a well-hidden storage area and the theft of an artifact of which even Sister Eva knew very little. I didn't envy the holy women. The responsibility was tremendous. And the repercussions of such a loss? Who knew?

I watched as he pulled his hand away and then passed it over the shelf beneath the first.

"I feel the same buzzing thrum of power as I felt from the other objects," he said. His fingers reached the far edge and then jerked back as though burnt.

"Jesus, Mary and Joseph…" he breathed, and I watched as he shook his hand vigorously as if he were attempting to regain feeling in it.

"What was it? What happened?" I was snapping at him, and I knew it. The phone with its flashlight was focused toward his hand as he examined his skin.

"The prickles radiated down my fingers and thumb, like before, but much stronger," Abe muttered. He was silent as he gave himself a moment before leaning into the cabinet to peer at what caused his discomfort, the cold illumination of the cell phone flashlight showing every sharp edge. Near the back corner, encircled within a few inches of an empty shelf, was a small black cylinder-shaped object. Abe's bare hand disappeared as he pulled out a white handkerchief, using the fabric to cover the piece before he lifted it out to get a better look.

The light from the cell phone washed over the slick black texture of the object revealing a slight tinge of a faded marbling so subtle it could easily be missed. He tilted it in the light, studying the faint curving lines before using the handkerchief to flip it over for a view of the other side.

"It looks like petrified wood. Black petrified wood. Less than two inches long and no wider than a centimeter." He narrated the description as he held the object close to the phone. He shifted it from end to end, and I noted no markings etched on either end. He tilted it in the light, examining the lone small hole on one side near what might be the top of the piece. The hole could have been a natural occurrence or a manmade feature by the use of a drill or awl. Either way, a length of chain, string, or leather could be easily threaded through the hole so the piece could be worn as a necklace or bracelet.

"What do you think it is?" I asked.

Abe didn't respond right away, and his break of silence told its own story. We were both in the dark about this one.

———

Declan hugged the wall adjacent to the door of the room. The shadow of a human form on the floor was holding something up. He focused on the object, a hard feat considering the constant buzzing hum which was drilling into his ears.

What in blazes was the noise? The hum of the thing's power?

He took a deep breath and held it. One. Two. Three. *Steady now.* A slow blink and exhale, quiet as a bloody mouse. One. Two. Three. *There, really look at what it's in the shadow's hand.*

It was the piece Lucifer described, at least in shape and size anyway. He wasn't completely certain of course, the object was just a shadow after all but the feeling of familiarity was stronger here, much stronger. And there was the buzzing of what he believed might be the power to consider. He caught sight of a subtle glowing outline around the artifact. Had it been yellowish or even one of the many shades of white, he'd have mistaken the radiance for a trick of the lighting, but the outline was more of a faded green like an unpolished emerald. He chanced a glance into the room and saw the emerald hue was absent, only the color one might expect from a cell phone the man held in his free hand. The fake metal cabinet stood with its door gaped open to reveal the hidden room and the tall lanky man standing in the near dark, holding the object in some sort of white cloth. He looked like the guy in the village square walking with the beautiful woman named Alex earlier. Declan inhaled deeply through his nose to try and pick up the man's scent; the smell of stone, drying lavender, and a musty odor of a closed-up room wafted to him. Beneath it, he recognized the smell of the cologne. He closed his eyes to concentrate, probing deeper. There was nothing, just as before; definitely the same guy but there was something more and it took Declan just a second to recognize what it was.

The familiarity he'd been feeling, first at the square, and now here wasn't from the artifact, not at all. It was from the man; the tall, dark, and fugly man with the glasses and the sour expression. He knew him. But where? He'd walked the Earth for a thousand years or more and had seen a hell of a lot of people, forgotten a lot of people, lived his own so-called life way past countless human lifetimes.

Declan stared for a moment, watching the man tilt the black cylindered object in the light, first one way and then the other, studying it. He turned his eyes back to the shadow on the floor and noticed the artifact's outline pulsed with the tilting movements.

An outline of light within a shadow? It's physically impossible, he thought. *Isn't it? This has to be what the old devil wants. It has to be. And who is this fucking git holding it? Why is he holding it? Why---*

The shadowed man lowered his hand and spoke again in a

low voice, barely audible in the velvet darkness. Was he talking to himself? What kind of lunatic was this? But no, he could see the screen on the phone was lit, and a second voice emerged from the shiny piece of technology, a woman's voice? Maybe Alex? And then the tall man angled away from the cabinet and began folding the object into the cloth before tucking it into the front pocket of his pants. The buzzing sound became muffled to barely a whisper.

Declan scooted further into the cover of shadow, thankful the irritating noise was dumbed down. He could actually hear tall, dark, and lanky's side of the conversation and when he forced himself to concentrate, the woman's voice came to him clearer.

"I don't know," the man said, "but I think it would be a bad decision to leave it here with all of the others."

"Get it to Sister Eva then," the woman's voice said. "If anyone knows what to do with it, she will. And you're right. There's so much residual energy in the room, anything could happen. Did you feel anything like it when we found the rose?"

Declan felt a wry smile on his lips, satisfied the red flower had been discovered. There was something mysteriously romantic about leaving one whenever he took something; an artifact, a life, something lost and something gained. It was a shot better than what was taken from him, where any payment which might be made was given in the currency of agonizing pain and misery. The man's voice yanked him out of his thoughts.

"Just the baseline of energy I would have expected," was the reply.

There was an aggravated sigh on the other end of the line.

"Then something or *someone* woke it up. Either way, it's no longer idle and definitely not safe."

A pause in the conversation allowed Declan another moment to think. What could have awakened the piece? It wasn't him, surely. He'd just gotten here. And he seriously doubted it was the man's doing, otherwise the thing should have been going all bells and whistles when he was in close contact with it the first time.

So, not him, not me, and highly unlikely it was the woman on the phone. Who then? A nun?

"I'm heading on up," the man said. "I doubt Sister Eva is asleep."

"Probably not," the woman said. "When you're squared away, I need you both here. Brother Joshua's people have arranged for the flight and they'll have someone waiting at Louisville International to pick you up."

The sound of metal rubbing against metal reached Declan's ears and drowned out the other side of the phone conversation. There was a click, probably the fake cabinet door latching closed, and footsteps coming out into the room in front of the hidden one. He moved away from the door and further into the darkness as the light was extinguished, leaving only the dull glow of what he believed to be the man's phone. The door shut and Declan waited, counting slowly in his head as the man passed on by him without a hint of notice, still carrying on the conversation which grew more muffled and incoherent as the phone went down the third-floor steps with the man. If Declan didn't intercept tall, dark and lanky before he reached this Sister Eva, the entire night would be buggered and there would literally be Hell to pay.

Declan moved silently down the corridor, waited until he heard the scuffing sound of a shoe sole against the stone...a pause...and then more scuffing indicating the second floor was reached, before taking the steps himself. Pulling upon his other-worldly resources, he covered the distance gracefully and without a sound. The third story cleared and then the second.

The man's shadow bounced along the wall as he descended.

Declan turned his eyes upward to the low stone ceiling where this section of the stairway was encased. He clinched the dagger's blade longways between his teeth like some storybook pirate diving off the gangplank to take on the Kraken and then sprung straight up, defying gravity and latching onto the stone above. With his legs splayed, his boots unnaturally fixed to the stone, and with fingers spread, he scrambled along the ceiling headfirst like some huge spider.

Overtop the man still talking on the phone and oblivious to what prowled above, Declan readjusted his grip on the ceiling and released his boots from the stone. Closing and straightening out his legs, he swung them out behind him and connected with enough force to the upper middle portion of the guy's back to send him careening off the remaining stairs and tumbling to the first floor below. There was a grunting gasp followed by the faint sounds of something heavy meeting rock and scuffing a few feet along before the momentum died and the noise stopped altogether. Declan swung his legs up and then back out again as he let go of the ceiling and backflipped into the air, landing right behind the sprawled out man. Dropping the dagger into his hand, he whipped around ready to grab the man by the hair, slit his throat, and retrieve the amulet. The woman's voice was coming from the cell phone still in the guy's hand.

"Abe? Are you okay? What's going on?"

The name gave Declan pause and his mind scrambled to put it to memory.

Abe...Abe...I knew an Abe once, didn't I?

Abe jumped to his feet and whirled around to face Declan as he put the phone back to his ear. "I'll have to call you back."

I have heard the voice before, Declan thought. *Where?*

Not waiting for a reply from the woman, Abe ended the call and set the phone down on the floor. The black-rimmed glasses were off, possibly flung into the darkness wherever physics took them, and there was a nice gash surrounded by an impressive friction burn on the left side of the guy's face just below his eye.

"Who are you?" Abe asked, backing up a couple of steps.

"Whoever you want me to be, mate," was Declan's reply as he flipped the dagger end to end in his hand as if he were tossing nothing more than a coin. "The real question is who are *you*?"

The man glared defiantly at him.

"What? No answer? Bloody shame." Declan took two steps closer and angled his position to Abe's left; the side which appeared to have taken most of the damage from the meeting with the stone floor, the weaker side. "See, I know damn well you aren't human."

Although the light was significantly dim, Declan could still make out the space of creased skin between Abe's eyebrows which were now downturned, furrowed. There was no mistaking the sudden hardness in the man's eyes, nor was there any question his body was readying itself for a fight. Rather than rigidly tensing up, Abe's form appeared to relax in a stance trained in martial arts, as if this moment was nothing more than an everyday occurrence. Subtly turning his wounded side away from Declan's advance, he lifted his arms up with his stronger right to the front to block any incoming blows and the weaker left to push the offensive should the opportunity arise, his fingers spread in a natural fashion and his stance shifted slightly to pull on core strength when the need called for it.

Declan stopped, snapped the dagger out of the air by the handle without so much as a glance to see what its position in space might be in the descending rotation, and pointed the tip of the blade at Abe.

"You've got no smell," Declan said with a wry smile.

Abe's expression grew more stern. "I say again, who *are* you?"

Declan ignored the question and continued. "Everything *smells*, mate; alive or dead, human or animal, from the halls of heaven to the bowels of hell there is always some odiferous imprint to tell who they are and where they're from. But you? Nope, not one measly trickle of a scent beneath your cheap cologne. So the real question is who the fuck are *you*?"

Abe said nothing and Declan feared this was going to be the standoff of the century, the man just kept matching his trek step by step as if he were contemplating something more than just their tedious little dance. If something didn't go soon, the blasted nuns were going to be up for prayer, chants, and whatever else they were known to do so early in the morning and they'd find them both still circling the drain. The last thing he needed was the sting of prayers upon him and if it did happen, he'd bloody well rather have them at his backside as he distanced himself from this overly righteous place.

Best get to it, he thought.

Declan charged forward, thrusting the dagger ahead of him. Abe blocked it from reaching the side of his body with a left arm but the point cut deep into his skin and then slid along the flesh until Declan retracted it, ready for another strike. Abe grunted in obvious pain and covered the wound with his hand, a reaction which seemed a tad dramatic for just a cut. Glancing down at the blade, Declan saw the blood coating the tip, no big surprise there but what really got his attention was the etched figure of the dragon near the hilt. It was moving.

What the hell?

When he looked up from the dragon whose etched eyes glowed a perilous crimson while its outspread wings beat against the air and its reptilian tail writhed, Abe was right there to take his opportunity. A fist drove into Declan's mouth and he could taste the metallic hint of blood on the man's knuckles when the flesh broke open from the blow. Declan's head whipped back, taking his body with it. His back hit flat against one of the stone pillars with enough force to comprise the masonry. There was a loud reverberating crack and Declan barely rolled out of the way of the collapsing rock. He started to get up and couldn't. The metallic flavor of Abe's blood grew more potent and suddenly the world seemed to be spinning, his vision was blurring, and his ears started ringing. He could just barely make out the tall man's retreat from the dimly lit and expansive room when he heard the sound of a door opening and pounding feet coming closer. The nuns most probably heard the commotion and were heavenly bent on being reinforcements.

Get up! Declan thought. *Get the fuck up and get out!*

He managed to regain his feet enough for a stumbling run to the cellar stairway. One step down, he lost his balance and tumbled along the first flight. Crawling on the landing, he pulled himself up to stand, wavered drunkenly, and continued. When he reached the tunnels, the dizziness was almost unbearable but he pressed on out the way he'd entered through the copse of trees and into the wooded area where he finally collapsed to his knees. The dagger was still in the grip of his hand, but he barely took notice as he bowed forward and vomited in great straining heaves. He could still taste Abe's blood in his mouth, faint, but there. The blackness of unconsciousness threatened to take him, but his mind whirled around a memory instead.

"Whoever did this knew what they were doing, Max. I'm certain of it. Look at her."

Max did and the sight sickened him. A large slash across her neck indicated at least one if not both arteries were severed. She would have bled out quickly, the better for her as the cutting didn't appear to have stopped there. He stared at the front of her dress, hiked up to reveal a gaping abdomen. Part of her intestine lay next to her while another two-foot section was stretched up and laid over her chest and neck like some sort of sickly twisted scarf; all of it smeared in shit.

"The bastard rummaged around inside of her," Max's partner said, "and I'll bet my last bloody Bob she's missing a part or two."

Max gave Abraham an intense look of disgust. He wasn't squeamish about blood and guts. One human year in the bowels of Hell relieved him of any such weakness. But he did find some of the things humans did to one another disturbing. There were demons who weren't as brutal as some human beings and he was a perfect example. Yes, he took his fair share of lives, but not like this. Inspector Declan Maxwell Faulkner of Scotland Yard found murder illegal and immoral. Declan Maxwell Faulkner the incubus, found murder necessary for his survival but brutality was extremely distasteful and unnecessary.

Max refrained from rooting around in the dead woman's abdomen to confirm Abe's suspicion. If this monster went to all the trouble to cut through several layers of tissue and pull out more than just a few feet of bowel, then it was safe to assume the killer was looking for something.

"I agree," Max replied. "The wounds are the same as the other victims."

Abe shook his head in dismay. "Ripe bastard, he is. It'll take all my reserve to keep me from strangling the man once we catch him."

Max gazed down at the woman's mutilated corpse and sighed.

"I'm afraid you'll have to get in line, mate."

· · ·

A fresh round of dry heaves convulsed Declan's body as sweat beaded on his skin, running trails downward until there was no longer space for it to run, gravity took over and pulled it off of him dripping onto the thirsty ground. The breeze, so warm earlier, now felt cold against him. He backed away from the pile of vomit as if it were something as dangerous as acid and swiped his mouth with the back of his hand. The small taste of Abe's blood still on his tongue.

"You poor bastard," Declan groaned, "you should've left well enough alone."

CHAPTER NINE

I couldn't help but worry even though I was pretty certain Abe could take care of himself. So could the sisters really, now they were wise to the danger which threatened them. Alex proved herself in battle, no longer to be classified as a damsel in distress as if she ever were. No, they could all handle themselves and I would just have to be patient; steep a cup of calm the hell down tea and wait. I put the katana back in the case and closed the lid. I didn't like it. I didn't like being so far away from Abe and Alex, but I needed to be here. This was the crime scene as much as the Abbey.

I made a few quick phone calls, reaching out to some of Brother Joshua's followers. After I was assured there would be back up arriving at the Abbey in the morning, hoping it would be some of Vic's posse, I felt much better about my request. I needed Alex and Abe to come home. The crime scene would have to be cleaned up soon and supernatural clues were not something left around for any poor schmuck who happened to be walking in the woods to come upon. Alex needed to see the body of Slyvie before it was moved, perhaps her medical background and workable knowledge of the supernatural world could provide some sort of insight on the young woman's death. Brother Joshua's people were equipped with the same credentials but I trusted Alex's opinion more; and Abe's. I wasn't sure what he could add to the mix but something deep in my gut said a helluva lot.

Abe's call came about a half an hour later. He and Alex were leaving the Abbey shortly to head to the airport. When I asked him what happened, he responded in his normally cool, calm, and collected way. He would fill me in when he arrived, not over the phone. Since there was a whole lot I didn't know about him, I respected his decision and refrained from badgering about the artifact even though I was really wanting to find out what Sister Eva knew about it.

Easing the katana back into its customary space, I stood and stretched. After a long flight and a long day, my body needed rest even if my brain didn't want to turn off. I would have felt better about it if my two canine companions were here. Fluffy and Bart were being watched by the local veterinarian who now cared for their medical needs. The clinic offered boarding, but I knew the vet took the dogs to his own home rather than leaving them in the small kennels. The two big dogs apparently got along swimmingly with his rescued greyhounds.

I put my overnight bag on the bed and took out the necessities before heading for the shower. With any luck, my partners would be back soon. In the meantime, I needed to discover what sort of monster made mummies out of his victims.

———

Ernestine was waiting for him when Declan finally made it back to the empty parking lot. He got in, shut the door, and just sat there in the driver's seat for a moment.

What the bleeding hell happened? It was a simple plan. Get in. Get the thing. Get out. Where in those three tasks, those short simple tasks mind you, could there possibly have been room for this shit? He glanced down at the hand which miraculously still held onto the dagger. Turning the handle, he studied it with eyes which were just now starting to clear. The dragon above the hilt was the same image as before, drawn into the metal as furious and threatening, but still a drawing nonetheless and unmoving. Did he imagine it? Possibly.

He set the dagger on the passenger seat, unconvinced it was the weapon which caused his what? Dizzy spell with bonus hallucinations of a past long fucking gone? He didn't believe it was the dagger, not all by itself anyway, but it wounded Abraham and in turn, the blood which repulsively tasted like copper put one hell of a whammy on him. Declan leaned back onto the headrest. And Abe, good old Abe, ex-partner, ex-friend, but was he an ex where their friendship was concerned?

"No mate," he whispered, " you just up and died. Now, what the hell are you doing on this plane of existence?"

No one answered of course.

Declan rubbed his face with both hands, feeling the dampness of sweat from his bout of vomiting, and started the engine, turning the air conditioning to full blast. His scent of lavender and amber wafted around the inside of the car as if he'd just stepped out of the shower.

He laid his hand on the gear shift ready to set Ernestine to rolling. To where? No idea, but maybe a drive would do him good, clear his head. Now wasn't the time to ponder over Abe. There were bigger problems. He'd left the abbey without the artifact which was bad news for him. Lucifer was going to be pissed. Declan glanced up as he depressed the brake and saw a dark-colored sedan coming his way. He paused, noting the two shadowed occupants in the front seat, and threw caution to the wind, quickly shifting his eyesight to his demon side. The two people were Alex in the driver's seat and Abe riding shotgun. There was an expression of intense determination on her face. Abe's eyes were closed, his head back on the rest as if he were sleeping, but somehow Declan sincerely doubted this was the case. The car sped on by curving around one of the many statues on the way out of the village.

He closed his eyes, shutting down the sight, and then reopened them to a substantially darker view of the lot and the winding road beyond. The woman on the phone, what did she say? He pulled his foot off the brake and drummed the tips of his fingers on the head of the gearshift in a slow rhythm. Louisville International, he remembered now. They were supposed to meet up with a driver at the airport in Kentucky.

Declan reached over, flipped open the glove box, and pulled out a disposable cell phone he'd stashed there for such purpose as this. He turned it on, pressed in the number from memory, and waited. The call was picked up after two rings.

"Yeah?" The voice was gruff and the accent midwestern.

"Do you have a plane ready in Paris?"

"Yep. Where to?" the voice asked.

"My old Kentucky home," Declan said.

The man gave him the gate number and told him where the plane would be. Declan hung up and tossed the phone back into the glove compartment, shifting Earnestine into drive and pulling out of the lot. He kept his speed at a reasonable rate so as not to overtake the sedan, nor to tip Abe off should he actually be awake with his senses on full alert. At one point, about ten miles outside of Paris, he caught sight of a sedan's tail lights. He slowed Ernestine down, putting a much safer distance between them and drove to catch the plane waiting on him.

As promised, the plane was there with the engine running. Declan wiped the dagger's blade off with a rag from the glove box and then slid it back into the sheath strapped to his leg. Later, he would try to find out more about the weapon but for now, he would keep it with him. Whatever Abe was now, the dagger may very well be his only protection should they come to blows again. Yeah, the dagger in all of its ominous glory was staying with him.

CHAPTER TEN

I woke up late, surprised I slept so soundly on such a night. But then, exhaustion got the best of everyone, and the jet lag was real.

I left the house to grab breakfast, going by the local Kroger to pick some things from the shelves in an almost mechanical manner. My mind was on other things, on other bodies. I would need to do some serious research once I got back to the house and fired up the supercomputer, compliments of a handy geek friend of mine.

And if it didn't work, if there was nothing to be found there? What then?

Well, Brother Joshua was looking into our strange problem already, and even with several hours of a headstart and numerous sources, he didn't have any hint as to what killed Slyvie. So I definitely didn't deserve the frustration I was dealing out to myself.

I rubbed my forehead slowly, aware of the headache pushing behind my eyes. I needed coffee, but first I wanted to pick up the

TONY ACREE'S ABSOLUTION • 89

dogs. Fluffy and Bart were as much a part of our strange little team as any human, and I knew I might need to rely on their sharper senses to keep me aware of anyone who might be tracking my movements.

Could the Infernal Lords be behind the body in the cabin? Brother Joshua didn't believe it was their work, and I knew he was familiar enough with them to make the call. But if not them, then who?

I turned the car toward the vet office where the dogs were staying, my mind playing out the possibilities.

Would Paul know? Just the thought of the man who wasn't a man, the clever Infernal Lord who managed to pull me into his plot to overthrow his master, made my head ache a little more. Paul was smart though, and for some reason, I believed he harbored some sort of strange affection for me. Likely not romantic, but Paul let me escape from his funhouse of horrors and it made me suspect of his feelings and intentions.

Dare I approach him? No. Not yet.

I ran into the vets and left with two fierce-looking Dobermans.

———

Declan slept on the plane. As an incubus, sleep wasn't necessary, but when he sank deep into the plush seat of the luxury jet, he found himself completely drained. Whatever happened and whatever the repercussions, if there were any, was a complete mystery to him. Never in all the hundreds of years he walked the planet did he have anything like this happen before and he found it confusing and extremely unsettling, like he was being played by some bigger entity. His eyelids grew heavy and he was asleep before he could think any more about the situation or offer any protest to slumbering on a jet with him as the only passenger. The pilot woke him with an announcement over the intercom, they were approaching Louisville International and should be landing in ten to fifteen minutes. Declan stretched as far as the seat would allow before strapping himself in and awaiting the touchdown.

He didn't believe the woman on the phone was ordering Alex and Abe to good old Kentucky for the hell of it. Her voice sounded urgent from what little he'd overheard and he didn't need to have ESP to figure out his cabin was most likely discovered, complete with two corpses left lying in the bedroom. He hoped he was just being paranoid, but he doubted it was the case. He'd been careless, leaving them out where human eyes could see instead of disposing of the bodies somewhere else, far away from the cabin or the property it stood upon.

What's done is done, he thought. *Scratch one Kentucky cabin.*

He wouldn't be using it again, which was a shame really. He'd liked this one, remote but in decent condition, the perfect place to feed.

Declan grimaced. He was going to have to replenish soon or he'd find himself too weak to do more than whimper in a corner somewhere. And with his hideaway gone, or at the very least too dangerously risky to use, his options were limited. A complete feeding was out of the question, true, but maybe a partial would tide him over. Gazing out the window, watching the trees and houses get larger as the plane descended, he waited.

The sun was just breaking over the horizon when his plane landed and the pilot met him at the head of the debarking steps. He was a tall and slim built man, his pilot hat pulled down so it obscured most of his hair, what little showed just below the back and on the area next to his ears was dark with short lines of silver threaded through it. The pilot introduced himself and stuck out his hand for a shake. Declan smiled, relieved no one else was around and took the man's hand into his own. The middle-aged man smiled back as he began pumping Declan's hand up and down enthusiastically at first. And then the movement slowed as the overly and quite possibly fake smile began to fade, the pilot's eyes appeared dazed and took on a slightly lavender hue.

The incubus inhaled, allowing his hand to relax with the man's loosened grip. The pilot moaned and Declan felt the shudder of orgasmic pleasure rush through the man as some of the wisping life force was siphoned off and replaced simultaneously with raw lust. Breathing out in a slow exhale, Declan forced his flesh to cease absorbing. It would be enough to get him through.

"Nice flight," Declan said, easing his hand away.

The pilot blinked. And then blinked again. The normal color of his eyes returning as the lavender lightened and then vanished.

"Uh, thank you," the pilot replied, swiping the back of his hand over his now sweaty brow. "Do, uh, do you need me to stay in town for a flight back?"

The question was unsteady and stuttering as the man glanced down at the front of his pants where a small but noticeable wet spot covered the area right next to his zipper. The pilot's cheeks blazed red as he lifted his eyes up in the guilty way a teenage boy might appear after being caught red-handed wanking off behind the door believed to be locked. To save the man undue embarrassment, Declan pretended not to notice.

"That won't be necessary," Declan replied. "I'll take a commercial flight back."

The incubus pulled a couple of c-notes seemingly out of nowhere and slid them into the guy's hand, being careful not to linger skin-to-skin too long. The pilot nodded dumbly and thanked him as Declan took the steps off the plane and onto Kentucky ground.

———

There was something more to the story. I looked at Abe, his face haggard and pale, a swelling and purpling area under one eye which matched the split lip. Whatever occurred before they left France, it wasn't a good sendoff party with well wishes.

I shot Alex a look. "How was the flight?"

Alex looked back at me, all wide-eyed innocence. She was good at playing dumb, but I knew just how sharp her brain was underneath the lovely face.

"The flight was fine," she responded. "Amazing how they just happened to find tickets for us at the last minute." Her voice hinted at something, but I couldn't rise to the bait. Brother Joshua and his clan were equipped with a long reach and roots reaching deep into the digital system of our world. Arranging for tickets would have been child's play.

"Lucky," I muttered.

As I nosed the car into its parking space next to my tidy home, my eyes went first to the windows, lit from within but shaded by curtains and blinds. I put out one hand. "Let me check around," I said.

There were shadows of figures blocking the light, an impatient quick movement of form and shadow. I checked the knob. Despite my comment, both Alex and Abe slipped out of the car. I scowled in their direction but continued around to the back of the house. The barks sounded then, thunderous alarms warning any intruder this home was under the protection of trained guard dogs. I felt my shoulders ease as I pulled open the rear storm door and used my key in the lock. The perpetrators of the shadowy figures burst into the kitchen, all doggy smiles as they recognized me from scent.

"Did you keep my house safe?" I asked, not caring my voice changed to the all ooey-gooey with relief tone.

"You didn't think they would let anything in, did you?" Abe was at my back, carrying the two suitcases he and Alex packed for the journey. Typical. He looked like hell, but he would insist on carrying the bags. Ever the gentleman.

"I was pretty sure they wouldn't, but I wanted to make sure," I tossed over my shoulder. I didn't want to let on how antsy I was feeling. There was something not right with the recent crimes, and it was getting under my skin.

"Where do you want these?" Abe asked.

Alex followed Abe into the kitchen and gestured toward the short hallway. The house was built with three small bedrooms, and she was growing accustomed to staying in the guest room.

Abe nodded wordlessly and went down the hall. He was moving slow, though.

"What happened to him?" I asked in an undertone.

"He got into a scuffle with an intruder in the Abbey last night," Alex said, but held up a finger. "Don't worry. Sister Evangeline is well aware, and at this point, she suspected whoever was behind it may have been coming after us. She said they might be safer with us away."

I looked quizzically at her, but she just shrugged as Abe came in.

"I'm heading out now," Abe announced. He looked bad and I wondered if he was in much pain.

"You're not going anywhere until I've checked those stitches," Alex responded flatly.

"You don't have your kit, do you?" Abe raised an eyebrow in

his characteristic expression of doubt, but he didn't have his usual stoicism.

"It won't take me but a minute to run-up to the drug store and get the supplies," Alex responded tartly. "I'll check you over, but I don't think you should drive." She snatched the keys from the counter.

"I'll have someone pick me up." Abe ran a hand through his hair and I noticed his knuckles were bandaged as well.

"Are you going to tell me who did this to you?" I asked, my voice sharp.

"Not who," Abe answered, his eyes cutting to me. "What."

CHAPTER ELEVEN

The air felt heavy as Declan made his way across the tarmac and into the airport proper. A cool blast from the air conditioning unit above the sliding doors slid over him, ruffling his inky hair, and adding an unwanted chill. Not wasting time, he moved through the building, keeping his sights out for Abe and Alex. He doubted he'd find them in this traveler's chaos, but it didn't hurt to keep a sharp eye out. When he reached the front entrance, the doors swished open, allowing him to pass through and back out into the sweltering air. It was a far cry better than conditioned air, which only added to the frigid misery inside of him. Moving out of the way of a passerby, he pulled out his cell and made a request on the Uber app. Confirmation of his ride was immediate and less than ten minutes went by before a van pulled up. Well, almost a van. Probably was a van about fifty years ago, now it kind of resembled a small beached whale with the rotten luck of having helped itself to a hearty serving of spoiled plankton and, consequently, turned a nauseous shade of green. There were wheels though, but no hubcaps; the bulbous lug nuts stuck out like metal warts against the rusty background of the naked hub. The windshield had a nice crack in the center which seemed to have begun as a minor hole near the bottom and then stretched up at an unsteady incline as if it were part of a squiggly line on a Wall Street stock broker's financial chart.

Declan winced as the brakes squealed at the burden of halting the big sick whale's progress. The driver reached across to the passenger door and shoved it open, producing a horrible rusty hinge noise that set Declan's teeth on edge.

"Are you Mister Faulkner?"

Declan just remained there for a moment trying to decide if he should lie.

"I know she doesn't look like much but she'll do the job and take you where you need to go," the driver declared.

He wore black squarish-rimmed glasses typical of a 3D moviegoer. The lenses were slightly tinted some off-shade of brown but still translucent enough to see the guy's big blue eyes. The man gave Declan a reassuring smile which displayed a perfect line of white teeth in between a rather scraggly looking beard and mustache.

"I think there's been a mistake--" Declan said, then stopped not because of what the driver said next but because he caught sight of a black SUV passing by.

"Suit yourself, Mister, but the closest Uber will be a half an hour wait if you don't feel Big Bertha is up to snuff."

Declan vaguely heard the guy, his attention still caught onto the SUV. The windows were darkened so he couldn't see anything more than a driver who looked more like an insurance salesman than a chauffeur and two shadows in the back seat. One of the passenger windows gaped open a few inches, and it was more than enough to catch a scent.

"Alex," he breathed.

"No sir. Name's Russell. Russ, if you're nasty."

Declan looked back at the driver and tried for all his might to stop a smirk from coming on. He failed and laughed out loud to top it off.

"Now, there you go," Mister Call Me Russ If You're Nasty said. "I'll win you over with my charm and Big Bertha will carry you to your destination."

Declan climbed onto the seat, cringing as the rusty hinges screeched in protest while he clunked the door shut and strapped on what could very well have been the original seatbelt the manufacturer put in when this dilapidated piece of shit was built.

"Where to, Mister Faulkner?"

"See the black SUV up ahead?"

Russ gazed out of the windshield for a moment and then nodded.

"Follow it," Declan said, "but not too close. A blind chap could see this shit-green monster coming from a mile away."

The driver, Russel, Rus, Russ If You're Nasty, gave out a good-hearted belly laugh and shifted the POS into motion. The motor was decidedly quieter than Declan would have predicted given the thing's horrendous outward appearance and there was no backfire, which was a relief.

Once they were moving along the interstate at a steady rate of speed with the SUV in sight but several hundred feet ahead, Russ turned to Declan and stuck out a hand.

"No offense, but I try not to shake hands if I can help it," Declan said. "Germaphobe."

Russ withdrew his hand and beamed. "No worries. You're like that guy on Netflix. Monk?"

"I suppose," Declan said with a shrug. He knew what Netflix was, and he had an account, but the only Monks he knew about were the righteous bastards who did time in monasteries, making wine, and chanting up all worries and complaints to the man upstairs.

When Declan didn't offer any further comment, Russ piped up, delighted to have a captive audience at his disposal.

"You probably don't want to talk about it. My Gramma has a phobia of spiders. She swears up and down they're the devil, won't let us talk about them while we're around her and near pees herself when she sees a picture of one or if there's one on the T.V. I think if she ever saw one in person, she'd have what the docs call a myocardial infarction."

Declan did a double-take. "A what?"

"Heart attack, Mister Faulkner, a heart attack. It's just the doc's fancy way of saying it."

"Can you stop with the Mister stuff? Call me Declan."

Russ paused and nodded. "Declan. Okay. I can do. Just curious, are you from England?"

The incubus took a deep breath and held it. Normally, he would silence annoying chatter like this with a simple touch. Maybe even take a little taste while he was at it, but there was something he found intriguing about Mister Call Me Russ If You're Nasty and he figured it would be poor form to do that to him. The guy was nice after all, and to feed on someone when his hunger was reasonably sated at the moment was rude in his mind.

The SUV shifted and veered into the slow lane. Up ahead, Declan saw the large green sign which announced the upcoming ramp for exit 23A to I-71 in reflective white lettering.

"It's going to get off onto the next exit," Declan said. "And yes, I live in England."

Russ steered the van to the slow lane between a white Ford

sedan and a candy apple red Dodge Ram as the SUV took the exit.

"How do you know?"

"How do I know *what*?"

"How do you know the guy's gonna take the exit ramp?"

"Call it a hunch," Declan replied.

"Mind if I ask why we're tailing these guys? Are you a cop?"

Declan paused, wondering if he should tell Russ to mind his driving and his own business. No, the guy meant no harm and all the questioning was merely a bit of filler to occupy the ride.

"Yes, but not here," Declan answered.

"So who's in the SUV?"

"An old friend."

Russ exited and drove on. Within twenty minutes, Declan had learned quite a lot about his driver. The guy claimed he had a couple of college degrees, one in computer science and another in business, and he'd just finished up an online master's program in computer engineering from Purdue. He lived alone in an apartment off Hurstbourne Lane and was doing some freelance work with a computer company in California.

Declan studied him as he talked, vigorously moving his hands around, shifting one from the steering wheel and waving it about, then replacing it and transferring the other; repeating the process several times within each chunk of chatter until Declan could anticipate exactly when the hand switch would occur. He was quite a character and for the first time in a long while, Declan started to feel a scant bit of comfort in someone's company.

"Looks like our guys are taking the next ramp," Russ said, interrupting his own story about a botched online date which turned out to be with a middle-aged woman who'd posted her profile picture from one taken thirty years ago.

We're not that far from Crestwood, Declan thought, *and it's too much to be a coincidence. They have to know about the cabin. Why else would they be here instead of at the Abbey comforting the nuns in their time of sorrow?*

"Go ahead and take the exit," Declan told Rus, "but don't worry about tailing them when you get off the ramp. We'll stand out like a sore thumb in this eyesore."

Russ shrugged, not seeming to take offense to the jab at his van. "Okay. So where do you want me to take you?"

Declan pulled his cell phone out of his pocket and glanced down at the dwindling power bar.

"Hit Walgreens if you don't mind. I need to pick up a power bank charger."

"You got it, boss."

The statement hit Declan as funny. Truly funny. He'd laugh but somehow the whole business just seemed right.

"Say, Russ, why do you drive for Uber when you've several college degrees. You could get a job anywhere."

"I'd rather freelance. My time, my terms, that kind of thing. As for the Uber gig, let's say I find it stimulating; loosens up the old brain cells."

Declan maneuvered around the seatbelt, reached in his back pocket, and freed his wallet. There really wasn't an actual need for the action, but he didn't want to freak the guy out by pulling cash out of thin air. Instead, he opened it and liberated five hundred dollar bills. Russ glanced over and saw what he was doing.

"Ah, dude. You shouldn't carry cash like that around. Someone will rob you blind."

Declan smiled. "No worries, mate. Look, I've got a proposition for you. I'm really too short on time to go to the rental store and pick up a car. Would you mind being my driver for a couple of days? I'll pay better than Uber."

Russ took the ramp and stopped at the intersection light. The SUV drove on and made a right onto one of the streets which fed into the many subdivisions within this area.

"You're serious?" Russ asked, turning to Declan.

"You betcha," Declan replied, sliding five hundred dollars into the young man's hand, careful not to touch his skin when he did.

"Righteous!"

"Um, yeah."

The van started to move forward and suddenly jerked to a stop as Russ slammed on the brakes to avoid being sandwiched in a head-on collision between a truck and a station wagon. Neither driver seemed to be paying attention, Declan noticed as he felt his seatbelt tug against him, both assholes were peering at their cellphones. Russ killed the van's engine as sirens blared off in the distance.

"Looks like we'll be sitting for a while. So, tell me about this job, and what you need me to do."

Declan told him, keeping much to himself of course, but enough to lure the guy into agreeing to the position. It was a good half hour before the mess was cleared enough to allow them to pass through the intersection and move on their way. When they approached the turn in for Walgreens, Declan spotted the empty black SUV parked at the front entrance.

"Dodge around to the back, mate," he suggested.

"Is that the one?" Russ asked. "Ye ole friend of yore?"

Declan nodded, noting the license plate number as they went by. Rounding to the backside of the building, Russ settled the massive green whale into a parking spot in the back lot reserved for employees.

"Stay here and wait for me," the incubus said as he shut the door, wincing at the squealing hinges as it proceeded to close.

"Sure thing, boss. Russ be waiting."

Declan glanced over his shoulder and saw him lean the seat back to get more comfortable, his eyes closed behind the brownish tinted glasses beneath the plain navy blue ball cap he wore. The bold white lettering on the front of Russ's black tee shirt caused Declan pause.

I WENT OUTSIDE ONCE BUT THE
GRAPHICS WEREN'T ANY GOOD.

Chuckling, Declan went around and tapped on the driver's side window. Russ opened his eyes and rolled the window down.

"Mind if I borrow your cap?"

Russ handed it over. "If you got cooties, don't return it."

"Wouldn't dream of it, mate."

The doors of Walgreens swished open and Declan walked in. He felt the conditioned air against his skin, sending a round of chills through him like the points of sharp knives. The lighting was bright and unnatural, the ceiling striped with the glare of LED bulbs. He could detect the many scents of all things new, the peculiar odors emanating from the pharmacy area, and the aroma of humans. Not all of them smelled delightful and he promptly moved past one overweight and quite hairy man who should have been doing a tour through the personal hygiene aisle but was quite fixed in front of a rack of magazines.

He found her in the first aid aisle, squatting down and studying the bottom shelf filled with rolled bandages and other fix you up quick items. There was a large brown bottle under one arm, probably hydrogen peroxide, and in one hand she gripped a package of Telfa pads and antibiotic cream; the other clutched a roll of cloth tape with the last two fingers of her delicate hand while she seemed to be weighing her selection. He stepped further into the aisle keeping his eyes on the products while watching her in his periphery, she put the roll back and then picked up another brand. Her scent became stronger as he grew closer, so sweet and alluring. Normally, the hunger would begin to rear its ugly head when something this luscious was so near, but for some reason, it didn't seem to care one way or another and stayed as a silent monster within him.

She stood and swung right into him.

CHAPTER TWELVE

I watched as Abe eased into his seat across the table from me, and I pushed the cream pitcher closer to him. The coffee was hot and strong, hopefully enough charge to get him home after Alex finished doctoring him up.

"Are you going to tell me what caused that?" I gestured to his face, the slow purpling under one eye, the puffy lip where he was struck.

He heaved a sigh and scooted the cream pitcher closer to him, carefully tipping it with hands that weren't quite steady.

"I would tell you if I could," he responded, finally looking up from his cup.

"What happened after our call?" I recognized something was up when the signal had been so abruptly severed, and it had been over an hour before I heard from him again.

He shrugged and took a sip of coffee, eyes closing in the faint steam wafting from the liquid. After a prolonged silence, his eyes met mine.

"I don't know what it was. Who it was," he answered, his tone quiet. "I was getting ready to head upstairs when something, or someone, hit me. The strike came out of nowhere. I didn't get a warning, and for me, that's highly unusual." He passed one bruised hand over his unmarred cheek. "He was a decent fighter, almost too good. I got the impression he had some tricks in his bag that most don't."

I cocked my head and studied him. He was being straightforward. I had watched him fight. His senses were sharp, and he didn't seem to miss much. I was a good fighter myself, and I estimated he could give me a run for my money. Not that he was invincible. The proof of that was all over his face.

"He had a knife. At least, I think it was only a knife. It was so dark, I never got a good look at him, but there was something so," he shook his head.

"So what?"

"Familiar. Like, really familiar. Eerily familiar. I felt like I was fighting someone I knew very well."

"A friend? Family?"

"I couldn't say."

I found it a little disconcerting that he didn't rule out those two possibilities. How close was he to the perpetrator? There was something he was holding back, much more to the story than I was going to get. I gave up on that line of interrogation.

"What was he after?" It was a legitimate question, but one I suspected neither of us knew the answer to.

"I don't know. I thought maybe he was trying to explore the Abbey, and I got in his way. But it felt more deliberate than that. I don't think he just stumbled upon me. I believe he recognized I was there, knew exactly where I was and what I was doing."

"Then he was watching you?"

Abe shook his head slowly. "As I said, I don't know what his original intention was, but when he came after me, it was purposeful. The only other thing that makes me a solid target is this." He reached into his pants' pocket and pulled out a handkerchief, unfolding it in front of me. Tucked inside was the small cylindrical object I'd seen before from the video chat we'd had before matters went extremely strange.

"That's the piece you found last night," I stated.

"Yes," he acknowledged. "I still had it in my pocket when he attacked." He smoothed his thumb over the surface. "If he wanted this, then he was sorely disappointed." His eyes held a glint of pride.

"Did you talk to Sister Evangeline about it?"

"I did, but only briefly. She maintained this artifact has been at the Abbey for as long as she can recall. Most of the specimens are cataloged in a text dating back several centuries. She wasn't able to do any research about it for me, but she said she would as soon as time permits."

"She didn't recognize the history of it or the significance?"

"That's what's so peculiar. This has been lying on the shelf for ages and no one thought anything of it. We don't know how old it is, where it's from, or why it is in the Abbey in the first place. Sister Eva said she hadn't heard anyone talk about feeling any mystical energy from it, but I am positive I felt something."

I looked at his hand, now steady as he held the object centered in the handkerchief. He touched it with one tentative finger.

"Do you feel it now?"

He shook his head. "When I pulled it from my pocket to show her, I didn't sense anything, but I wasn't about to leave it there. And Sister Evangeline asked if I would take care of it."

Wise woman. I figured after the deaths, the nuns wouldn't

want any troublesome objects left behind. But of course, that was assuming these were normal sisters living in the convent, and that was a fallacy. These were finely trained warriors, meant to battle evil and halt the spread of it. There wasn't a battle born of faith that they would refrain from entering with full force.

But I could tell from what Abe wasn't saying, he was still thinking about the attack. Who had it been?

———

"Oh gosh!"

The brown bottle struck the floor, but its squared body stayed put instead of rolling away like the rounded peroxide bottles of old. The rest of the bandage material remained clenched in Alex's hand becoming a barrier between them as she reflexively put her hands up in front of her when she turned. He could smell everything about her now. So beautiful. So...innocent? No. That wasn't it. Alex's essence was filled with strength and determination. He'd seen Jasmine growing against a massive stone retaining wall once when no other flora dared, and that was the only thing he could compare her to. She teetered into him a bit and he forced himself to touch her upper arms to hold her steady. The sensation of her skin on his was like nothing he'd ever felt before and his breath caught in his throat, the only reaction his body could manage at the moment.

"Oh gosh, I am so sorry," Alex said.

If she felt anything from his touch on her bare skin, she didn't let on, and when his eyes met hers, he could see no change from their original bluish-gray color. His heart sped up and his mind began racing.

What the hell is going on here? She's human. I know she's human. I can smell it on her.

He felt her regain her balance, her body shifting to take a step back out of his reach and he let her.

"Just call me Grace," she declared with an embarrassed laugh as she readjusted the bandage supplies in her hands to retrieve the bottle off the floor.

"No worries," Declan replied. "Allow me, please."

He bent down and picked up the downed bottle of peroxide, handing it to her.

"Is your name really Grace?"

Alex chuckled. "Uh, no. That's just a saying some of us use here. It's a nicer way of saying I'm a clutz. Are you from Australia?"

"England," he replied.

"Love the accent," she said. "Bet you've never heard that one before, huh?"

Declan smiled. "Maybe once or twice."

He extended his hand to her, not just formality's sake, but because he needed to be certain something wasn't missed and another touch of her skin was the only means to achieve it.

"Thanks," he replied. "I'm Declan."

Alex shifted the bottle of peroxide back under her arm and extended her other one, taking his hand into hers. "I'm Alex."

He felt the nice firm grip of a woman who knew how to shake hands, the soft and supple skin against his own, and the heat that the contact between them gave him. It surged through him, quickening his heart into a pounding rhythm, tingling every inch of his skin and settling into a hardness in his nether region. Yes, he was attracted to her, that was obvious. And? And nothing else. *Dare he try to test this?*

"It's nice to meet you," he stated, making just the slightest effort to pull something from her. "Are you from this area?"

"No, but a friend of mine owns a house here. So, what brings you to this side of the great salty lake?"

Declan got absolutely nothing from his little trial, not in her life force anyway, but she was talking to him; questioning him. Why was he here? He reached into the back pocket of his jeans, liberating his leather wallet and showing her the credentials inside.

"Inspector Declan Faulkner," she read. "From Scotland Yard?"

"On holiday, actually. I just thought I'd do a bit of a tour through Kentucky. I should be in town for a couple of weeks. Would you mind getting together with me for a cup of coffee some time?"

Alex laughed. "I thought the English drank tea."

Declan smiled. "Some do, but I find coffee tastes better."

He reached into his wallet and plucked out a business card, handing it to her.

"My cell phone number if you decide you'd like to join me sometime."

"Inspector Declan Faulkner, Scotland Yard," she read off the card. "Any chance I might entice you into a less than a social meeting?"

He raised a brow.

"Strictly business, I assure you. And since you are on vacation, no is an acceptable answer."

Declan felt his heart speed up again. His brain felt itself whirling on a good tantrum.

What the bloody hell are you doing? Get too close and you'll bugger it all up.

"Absolutely," he replied with a slight gentlemanly faux bow. "Call me anytime."

"I will," she replied, pocketing the card into her jeans. "It's been nice meeting you, but I've got a friend who is in need of these things."

Declan stepped aside. "The pleasure is all mine. Give my regards to your friend for a speedy recovery."

"Will do," Alex said over her shoulder as she headed to the checkout counter.

CHAPTER THIRTEEN

By six the next morning, Abe pulled in the driveway to pick up Alex and me on our way to the crime scene. This time, he drove an antique Jaguar, silver, and sleek, but the knocking and wheezing sounds made me squirm. We needed to get to the cabin before they destroyed the area so this wasn't a good time for car trouble, as if there ever were a good time. Time was of the essence. This was not an ordinary murder. Due to the supernatural nature of the crime, after Brother Joshua's people finished their examination, they would eradicate the place. I wasn't certain precisely how they would do it, but since the cabin was remote and not well known, they might just burn it to the ground for all I knew.

I gave directions once we exited off I-71 and turned onto some of the rural roadways. I wasn't raised here, but since my father once worked in the area as part of a bogus church with Satanic leanings, I knew the geography well.

I winced at the thought. I tried not to visualize my father, attendant of the devil. When I worked for the Church of the Light

Reclaimed, it was presented as a farce to me. My father, I estimated, ultimately lost his mind completely along with this totally perverted organization. I didn't know they were indeed getting directives from the Devil himself.

As we pulled up to the cabin, I shook my head as though to jar the thoughts loose. God and the Devil, it was all part of fairy tales for me, along with unicorns and the boogie man. Damn, but I had been so wrong.

"It looks like the place is abandoned," Alex murmured from the backseat. None of us were eager to run into the building. It looked haunted as it was, overshadowed by the lush trees around it, the air thick with humidity. I knew they moved the bodies. There was no way they would leave them in this heat. I wasn't altogether certain where the remains were taken, the broken nun, and the dehydrated Slyvie.

"It won't be," Abe responded. "I am confident they have this place under surveillance, in case the murderer comes back, or to prevent anyone else meddling in their business."

I didn't respond but climbed out of the car. I kept my handy gun tucked into a stylish shoulder holster under my layered shirt. If there were people here who shouldn't be, I was ready. If they weren't people, but some new kind of horror, bring it on. I was in a mood and all the coffee in the world wasn't going to make the morning any better.

"Let's go," I said.

Abe followed me closely, his injuries not slowing him down. I saw his multiple bruises and lacerations last night. He boasted a nice line of stitches due to the wicked slice from a blade. Alex stitched the wound closed with the sister's first aid supplies, but she was insisting on keeping an eye on it. Once healed, it would match the several other scars decorating his skin.

The sight of Abe's naked chest and back gave me pause. Not

because the lean rippling muscles were a nice distraction, which they were, but because I could tell Abe was not what he seemed. I knew he was a fighter, but I didn't understand the extent of his history of battle. The scars were varied, a tale of blade and bullet. Like his Clark Kent glasses, he was losing some of his accountant mystique.

I reached the doorway a second before him and stopped, the fingers of my right hand hooked into the handle of the frail screen door. The front room appeared darker through the screen mesh but I could make out the downed front door propped against the bulky shadow of a couch. My eyes shifted downward at an angle where I could see cracks in the wooden door frame and chunks of wood missing from where the hinge would have been; leaving only small holes where screws once held the hinge tight into the frame. Above me, a battered hinge hung perilously from one lone screw. Abe was close behind me, and when I nodded, he and I swung it open and stepped inside.

Even in the full morning light without seeing it through the meshed material, the room was murky; the air within it was dense and heavy like some old tool shed left sealed up in the late August heat of summer. I could feel the sweat beading up against my skin. Whatever or whoever used this place certainly didn't seem to mind the extremes. From what I could tell, there was no air conditioning, and as I scanned over the walls, no thermostats for either air or heat. The couch, one of those overstuffed ones you could plunge into, was littered with dust and what looked like wooden splinters. I glanced down at the floor in front of it and saw much the same, indicating the door landed in this spot. It was an unsettling observation; there was at least thirty feet of space between the front entrance and the couch. Whatever hit it, hit it hard. I stopped when I heard footsteps coming from the rear of the building, then the sound of a door opening, and more footsteps. A thin wiry man with a sallow complexion paused in the doorway.

"You're Samantha?" His voice was reedy, giving the impression if the wind blew hard, he might take flight on the gust.

"I am." My hands were by my side, but I could draw a gun if needed. "And you are?"

"Doctor Bandish," he said shortly. "I'm just taking some samples from the area. I'll clear out in a few minutes, but I was to wait for you to arrive." He cast me an inquisitive look. "The cleanup crew will be here as soon as you're finished."

He wanted to know who I was and why they ordered him to wait on me. I wasn't going to satisfy his curiosity. He was a scientist. Let him gather his test tubes and samples. I doubted he would learn much.

Abe entered the chamber behind me with Alex close on his heels, collectively we moved past Bandish and into the room from which he emerged. Bandish graced the threshold as I stepped towards the center of the space and looked around. The bodies were removed; the bed was empty and the restraints which held the desiccated corpse in place were dangling free. They also packed away the linens from the mattress, but the mattress itself looked in good condition, with no bloodstains or obvious signs of a struggle. Whatever happened on the bed didn't have anything to do with blades.

The broken chair lay on its side, and further signs of a scuffle showed in the indentations in the wall, the broken plaster pieces with flecks of blue paint mixed among the white dust, and the blood spatter. Lots of blood splatter. The nun gave her all in the struggle, but it wasn't enough.

I shook my head and observed with interest as the good doctor knelt down and took blood samples from the floor. He was meticulous in his movements, and I saw Alex stopped as well.

"Do you think this is all from the victim?"

When the doctor tilted his head up to respond, he looked a little like a mole who climbed from his hole a little too early.

"We anticipated there might be a mixture. But here, the blood shows some extraordinary signs of a chemical process. See this stippling? It makes me suspect the blood came in contact with something very potent, acidic, right about here."

I could see the wheels turning in Alex's formidable mind. I liked chemistry in school, but the knowledge didn't stick, which was one reason for my assembled team. I could fight. I was smart and plenty able to go after the scum who killed them. But I needed help to track them down.

"Any theories?" I glanced toward Alex, but she silently shook her head.

"What is your opinion?" She was peering at the doctor as he studied us.

"I don't know. There were no signs of any chemical weapons, nor were chemicals used to try to clean up the scene. It was left as is."

"Fingerprints?" I demanded of Bandish.

"Plenty. There were prints from both victims, but several other unidentified sets as well. We have palm prints, a few thumbprints, lots of partials." He studied Alex over his glasses. "I assume you're going to see the bodies?"

"We are heading there next," I supplied. I didn't like this little man although I couldn't convey why.

"You will understand the scene much better after you have studied the remains," he informed Alex, his expression indicating his understanding. He recognized she was a medical person and preferred to share his words of wisdom with someone of a similar ilk.

I turned away and stalked around the room, my mind considering the remoteness of the cabin. It was the perfect getaway for someone to step out of the public eye, to get a little peace and quiet, to remove oneself from the constant buzz of humanity. For the same reason, it made a great place to hold the women captive, to question them leisurely, and to end them.

Bandish left the room and I heard the sound of the screen door at the front of the cabin shut. Abe stood in front of the one window in the bedroom. His facial expression was drawn; he looked intense and distracted as if he were struggling to remember something. I started to step over and tap him on the shoulder but thought better of it. The look of concentration was likewise one which suggested he was far from here. A touch would probably startle him. Instead, I remained where I was.

"Abe?"

He didn't answer and Alex glanced over at me. I held up my hand, calling her to a halt when she started to step forward and shook my head. I called his name again a little louder, but still in a questioning voice. He blinked and suddenly swung around.

"Yeah?"

"Do you feel anything?" I asked.

Abe looked down at the floor for a moment and I saw him swallow hard as if he were trying to work himself up to answer. I waited.

"Maybe deja vu?" he said finally. "It's the same sense of familiarity I felt at the Abbey, but--"

"But what?"

Another swallow and I caught the troubled look in his eyes. Abe was usually the unflappable one, like the sisters, he always appeared to be a step ahead in his knowledge. I didn't like this uncertainty.

"Sam, I feel like I've been here before."

"How so?" I asked, not sure of any other way to reply. My stomach flipped over uncomfortably.

More and more, things were seeming different than they appeared on the surface, and although I didn't believe in something like reincarnation (didn't even see how it could be possible) I was rapidly learning nothing should be discounted. If Abe felt like he'd been here before, then I needed to trust his feelings and go with it. To ignore it would be not only stupid but could possibly be detrimental to this whole messed up affair.

"I can't put my finger on it exactly," he countered, "maybe a memory?"

I thought about the bead session with one of the sisters and stepped towards Abe.

"Close your eyes for a moment," I suggested.

He furrowed his brow and gave me a sideways smirk but his shoulders relaxed a bit. "Tapping into your inner Freud, are you?"

Alex laughed faintly and approached him from the opposite side.

"Trust me," I told him. "I want you to close your eyes and forget us for a moment. Just think about this cabin. Focus on how it feels to be here. Don't fixate on the murders, okay? I know it sounds ridiculous, but as you shut your eyes, I want you to block them out and focus on what this place reveals to you."

Abe gave a shrug and closed his eyes. "I guess it can't hurt."

"Now concentrate," I suggested, giving him a moment of silence before continuing, "and explain to me what you sense here."

I could see his eyes shifting back and forth beneath his lids in short, quick jolts as if he were dreaming. I knew he wasn't under hypnosis because it was beyond my expertise, but he was deep in reflection and narrowed in on something. A minute passed. And then another. Alex waited patiently alongside him, silent.

"I feel comfortable," Abe said finally, "cared for. Not the romantic kind but love like brotherly friendship."

I hesitated. "What do you smell, Abe?"

He inhaled a breath through his nose slowly. Alex shot me a look of uncertainty and I knew what she must be thinking. Anyone could detect the stench of death all around us, death, and decomposition. Abe flinched in surprise, but kept his eyes shut.

"I smell wood smoke," he responded, "from a fireplace."

I glanced over at the far wall in the front room where a stone-fronted fireplace stood. It appeared vacant and desolate. The charred remains of what once fueled a cozy fire were now long gone and covered in a layer of settled dust.

"Focus," I said again. "What do you see?"

Abe's expression faded with a much longer pause. I started to say his name again, get his attention, get this moving along, but when I glanced over at Alex she shook her head as if to tell me I needed to be patient. I nodded in reply and waited him out.

"I was here," he declared, his eyes moving quickly behind the lids as if watching the memories slide by, "but I wasn't, you know? Maybe like a dream? I was sitting on the hearth watching the flames dance around like they do and wondering...I was wondering why I felt bad about something I did. Why I...I felt guilt, a lot of it. And someone else is here. He says, "You did what you felt you needed to. There's no bloody guilt in it, mate. You probably saved many a whore from the same nasty fate." He can't see me, though. There are tears in his eyes, but his face is too blurry to make out. He sits down next to me, as if he's all alone, just watching the flames before he says something else."

I remained silently waiting, wondering if reincarnation was something real when he spoke again.

"He says, "Take it from your old chum, Max. You did this bastardly world a favor. One less butcher stealing his flesh from the Whitechapel district. I'd give you a bloody medal myself if I could," Abe said, opening his eyes. "That's all I remember."

I stood there for a moment, contemplating the questions which weighed heavily on me since I met him. Who are you? What are you? But this was not the place for a discussion.

"Do you think these are real memories?" I asked instead.

Abe shrugged, his expression was unreadable. "You asked. I answered. That's all I know."

I chanced one more question. "Do you believe in rein-carnation?"

Bandish burst through the door and I realized I recognized the expression of relief wash over Abe's face.

"I think you need to see this."

I followed him outside to the front of the cabin, just off the tiny front porch near the stacked logs of the wall. There was a small puddle, dwindling down to nothing in the dry August heat, and in the center sticking up at an angle was a glimmer of silver. I crouched down but couldn't get a better look.

"May I?" I asked Bandish who gave a nod and handed me a latex glove.

I slid it over my hand and gently pulled the silver pentacle free of its muddy prison.

Visiting a bloody crime scene always affected my appetite, but my companions were a hardier sort. We stopped at a local chain restaurant on the way to our next destination. Abe drove and I kept a sharp eye out for anyone who might be tailing us from one site to the next.

I didn't notice anything obvious, but I encouraged Abe to use a little of his clever handling of the sedan to help us melt into the traffic. He gladly complied and I was distracted away from my grim thoughts with the weaving and close cutting turns of his driving.

By the time we drew close to our destination, I was itching to get out and get some air. I needed action, needed to walk, needed to feel the heat of the pavement beneath my feet just for a moment. When Doctor Bandish told us where to meet him to view the bodies, I just stared at him.

As a periodic resident of Louisville, I was aware of the old building which now housed Kindred Hospital. The original Saint Anthony's hospital was built over a hundred years ago and staffed by many from the religious order during the following years. It remained open and functioning until the mid 90's when financial stressors caused it to fail. It reopened under other management, and now was a medical facility focused on meeting the needs of patients on ventilators.

I passed by the building many times when I was in Kentucky but never went inside. Now I frowned as we pulled into a parking space to the side of the building and approached the flat brick wall. A recessed metal door was sunk into the façade, unnoticed for most unless perhaps you were an employee of the hospital.

As we approached, the door swung open and the grey-faced Doctor Bandish slid into view. I stifled the urge to draw away.

"Come in," he hurried us, and we filed into the building, the frigid air conditioning blowing the smell of chemicals and age with it. The doctor closed the door behind us and I heard the lock catch with a solid sound. No one would be following.

He gave us a hasty signal to follow, rushed down the hall, and stopped at the end where a heavy barred door blocked the stairwell. There was a keypad set into the doorframe, and

Bandish typed in a few digits before the door gave an audible sigh and pulled it open. Again, we proceeded into the tight space, a small landing with utilitarian concrete steps leading up and down.

"This way," Bandish muttered as he started down the stairs. I looked up, hearing the vast emptiness of the stairs above. I never enjoyed visiting hospitals in general, but this seemed even more uncomfortable, as though the floors above us were abandoned and we were alone in the building. The sounds of our steps seemed magnified and echoed ominously.

I let my hand slip to my side where the little handgun rested, small and deadly. It wasn't my only weapon but bringing the katana into the hospital didn't seem practical. Now I missed its weight and the deadly blade.

The steps ended abruptly at a wooden door, older and different from the ones above. I assumed this was part of the original building, untouched since the early 1900s. Bandish used a key on the lock, and the door opened silently. It might have been old, but someone was taking good care of the space.

"What is this place?" I asked, breathing in another smell now, something older, more earthy.

"This is the morgue," Dr. Bandish replied with a little more enthusiasm than necessary. "It isn't currently being used for the facility. These lower levels were put out of commission after the hospital changed hands. This section, however, continues to serve a purpose."

We followed him down the hall, Alex leading the way with the doctor at her side. She managed to engage him in a conversation, something about the equipment used in the processing of the bodies. I was glad his attention was turned away from me. I exchanged a glance with Abe, and he merely raised one eyebrow.

I shrugged. We passed through the first door leading into a dim office lit by a single gooseneck lamp.

"A moment," Dr. Bandish said quickly and went through the double doors opposite the entrance. I saw the blink of lights coming on, the shaky flicker of fluorescent bulbs so classic to the atmosphere. When the doctor reappeared and held open the door, I felt my hand slip to my side again, feeling the reassuring weight of the weapon.

Inside, the room was the stereotypical morgue from any hospital in the country. The floor was tile squares of neutral color. The cabinets with drawers for the storage of bodies were stainless steel and lined on one wall to our right. On the left was a wall of cabinetry and plumbing, sinks and drawers, many shrouded in white clothes or blue surgical material.

There were long-necked lamps to angle over the unfortunate occupants of the metal slabs, and the doctor hurried to hit the switch to turn them on. No one in charge here scrimped on the lights, and the powerful illumination lit up the smooth line of the white sheets, barely hinting at the shape of the bodies beneath. I suspected the doctor was enjoying this, the build-up to the big reveal.

Alex must have felt the same because she casually went to the first table and gently folded back the sheet revealing the marble-white face of Sister Mary Carmella. Her limbs were now eased back in their proper placement, the unnatural bends straightened until she looked like the statue of a corpse, pale and still. Without the spirit, this body was merely a shell. And while I wasn't sure I believed in any God or formal religion, I believed completely in death.

Doctor Bandish seemed disappointed Alex reached the victim first, so in a petulant move, he threw back the sheet from the second corpse. Under the bright lights, the body was even more jarring, the skin an even tanned shell with stains of deep black. He left the body covered to the waist, but the rest of the woman was exposed. Her face was still drawn in the travesty of a smile, too many teeth showing through thin lips and receded black gums. Her eyelids were paper-thin shields over deflated orbs; her hair was dry strands like corn silks. She seemed to have shrunk more, her skin clinging to ropy muscles and knobby bone, a crack parting her face from her jawline under her ear on the right over the bridge of her sunken nose, and into the hollow of her eye. Another similar crack traced from her concave belly to her right collar bone.

"Has she been cut?" My voice was sharp and angry in the silence.

"No," the doctor said, seeming to relish the word. "She continues to deteriorate at a rapid rate. I suspect if we didn't find her when we did, she might have been unrecognizable in a few days."

"Dry," Alex's voice came from the head of the platform. "She's so dry. It looks as though she was deliberately mummified."

"I agree," the doctor replied, clearly pleased. "But I can assure you, she has not. We have tested her skin. There is no chemical residue to explain the condition of the body."

Alex drew closer to the body as I thought about the pictures I saw of the young Slyvie in life, her dark hair gracefully falling around lightly tanned shoulders, eyes alight with life. The only similarity between the young woman and this creature was her hair, but even this lacked luster.

"Cause of death?" Alex's eyes shot to Dr. Bandish.

"We haven't started the formal autopsy, but preliminary findings are inconclusive. There were ligature marks on her wrists, but of course, she was bound when we found her. We believe we have found some signs of bruising on her arms where she might have been restrained, but with the condition of the skin, it is unlikely we will ever be able to make a positive conclusion."

"I'd like to be here for the autopsy," Alex said, her voice flat. She was in her element now, and I could imagine her mind was racing. This part of the mystery, the odd paranormal slant we tumbled into, was suddenly tossed in her court.

"I was going to begin this afternoon."

"Perfect," Alex said. "What time?"

"We can begin now if you'd like."

I glanced toward Abe. Seeing the body was plenty. I didn't want to watch them dissect her. I wasn't particularly squeamish usually, but I didn't see the value in staying around and watching over the shoulder of the medical professionals. I forwarded the pic taken of the silver pentacle found earlier on to the Abbey for Sister Eva to examine and received a response within the same hour which confirmed my suspicion the pentacle was indeed the stolen artifact. I replied back and told her the piece was now with Bandish and his forensic team, so she should contact Brother Joshua to arrange for it to be returned. Although I wasn't surprised the pentacle was at the murder scene since the acts on both women were grizzly enough to have warranted such a thing, I was surprised to find a chain on the ground nearby. It was broken and the links, where the chain was severed in two, were stretched and bent as if it were yanked apart. To me, it looked like the poor victim of our killer's frustrations or possibly even a celebratory move for a job well done like a football player slamming the ball to the ground passed the goal line. But since we didn't know what the piece was really supposed to be used for, it was just a big pile of assumptions. I decided to take the time and pursue another lead while Alex did what she did best.

"I have another errand I'd like to run," I told Abe, shooting him a meaningful look. I didn't want Alex to be alone with the creepy Bandish, but I couldn't stay to mind the team. There were alarm bells chiming in my brain. There was something other-worldly afoot and I wanted to get more details. Besides, there was also a chance there could be other victims, and just the condition of the body would be enough to link the murders.

"Do you need a ride?" Abe was standing at a distance from the body, but his eyes kept straying in its direction.

"No," I responded, although part of me wanted to tell him yes just so he'd answer the question I'd posed to him about reincarnation. "You and Alex can cover this, right?"

He gave me a short nod and I could see another look of relief wash over his countenance. We were going to have to have a conversation soon but now wasn't the time.

"Okay. I'll keep in touch." I turned on my heel, striding out of the tiled room, the place of the dead, and into the light.

Uber is a wonderful thing, and my driver was a middle-aged woman who looked like she might have been toting kids to soccer practice just the week before. The faint odor of teen sweat and dirty socks seemed to have permeated the foam cushions of her minivan. She dropped me off at the corner, close to the local grocery but within walking distance of my home. I didn't want anyone following me here. Once in the parking lot, I threaded my way between cars and through the backlot of the shopping center, crossing through the snaking streets of the subdivision until I came close to my property. I waited for a moment, watched before I pulled out my keys and continued to my waiting car.

I could hear the energetic barks from within the house. The dogs, Fluffy and Bart, took their job seriously. I didn't have time to stop by and check on them. I called a connection, a friend of a friend, who agreed to meet me at the police station. He was already pulling a few strings just to get me in there. I wasn't going to make him wait.

I drove with caution, my eyes focused ahead while my mind spun like a hamster on a wheel. The cause of death for Slyvie was a big mystery but I felt as soon as we knew the answer, we might have a bigger insight into just who could have done it. Her remains were obviously proof this was no ordinary murder, but it wasn't the only source of information. I pondered over the fine line which separates the heroes from the monsters. If Sister Evangeline and Brother Joshua didn't know what we were dealing with, I figured I might know someone who would.

I tried to dismiss the idea. To call upon an infernal lord, even one with a strange affinity for me, was risky to the point of stupidity. But if all else failed...

I pulled into the hole-in-the-wall establishment and checked my watch. I was ten minutes early. I pulled the thumb drive out of my pocket and studied it. It was another of the digital gadgets I acquired along with my computer and surveillance equipment back when I was in Florida. It would hold as many files as I needed.

I saw the cop slide out of his sedan and lean over to grab a faux leather satchel. He locked the car door with some deliberation and paused to straighten his rumpled suit. There were a few days' growth on his face, and the signs of exhaustion or alcohol weighed down his cheeks until he looked like he was melting.

I followed him into the darkened bar, eyeing his choice of position with approval. He sat with his back to the wall, his attention on the patrons around him. As soon as I approached, he stood, an old fashioned gesture I appreciated. Just because I could probably beat the crap out of him didn't mean I opposed his chivalry.

"Thank you for meeting me," I said, my tone even.

He raised unruly eyebrows, pulling his face into a disbelieving mask. "I wasn't aware there was much of a choice."

I gave a curt nod. Like any organization, the cops were riddled with tiny holes, each error or misstep tied to a tiny string that would loosen when pulled. My information on this guy wouldn't send him to jail. It might not even get him fired. But it might stain his record, and by the look of him, he was living for retirement.

"I got what you wanted," Augustus said in an undertone. He pulled the satchel onto the table, pushing back the requisite napkin, fork, and spoon. The laptop computer looked like it was built sometime just after the invention of plastic. Time and heat warped the gray top, and the insignia which once proudly showed a brand name was reduced to a slightly glossy smudge.

I pulled out my thumb drive and handed it over. After an eternity of booting, the computer finally showed the first screen, and the man tiredly logged into the system. A moment later and he was ejecting the drive to hand to me.

"Some of this stuff never even made it into our computer banks," he said in a low voice. "Some are just some notes I've gathered along the way. None of it is signed. If anyone asks, I never heard of this." He gave a nod to the device in my hand. I knew as a member of the state police, he would have his fingers in more cases than most, which was why I was here. If I wanted to keep him as a source, I needed to at least respond with more than a growl.

"I understand," I answered. Before he could move, my hand darted out to catch his arm. So much for the flies and honey approach. "I get this, and I appreciate the risk, but I need to know what you know, what you think of these cases."

He gave a loud sigh, chest expanding with the extra air.

"Look, there are only three we've found in this area." He glanced around and leaned forward. "I saw the first one. And it was just," he stopped, seeming to search for words to match his emotions. "It was surreal. It was like something out of a movie, and I kinda thought it was a movie prop at first." His elbows thumped on the table. "This woman, the victim, well, her purse was still with her. All her id, her jewelry, everything."

"She was found…" I prodded.

"Bernheim Forest. We were called in when the local force got stretched too thin." He ran a hand over his jaw, the stubble making a rasping noise against his palm. His sad eyes grew darker. "Locals thought it was a prank pulled by some high school kids. She was wrapped in a sheet, dressed in a long glittery evening gown, her high heeled pumps still on her feet." He shook his head as though trying to shake off the memory.

"Cause of death?"

The older man shrugged. "Doc couldn't tell for sure. The remains couldn't have been there long considering the condition of the clothes and the covering, but damned if the woman didn't look like she died a century ago."

I looked up to see a waitress heading our way, her dark hair tied back with a red handkerchief, and her nose sporting a bull piercing. My cop friend seemed to welcome the distraction. He ordered a double scotch on the rocks, I opted for an ale, figuring anything in a bottle would be safer than drinking from the glass.

"But the murder is unsolved," I said after the waitress left.

"We went to inform the family. They were in shock. They lived out in Prospect, in a mammoth house with an indoor pool. The girl was the daughter. Twenty-six and still in college taking a few courses at U of L." He shrugged. "By all accounts, she was wealthy, a bit of a partier. She was last seen at a bar in downtown Louisville just before midnight. Sometime after, she left the bar, but no one recalls if she was alone or with someone else. Next morning she's found by some poor day campers tromping through the woods."

"The next day?"

"Oh, yeah. She wasn't even reported missing yet, parents didn't know she was still out."

I turned over the facts in my mind. The online records told me much of it. The young woman held a reputation for enjoying a good time, and the reports all summed it up as a lover's quarrel. What wasn't thoroughly explored was the mummification of the body, something better suited to be seen under glass in a marble and polish museum than in the middle of the woods.

"And the case is still open." It wasn't a question. I knew for a fact the killer was never found, not in the three long years since the woman's discovery.

"What about the others?"

The waitress came by with our drinks, the bottle, and glass already sweating in the humidity. She put them indelicately on the table and turned before we could ask for anything more.

"The old lady was different. She was a greedy son-of-a-bitch who hung out at the casino over in Indiana. Get this, her pockets were full of chips when the body was found. Worth some money, ya know?"

I nodded. I did know. I wasn't a big gambler, but I visited the casino a few times with friends or failed dates. Especially when I worked for the 'church', and money was plentiful.

"And the place is bristling with cameras. Can't pick your nose without someone catching it on film. So we have plenty of footage of the victim. Weird thing, this lady literally wandered alone through the whole place, talking all the while, but looking at nothing. It was like there was a ghost at her elbow. We figure she must have some mental problem." Augustus tapped square fingers on the tabletop and took a slug of his drink. "Plain as day, you could watch her weave out of the casino and head into the parking lot. We saw her car drive off camera. It was found the next day on the side of the bridge."

"What kind of car?"

"Mercedes G class. If it wasn't for the car, we wouldn't have known the lady was missing."

"Her body was found in the river?"

Augustus nodded. "She got caught up by the shore on the Kentucky side. When we fished her out, no one knew what the hell we were looking at." He took another generous sip of his drink. "She was like the other one, still dressed to the shoes, but one fell off in the water. The body was," his face twisted with disgust, "brown and stringy. One of her arms dropped out of the sleeve while she was being moved."

I frowned. I supposed a wet mummy didn't have the staying power of a dried one, but it wasn't something I wanted to mentally picture.

"Same story though. Even after questioning everyone at the casino, no one seemed to be able to remember if she was with anyone." He sent me a look. "And yes, the case is still open. But it's dead. Considering this lady and her reputation, it's crazy nothing has come out about her death."

"The last one was a drug dealer?"

"Mmmm, yeah, almost creepier." He glanced toward the door. I saw a ripple of emotion cross his face, and he stood abruptly.

I stood as well, turning to look toward the door. There didn't appear to be any newcomers, but something obviously spooked Officer Augustus.

"I gotta go," he muttered, heading away from the table, the computer shoved under one arm.

I didn't stop him. There was something he was running from, and it wouldn't have been sporting for me to put him in danger. Instead, I kept my mouth closed and watched him push out the door, head down.

I paid the bill with cash.

CHAPTER FOURTEEN

Declan took a room at the Holiday Inn Express in La Grange. After his meeting with Alex, he was surprised he'd the presence of mind to pay for an adjacent room for Russ since he needed to go back inside Walgreens a second time to get the charger pack he went for in the first place. The woman was definitely messing with his head.

Russ was thrilled at the prospect of more cash for his trouble and even more elated to drive the car Declan rented, a silver BMW 5 of all things, instead of the nauseous green whale monster van which Russ seemed a little disappointed to leave behind at the rental lot. When he climbed in the driver's seat of the Beamer, however, some of the disappointment faded.

"Okay Boss, let me first say this is classy as hell."

Declan inclined his head and raised an inquisitive brow at the young bearded man with absolutely no base for comparison in the statement he just made. For anyone who has been to hell before, in the pits, in the lakes of fire, the muck, mire, and the polluting stench of brimstone and rot, classy is not even remotely the word they would use to describe it; not even in jest.

"But," Russ said, pointing his index finger skyward as if he were experiencing some life-changing epiphany, "don't you think something like a Dodge Viper or a Ferrari might have been a better choice? I mean, a Viper would have been seriously bitching."

"Bitching," Declan repeated as he strapped on the passenger seat belt to silence the beeping-dinging sound the car was making. "Yeah, well, we will not be seriously bitching this time around. I need a vehicle a little less conspicuous than your van."

This time it was Russ who raised a brow. "Dude, it's a BMW. It's *going* to attract some attention."

The incubus shrugged. "Look, I was compromising. I take your Moby Dick monster away for a few days and give you a nice, clean, and less smelly luxury car to drive. See? Compromise."

Russ shifted the car into drive and pulled out of the lot.

"You didn't have to insult my baby like that. I mean, you hurt me, man. You hurt me deep. You could have just said you preferred to ride around in this uppity mound of German engineering and I'd been like, 'Okay, Boss. Your dollar, your choice.' But no, you have to take a jab at the love of my life like she ain't nothing but a--a--"

Declan grinned. "A dilapidated vehicle which you trust to take you from point A to point B?"

"Dilapidated? Oh, it's on bro. You done angered the Russman. See if I allow you to ride in the most comfortable van again. No. Your uber is out. So don't even ask."

"Are you finished?" Declan asked with a laugh.

Russ narrowed his eyes playfully.

"Good," Declan continued, "cause I thought you might be a bit peckish."

"Ah, no way Boss. I will drive for you. I will help you get your property back from your old pal. And I will even put up with your insults on the love of my life. But I do not do peckers. Not now, not ever."

Declan's eyes shifted from the windshield to Russ. "What the bloody hell are you going on about? I said peckish. You know? Hungry. I didn't say anything about--"

"Peckers," Russ said for him. "Well, Boss, here in Kentucky we say hungry when we mean hungry. You start talking peckers to some people--"

"Peckish."

"Peckish. Peckers. It doesn't matter. Point is, most people don't find your P-word all that appetizing."

Delcan's brow furrowed. "It's not my P-word. It's just a word."

"Uh-huh, well you're in the good old USA, pardner. So, speak English."

"I--oh, fuck me. Just pull into the restaurant where you want to eat, will you?"

Russ smiled. "Can do, Boss. And just for the record, best not say fuck me out in public unless you mean it either. And probably not even then. A lot of folks around here don't take too kindly to that kind of talk."

Declan groaned.

Russ parked the BMW in the lot for Applebee's and killed the engine just as Declan's cell phone rang.

"Hello?"

"Is this Inspector Declan Faulkner?"

Declan sat up straight. "Alex? Uh, yeah, I mean, yes it's me, Declan."

Russ let out a low two-tone whistle and wiggled his eyebrows up and down. Declan flipped him the bird.

"What can I do for you?" he asked, turning around so he couldn't see Russ's childishly crude hand signals.

Alex laughed lightly. "I'd say start by telling me how you knew it was me calling, but I need to keep it short. Is there any way you can come off vacation for a couple of hours and lend me your opinion?"

"Sure, what do you need my opinion on?"

"First off, I'm a doctor. I didn't think I told you. Second, I've got two bodies. One I know the cause of death. One I haven't the foggiest. I would really like some fresh eyes to have a look, maybe catch something I've missed. Still interested?"

"Of course," he replied. "Give me the address."

———

My mind was still on the officer and his strange behavior when I stepped out of the bar. There was no one on the street. At least, there was no one who raised my suspicions. Who the officer might have caught sight of, I wasn't sure, but I knew I'd have to track him down at another time. There were more victims, and the more we knew about them, the more we could extrapolate additional information about the perpetrator.

My car was close by, but there was something unsettling in the air. I approached the vehicle with caution. My senses were buzzing. I discovered after my injury, the heartrending moment when Vic McCain put a bullet in me, there were some things about me which changed. I wasn't sure if it was because of the possession by the devil's spawn or the subsequent recovery with the nuns at the abbey, but I was given an additional talent which was proving itself to be handy. Whenever someone with a connection to the satanic church my father helped rise to power was in the vicinity, I got a telltale hint. It was enough to give me some forewarning of an incipient confrontation.

I flipped the side hem of the jacket away from my body exposing the gun holstered there. It wasn't my only weapon, but it was the first at hand. Bullets wouldn't stop these bastards, but it would slow them down. Then came the blades, blessed and sharp as razors. My katana was at the house. Wandering into a hospital with a sword strapped to my back was likely to draw some attention. But it was my weapon of choice and I was pissed I didn't think to at least put it in the trunk.

I saw the movement in the alley. With my senses on high alert and my hand already easing the gun from the holster, I headed into it. But this wasn't some poor drunken bum hiding out in the alley or a fatted rat waddling through the garbage. My heightened senses told me this was a servant of an infernal lord, a mini demon, a creature of the night.

I stopped at the mouth of the alley next to the bar, smelling a bouquet of old beer, sour garbage, and something else, an unmistakable stench of the otherworldly. I scanned the narrow way, noting the sizable dumpster, the open doorway, the stacked boxes slowly collapsing in on themselves. Nothing moved.

A car horn blared at my back, but I ignored the sound. Losing attention could make you lose your head, and I was fond of mine and preferred to keep it where it was. I took a slow step into the shadow of the building and heard the shuffle. I launched myself in the direction of the sound, using a free hand to rip away the cardboard covering a huddled figure. The bloodshot eyes of an old woman, hair wild with tangles and rags, stared up at me.

"Move on, Grandmother," I said in a low voice. "You don't want to be here." She must have read something in my face, or my tone cut through some of the other voices ringing in her head, because she gave a quick nod and started away, body hunched over in self-preservation.

With her movement, a second figure caught my eye, a lean feral shape. I couldn't tell its sex, not at the speed it was moving, but I took a few milliseconds to plan my move. Guns make noise; noise draws people. It was one reason I often preferred the blades. I dropped the gun back in the holster with one hand while I snatched a knife from the sheath with the other. I didn't start out ambidextrous, but the nuns insisted I fight two-handed and trained me to do so.

The blade was flying as my adversary launched its body at me and the tip of the blessed metal hit true, burying itself hilt deep into the creature's throat. Momentum kept it coming. As it emitted the gurgling keening sound brought on by the struggle to breathe, a second figure strolled out from the open doorway. A second blade was in my hand before my mind could process the other person. He was in a man's form, standing very still; intent on watching the show and no more human than the beast I'd just tagged with a knife.

The first creature made a furious hissing sound, black stringy hair whipping around a gray face, teeth exposed to show black gums. The blade was set tight into the wound. It wouldn't immediately bleed out which was unfortunate since I knew many of these demonic creatures needed to lose their heads to go down. If I could just get the blade, this one would be finished.

Going with my suspicion, I swung my right leg high in a roundhouse kick and the heel of my boot struck the thing's jaw, catching the blade as it went, and knocking it loose. There was a second gargling squeal and the creature dropped to its knees, blood as black as used motor oil gushed out in a thick spew almost like pus from the wound, splatting against the asphalt.

I heard a slow clap start as the creature sagged to the pavement. I looked up from the body, away from the slowly blackening skin and ashy eyes, to the man-shaped creature who stepped out further; his bald head a burnished black, his wide eyes distinctive in his dark face. He wore gloves over his long-fingered hands, and he wore a duster like some cowboy from a bygone era. He was exotic and attractive, and wow did he stink of evil.

"That was impressive," he said, his tone easy. "And before you stick one of those knives in me, might I have a moment of your time?"

"Stand very still, pretty boy," I replied through my gritted teeth.

He did as I asked, holding out his hands to show no weapons. Not as if his kind needed any. I suspected he could top most men in hand to hand fighting without breaking a sweat. Of course, I know his capabilities. And his weaknesses.

"Shame you destroyed my pet," he said, his eyes dropping to the heap at my feet. The creature looked more like a fallen statue now, limbs hardened into rigid lines, seams of red embers threading through its face like burning tears.

I was witness to the gradual deterioration of these hellish corpses before and felt no need to see it again. Before long, the body would begin to disintegrate, taking flesh and hair, fabric, and bone, all flaking off into a wave of ash and dust. I shifted my eyes from the carnage at my feet to the new visitor who still stood at a distance, legs braced, but still maintaining a casual air of someone just dropping by for a visit.

"Sorry about ruining your fun," I answered. "Why are you here?"

"I am merely a messenger," the demon continued, giving me a small bow. "I come bringing greetings from a friend."

"Fine, greetings received," I snarled. "What is your name, *Messenger*?"

"Oliver Hardy," he replied. "I would shake your hand, but I'm afraid you might cut mine off at the wrist." He cocked his head. "Love the knives, by the way. You've got a substantial aim."

"Yeah, thanks," I agreed. "Now, who sent you?"

"My master goes by many names, but I believe you know him as Paul." A half-smile quirked his lips showing very white teeth. "It appears you and he now have a common adversary. He wishes for a meeting. He would like to discuss--" he paused, his lips puckering as he thought,"he hopes to provide support in your attempts to apprehend the one who has murdered your people."

I felt a shiver slide up my spine like the cold blade of a knife. "What does Paul know about the murders?"

Oliver flashed another smile, but it was grim. "He knows enough to know it is a problem for us," he began, "but he also knows it isn't from our hands." He bowed his head. "Paul sends his respects."

I gave a curt nod. Paul was a true Infernal Lord, one of the twelve disciples of satan. I witnessed his act which usurped, and beheaded, his predecessor. No, Paul wasn't someone I would ever underestimate. Not if I wanted to remain on this side of the blade. Almost worse, was Paul's insistence I join him. He believed I was meant to be a paying member of the Church, and paying meant the price of my soul.

"Aside from the obvious, what does Paul want from me?"

"He would like to arrange a mutually beneficial meeting of the minds." Oliver gave me another smile. "He believes he might be able to assist you. I understand one of the nuns was murdered, along with her unfortunate companion?"

I nodded. It wouldn't do to lie. Paul would already know

almost as much about the case as I did. He held far-reaching associations, as did the rest of the Church.

"He will send a message to you when he is able to meet," Oliver held a cell phone out to me, all glass and metal.

"And he can track me with this," I said, nodding to the device.

"He wishes to assure you he would not."

"Tell your boss I will contact him when I can meet up." I slanted him a glance. "He's on the web, right?"

Oliver gave me another half-smile, amusement evident on his face. "Yes," he agreed.

"Good, I will get back with him later."

Oliver took a breath, a sigh really. My grip on the second knife tightened, but I didn't show the tension on my face. There was no way I was going to let on how twitchy this guy made me.

"I will relay your message," Oliver agreed. Without another word, he spun, his long jacket swaying around his legs. "'Til we meet again," he said. Then he picked up speed, going from a walk into a sprint in half a second, and before I could take another breath he cleared the far end of the alley.

After a long moment of silence, I looked down at Oliver's pet. What remained was an ashy smudge and the vague outline of something which was no longer.

CHAPTER FIFTEEN

I met Alex and Abe at a restaurant of Abe's choice. Goose Creek Diner catered to a sedate crowd, a fair number of them blue-haired or harried mothers chasing around toddlers with sticky fingers. I wasn't exactly sure why Abe chose the place, but I was distracted enough by my earlier encounter not to care.

We were ushered into a booth and a plastic basket of corn muffins was put before us. I wasn't shy. It took some calories to fight the bad guys. I took a mini muffin and a blob of butter and looked at Alex.

"What happened during your autopsy?" I kept my voice pitched low. There weren't a lot of people who would want to hear those details, especially when they were sitting down for a meal.

Alex shook her head and her gold curls caught the lamplight. "I know you guys have gotten used to the weird stuff going on," she began, "but this is way out of my paygrade."

I shrugged. Alex was a physician, and a good one, working at one of the public health clinics located in the low income and sketchy part of town in Atlanta. For the time being, she traded her gritty work and peach-scented cottage for my little home and work which required even more grit. In our last run-in with the other side of reality, her eyes were opened in an abrupt way. Now she knew what lay behind the mask of the mundane during the day and what hid in the shadows at night. I could see it was a struggle to find where she fit into the pattern.

"Then I guess the murder was significant. What was the cause of death for Slyvie?"

Alex's eyes narrowed, the green glint of them her only sign of distaste. "It wasn't like any of the mummified bodies I've ever seen. All the bodily fluids were drained, but it's where the comparison ends. The soft tissue atrophied more than a normal mummy's, and," she made a vague gesture with her hand, "they seemed to have lost all their elasticity. Everything crumbled when Bandish touched it and by the time we shifted the body, it was already starting to disintegrate."

"Then no cause of death." I glanced between the two. Abe's expression was grave but impassive. Alex looked like she was still trying to comprehend what happened during the procedure.

"Sorry. I don't have one for you. As for Sister Mary Carmella, she clearly died in a fight. There were multiple contusions, and it appeared she was strangled. The final death might have been a tremendous blow to the back which severed her spinal cord. But even without that, the shock would very likely have gotten her anyway." Alex looked at me. "I'm sorry, Sam. I know she was a friend."

"She was. And she was a good woman."

We were all silent for a long moment. The waitress in her torn blue jeans and shopfront tee came and took our orders. The dining fare was mostly home cooking, and when we got our full plates, I realized why Abe decided on the place. It was homestyle like mama used to make. Well, most mamas, my mother died when I was very young so there wasn't anyone to make meatloaf and mashed potatoes for me.

"What did you think of Dr. Bandish?" I asked at last.

"He knows what he's talking about," Alex replied, her words cautious.

"He is an unusual fellow, but he does good work," Abe agreed.

I slanted him a look and he arched a brow. He had replaced the dark-rimmed glasses, and although the jeans substituted the slacks, he still sported the just-walked-out-of-the-office look.

"What will happen to her? To the bodies?" I asked.

Abe tilted his head. "Slyvie's remains won't stay intact much longer," he noted. "After the post mortem exam is complete, what remains will likely be cremated and sent home to be interred. Perhaps the same will happen to Sister Mary Carmella."

I nodded. There was no way either family should be subjected to seeing the bodies as they were. And considering how quickly Slyvie's was disintegrating, it probably wouldn't survive the transport anyway. Cremation was the best choice.

"Have you ever seen anything like it?" I looked between the two people I trusted most. "What could cause this?"

"I have never," Alex responded quickly. "Did you speak to your source? The cop?"

I nodded. "This is not the only case of spontaneous mummification."

Abe looked up at me in surprise, his expression quickly going to a blank. It reminded me once more that although I trusted him, there was a lot I didn't know about Abe.

"What did you learn?" Alex again spoke up although I

suspected it was only because she wasn't lost in some other thought.

"There have been three reported cases in this area," I answered. "I haven't gotten a wider scope. Cops don't exactly like discussing these things with independent investigators."

"Then three may be the tip of the iceberg." Abe's expression was a study in introspection.

"This is sending up alarms for you?"

His eyes focused on me and his expression cleared. "Not the MO, but the possibilities are a little concerning."

"I'll have someone to get the total number for us," I continued. I knew of just the right computer geek who could get the info for me.

"I have a meeting set up too," Alex volunteered.

I gave her a sharp look.

"Don't get all Rambo on me, Sam," she said, shaking her head. "This guy is a member of law enforcement. And he's from Europe. I thought he might have some insights since our creep has gone international. He's meeting me back at the morgue."

"How are you going to bring in the little fact that the bodies were mummified?" I asked, arching a brow at my best friend.

"I can feel my way through the conversation," she replied. "I've got this."

"Are you going armed?" The question came from Abe.

"Of course," she answered. "The guy might seem trustworthy, but I'm not betting my life on his honesty."

———

Declan got out of the Beamer and crossed the small lot with Russ walking alongside him. He had no intention of taking the guy into the autopsy room with him, but only into the building where he could sit and wait. Russ could put away quite a bit of food and he demonstrated this ability at Applebee's while Declan only picked at his. As an incubus, food wasn't a necessity for life but Declan found partaking in a meal now and then pleasurable. Most of the time. This time, however, he just didn't seem to have the appetite for it and Russ devoured two plates of his own while finishing off what his Boss didn't eat.

When Alex called needing his help, Declan was both surprised and elated. There was just something he couldn't shake off about her, aside from her beauty, of course. The fact he couldn't seem to pull from her was curious enough, but a touch of her skin didn't increase his hunger for sustenance at all. The more attractive the human was, the more his hunger raged, which was the way it was, until now. Until her. Then the call ended and he began processing what Alex did for a living and what she needed from him. A sense of foreboding began clouding his thoughts. He didn't doubt the bodies she asked him to view would be the nun and Slyvie. There were just too many coincidences for it to be any other way.

As for the nun, he held no remorse. She was a member of the righteous and there was no doubt in his mind she was a cross-carrying member of the righteous army. He'd felt it as soon as the first punch was thrown. Instead of cowering on her knees and chanting those pleading prayers, she fought, and she fought well. Her death at his hands weighed not on his conscience, if he even possessed such a thing, for all is fair in love and war. No, no remorse, and no second thoughts about it. He won the fight fair and square and she lost. Simple as that.

Slyvie, though, was another story and he knew when he set his eyes on her dead body self-hatred would once again rear its ugly head. Her dried and deteriorating corpse, devoid of life, were what was left over, *his* leftovers. To look upon her again would be like someone opening the refrigerator and staring at the desiccated remains of a Thanksgiving turkey which sat forlornly in its cold coffin for many months past the meal in which it made its debut. This thought sickened him. The thought of what he *was* sickened him. And the thought he would have to feed again, and again, and again, leaving many dried human shells behind made the plate of food set in front of him all the more unappealing. So, when the bearded Uber driver asked if he was going to eat, Declan was more than happy to hand the plate over.

From the Beamer and through the small parking lot, the incubus was silent, his face set in grim anticipation as he approached the side entrance of the building. He pulled open the door and stepped inside. The smell of death hit him straight on. It was mixed with scant traces of his own scent, confirming his suspicion as if he'd just cracked open the door of the refrigerator and the bloody light blinked on bright as you please, and there layeth the leftovers.

"I need you to wait for me here," Declan said, pointing to a line of plastic and metal chairs lining one wall. "I shouldn't be long."

"It's okay, Boss," Russ said. "I'm a big boy now. I have no problem coming with."

Declan shook his head. He wasn't ready for someone like Russ to see what was leftover from his work. It was going to be bad enough having Alex staring at him while he viewed Slyvie.

"Wait here," Declan said. "The last bloody thing the Doctor needs is you tossing the massive amounts of your Applebee's all over her bodies of evidence."

It came out harsher to Declan's ear than to Russ's, who just shrugged and plopped down in one of the chairs. He swiveled around and propped his well worn sneakered feet on the third chair over, his long legs extending well over the second and crossing at the ankles in the third one.

"Your dime. Your time," Russ replied. "I'll just do a little resting of the eyes until you get back."

"Thanks," Declan said as he pushed the bar on the door and went through, leaving it to close on its own.

It could have been the lighting, fluorescent bulbs could play tricks on the eyes, but as he walked, things like the walls and the tiled floor seemed to shimmer, and wave, and fade. Declan stopped and shut his eyes, giving them a moment to readjust. When the normally solid darkness appeared, he opened them, and…

He was standing inside the stone archway. The oil lamps flickered around as if caught in a gale, casting fleeting shadows all over the room before him. A rancid smell like rotting meat permeated his nose and left a tanged distaste in his mouth.

"Good for you to show," a man with cherub cheeks and rumpled blondish-gray hair grumbled. "And about bloody time too. I was beginning to believe the Yard didn't give a damn about the death of a whore such as this."

Declan blinked. He could see the man wiping his hands down the front of a stained white apron. The sleeves of his white shirt were rolled up past the elbows and all of the skin below was coated in blood; some of it dried and flaked where the coating was thinner as if he'd been at his task for a while now. The source of the blood lay stretched across the wooden block table on her back, naked and already beginning the process of decay.

"And they sent two of you I see."

Declan found himself opening his mouth, talking, as if he were both inside himself and outside at the same time.

"I'm Inspector Declan Maxwell Faulkner and this is my partner Inspector Abraham Shepherd."

"Pleasure," the man smiled, revealing a row of crooked yellow teeth. "I'm Barker, the local butcher it appears, appointed by the Lord Mayor over this sodding mess. Well, I'll not offer a hand, unless of course, you've no qualms with a bit of rotted gore to grease your palm."

"It's alright, Sir," Abraham said. "That won't be necessary."

"Good," Barker said. "I'm not a man for frills and formality anyway. So, let's get to the meat of the matter, shall we? No identification on this one. The most immediate cause of her death was most definitely blood loss from the gash she has across the entire width of the front of her neck."

Barker pointed his plump and bloody index finger at the killing wound as if neither Declan nor Abraham could see it for themselves.

"Her liver is missing, but she was dead to the world by the time it was taken from her."

Both Inspectors approached the table leaning over to follow Barker's points and explanations.

"It's just like the others," Abraham said. "Same cause of death, missing organ, and the same type of victim."

Declan gave a slight nod and then turned, noticing a pile of clothes on the floor next to one of the wooden table legs. He glanced back up at Barker who was starting another rolling description about the victim's spleen.

"Excuse me," Declan said. "Sorry to interrupt. I see you are still in possession of this woman's belongings. I know you said there was no identification found, but did you find anything else on her besides her clothing?"

"A couple of shillings," Barker replied. He stepped over to the pile, picked it up, and then set it on Declan and Abraham's side of the table. Moving one ruffled cuff of the victim's dress sleeve aside, he revealed the money pieces. "There's also a

pawn ticket here. You might be able to find out who she was with it."

Abraham lifted the ticket up and studied it for a moment. "I know this place. It's just a few blocks from here."

Barker nodded and then lifted something else from the top of the pile. "Most unsettling was this."

Declan leaned over and peered into the man's blood smeared palm at the small cylindrical object which laid in the center. The chain, broken but still threaded through a hole near what could have been the top of the piece, was grimed up with something more dark and sinister than just tarnish. It lay limp and draped over the side of Barker's hand. Declan reached over to take the object from him and then thought better of it.

"What's so unsettling about a piece of jewelry?" he asked, retracting his hand.

"Not the piece, per se," Barker replied. "Just where I found the blasted thing."

"Oh," Abraham spoke up, "and where was that?"

Barker's mouth stretched in a disgusted grimace. "Her nether regions, Inspector. Her nether regions. It was tucked half an arm deep into her vagina, all the blasted way from her cervix to her womb."

Declan blinked again and the hallway was just the hallway. He swallowed down the need to retch and wiped the beads of sweat from his forehead. At the time, he'd paid no real mind to the jewelry. It was truly where it was found which mattered to the case, and who put it there and why. At the time, it was just a sodding piece of weird jewelry. At the time…

Declan felt a hand land lightly on his arm.

"Inspector Faulkner?"

Alex was standing next to him with a concerned look on her face. A blue mesh bouffant cap covered her head, framing her heart-shaped face and highlighting the slight bluish tinge to her gray eyes. Declan glanced dazedly over the blue paper gown she wore over her scrubs and onto the little blue mesh booties covering her shoes.

"Are you okay? You look like you're about to pass out."

"I'm fine," he replied, lifting his eyes back to her face. "Sorry. Morgues always make me uncomfortable."

Especially when the bodies inside them were the ones I caused to be there in the first place, he thought.

She smiled and her whole face seemed to light up. "If you don't want to go in there, I'll understand."

Declan rubbed his face in his hands and blew out a breath. "No, it's okay. I've got this."

Alex simply nodded and led him down to the doors leading into the autopsy room. Here, the fluorescents glared and buzzed ever so slightly, the lighting multiplied by two large surgical lamps attached to arms that were anchored into the ceiling. They shone brightly overtop two side by side autopsy tables where the last remains of the nun lay on one and the dried mummified corpse of Slyvie on the other.

The young woman reached into a small box next to one of the tables, plucked out a couple of green latex gloves, and slid them onto her delicate hands.

"There's a stool to your right, Inspector. I suggest you make use of it."

"Thanks," he said, sitting down.

"Now," Alex continued, "the body on this table is a no brainer. She died from obvious trauma, so I don't need help there. But this one, as you can see for yourself, is a whole other matter."

"Mummified," Declan mumbled.

"Yep, and this isn't your run-of-the-mill mummy either. This woman died at nearly the same time as the other one. The doctor who did the initial autopsy couldn't make one single cut without compromising the tissues; they were so dry."

"They disintegrated?"

Alex nodded. "One cut of the blade and poof. Dust. She can be moved with little damage and we were as careful as we could be, but any other invasive measures are out."

Declan stood up unsteadily and stepped over to Slyvie's table.

You did this, he thought, *you and your bloody hunger. It serves you right to have to look at her. Look at her face, her neck, her body. Look at it all and look well. This is your work!*

"Have you ever seen anything like this? I mean, seriously, mummification takes a long time, not just days." She paused. "Inspector?"

He swallowed hard, his mouth tasting of something foul like bile. The beads of sweat made another appearance on his forehead, the sides of his face, and under his arms. It ran rivulets down his skin, cooling his body until he felt a shiver. He gripped the side of the table with both hands, clenching his fingers tight against the metal, wishing he could find some small bit of relief and just rip the bastardly thing out from under the mummy. Perhaps it would hit the tiled floor and explode in a cloud of dust, making this entire thing go away.

You did this to me, Asmodeus, you ripe bastard. You gave me this hunger and set me loose in this realm. No, you are the real reason she lays here on this fucking table and you should be here to witness your handy work. But you'd like it, wouldn't you? Nothing would give your sick and twisted self more pleasure than seeing the damage you are ultimately responsible for…

"Inspector Faulkner?"

The sound of Alex's voice yanked him out of the poisonous

thoughts and thrust him back into their conversation. He ignored her question; to answer it would be to either incriminate himself or bald-faced lie to her. Changing the subject was a better option. Offering a possible solution to one of her problems was even better.

"My suggestion would be to try rehydrating the remains," he finally managed. "Not water though. Maybe something more viscous like liquid fabric softener?"

Alex's smile returned and broadened. "We've been so locked on trying to cut through the tissue, we never even thought about rehydrating it first. Fabric softener? Brilliant. You are a modern-day Sherlock, you know that?"

Declan met her eyes with his, holding them for a moment and she didn't look away. He did.

CHAPTER SIXTEEN

Fort Myers Florida was hot, no big surprise there. I stepped off the airplane and the humid saltiness of the air hit me full force. I was sweating slightly by the time I walked down the steps pushed up to the side of the airplane like some kind of traveling carnival ride. But this trip was on my dime, and I needed a flight I could take immediately and cheaply.

The rental car building was a low 70's joke, all concrete and no thought to aesthetics. The woman behind the counter looked like she'd rather be anywhere but here. The air conditioning was blowing full blast, but a puff of humid air breathed in each time the doors swung open as though a dragon was lying in wait just around the corner.

I got my rented compact sedan from the lot and left the airport. I didn't want to be late for my appointment. Rob Castel was a little on the nervous side, and making him wait for me was not a good idea. I got his name from Kurt, a close friend of none other than the Hand of God himself, Victor McCain. And while Kurt was an easy-going, surfer wanna be with a heart of gold,

Rob was an uptight worker bee with a brilliant mind but limited tolerance for chaos.

Chaos tended to be my steady date, so my arrival was not always a happy event for Rob. But if I wanted to get something done, and without the long arm of Vic McCain reaching in to dabble in my problems, I needed to go to Rob rather than the more affable Kurt.

Rob's home was situated in the palm-shaded neighborhood just a few streets away from the famed Edison Ford Winter Estate. While the renowned inventor moved to Florida to enjoy the climate and the fantastic view from his lush gardens, Rob chose to remain locked up inside his ultra tidy home. When I rang the bell, it took him a few long minutes to answer. I figured like any other tech-savvy geek, he was likely to have a camera installed by the door to observe his visitor. He knew enough about me to realize heading for the back door wouldn't have been prudent. He also knew I carried cash.

When he answered, I saw his eyes drop to thigh-high level, not because he was checking me out, but because the last time I arrived at his door, Bart and Fluffy were with me. If I thought I could have, I would have walked them on the plane for this ride since they truly loved Florida, but my cheapo tickets didn't include pets.

"Rob," I greeted him. I didn't hold my hand out for a shake. He wasn't a handshaking kind of guy, and touching me would make him doubly nervous.

He gave me a slight nod in return, and tried to smile, but failed with a half grimace.

"Can I come in?"

He hesitated at the door. I was pretty sure he knew he didn't have a choice, but I wanted to give him the impression he might.

"I have a job for you, purely research," I added.

Rob stepped back and allowed me into the dim interior. For someone who lived in sunny Florida, he certainly liked his shade. I studied his narrow back as I followed him through the orderly living area into the larger space he used as an office. A massive shelving unit was installed since my last visit here, and the tools of his trade filled the spaces with wires, black boxes, keyboards, flat-screen monitors, and other things I couldn't identify.

"What are you looking for?" Rob wasn't much for small talk but the directness was good. I didn't have a lot of time to waste.

"I have a computer search for you. It's information I couldn't exactly get myself." I gave him a meaningful look and was happy to see the flash of interest in his eyes. He pulled out two chairs next to a desk which held no less than four monitors and gestured to me to sit down.

"Okay," he slid into the seat closest to the keyboard, and under the rapid clicking and typing, the screens lit up in all their technicolor glory.

———

Alex followed Declan out into the waiting area where he'd left Russ. He was in pretty much the same position, only asleep with his head lolled back and tilted against the wall. His mouth was agape and he was snoring loudly.

"Wow," Alex said with a laugh.

"Bloody chap sounds like a congested lawnmower," Declan said, nudging Russ's leg with his knee. "Come on now, sleepy time's over. Look alive."

Russ cracked open an eye and shut his mouth, smacking his lips a couple of times before he lifted his head. His long legs spilled out onto the floor as he set upright, stretching, and yawning.

"Feel better?" Declan asked with a sardonic grin.

Russ rubbed both eyes with the heels of his hands and then pried the heavy lids apart to look up at Declan and then over to Alex.

"Sorry Boss," he said with another yawn, "a full belly makes me sleepy. Who's the beautiful lady?"

"This is Alex, the doctor I was telling you about. Alex, meet Russ, my Uber driver slash assistant during my stay here."

Russ stood up and shook Alex's hand. "Nice ta meetcha," he said with a boyish grin. "Do you come here often?"

Alex giggled.

"He also moonlights as a comedian," the incubus said with a roll of his eyes.

"I see that," she said to Declan and then turned to Russ. "And no, this isn't my first time here in this particular morgue."

Russ raised a playful brow. "Hang out with the dead often, do you?"

A sly smile touched her lips. "Much too often I'm afraid, but I prefer the living. Say, since you guys are a little less dead than my normal homies these days, how about joining me and a friend of mine for dinner? I make a mean burrito."

Declan opened his mouth to decline the offer when he felt Russ's sharp elbow jab into his ribs.

"We'd love to," Russ said, giving his boss a look which screamed not to turn down free food, especially burritos, ever. "Just name the time and place. We'll be there with empty stomachs, a hopeful smile, and a case of beer."

"Oh for crying out loud," Declan mumbled under his breath.

Alex laughed. "It's okay. I could definitely use a beer when I'm finished up here."

She reached under the gown and pulled out a small notepad

and pen, scribbling furiously before ripping off the page and handing it to Declan.

"Here's the address where we're staying. Dinner is at seven."

Declan and Russ strode back out into the parking lot and climbed into the Beamer.

"Why the hell did you do that?" Declan asked.

Russ shrugged and strapped on the seatbelt. "Because you weren't going to. Oh, and you're welcome."

Declan gave him a stern look.

"I mean it's pretty obvious you like the lady," Russ said, starting the car and pulling out onto the street. "And forgive me for saying so, but you don't seem suave with the ladies if you know what I mean. But don't you worry, good ol' Russ is here to bridge the gap of your social awkwardness."

Declan just sat there, speechless.

———

I couldn't sleep. I sat up in bed, pushing the rough white sheets with the requisite ugly bedspread to the foot of the bed and standing. My eyes automatically went to the little table next to my hotel room bed. The gun was still there, the handle in my direction, the black beady eye of the muzzle directed toward the door. If anyone decided they wanted to visit me, I would be ready, and they would regret the impulse.

I slid off the bed and padded barefoot to the bathroom. The fluorescent light was not flattering to my pale complexion, and it gave my red hair an orange tint. Attractive. I glanced toward my phone and pondered again what my next steps should be. Should I contact the nuns? Should I put out a call to Brother Joshua? Should I call Alex and Abe to warn them?

I switched off the light and shuffled blindly to the round table set strategically in front of the single window. There were lights pressing at the curtains, street lights glowing golden through the thick material. I ran a hand down the length of one panel and pulled back the fabric. My door faced the road. I retreated to Estero Boulevard when I left Rob's tidy home. With a full flash drive full of nightmares, I wanted somewhere safe and familiar to run to. The hotel was cheap, on the beach, and fairly clean.

Through the glass, I could see the street was quiet. There were a few inebriated co-eds staggering along the sidewalk, and a few hardened souls who lived and worked in the night venturing to their work establishments. But for the most part, the residents and tourists on the beach were tucked in their beds, believing for all the world they were safe. Safe from the monsters bumping around in the night.

They weren't.

Now I moved away from the window, grabbing my weapon and putting it in a pocket I sewed into the comfortable sweat shorts. It was sad I always felt the need to be armed, but since learning the Devil was a personal family friend, I didn't trust many people.

I put on flip flops. If I was going to the beach, I wanted to be comfortable, and besides, I could kick them off if I wanted to run. I locked the door behind me as I slipped out into the night. My eyes skimmed the darkness, the heat, and moisture like velvet against my skin. Nothing to fear here. Correction. There was nothing here to be afraid of which I couldn't or wouldn't encounter elsewhere. And from what Rob discovered, it would be good to be fearful wherever I was.

Dozens. There were literally dozens of mysterious deaths, leaving bodies as mere husks. It was staggering, so many people could be victims and an alarm not sent up among the ranks of some law enforcement agency. But the truth was, many of the

cases were buried before they ever came to life, the investiga-
tions snuffed out before they ever reached the cop on the street.
And it wouldn't count the others, the many murders gone unnoticed by the all-seeing cyber eye.

I ducked behind the hotel and stepped onto the wooden
planking leading to the beach. The moon was a buttery drop in
the sky, the stars like glittering bits of glass. The waves licked at
the sand with a peaceful repetition, and I turned to gaze out over
the flat expanse of the Gulf.

My world was like a broad hallway with closed doors that
swung open at unexpected times, revealing unbelievable things,
mysterious things, terrible things.

This new kind of murder made me shiver. The victims
stretched across the United States and beyond, touching upon
every continent, every region. Age, sex, socioeconomic status;
nothing seemed to matter. Death was again the great equalizer,
and it came for each of them in turn. But these deaths weren't
prevalent enough to raise too many alarms. A body found every
three to four months, here and there. And the condition of the
bodies wasn't exactly the same. I closed my eyes to shut out the
visions.

So, why now did they show up on searches? Rob couldn't
say for sure except to note many of his files were tucked in
obscure records, buried. And the families of the victims? What
were they told?

I pressed one hand to my chest. There was a lot of grief in
those pages. There was sorrow woven into the reports for these
victims, sorrow for someone's mother, brother, father, son, sister,
well-loved, now missed. And the photos flashed through my
mind, some in the pencil sketched black and white of early
photography, some technicolor high density, supersaturated
snaps. But the condition? Always the same. Dust unto dust.

———

Declan slid the key card into the slot at the top of the lock and then pulled it out when the tiny light next to it turned bright green. With the other hand on the doorknob of his hotel room, he paused, glancing over to see Russ grinning at him with a whole lot of teeth like some proud Tom cat who just snagged a prized mouse. Declan knew good and well the satisfied smile was due to the fast one he'd pulled regarding dinner with Alex and her friend, but there wasn't a need to be a prig about it. He paused, waiting for Russ to finish his gloating and go into his own room, then thought better of it. The guy might get a bit more satisfaction foregoing his own quarters for the moment and following Declan into his, probably to offer more advice of the romantic nature or to add in a few more tasteless puns aimed at Declan's supposed awkwardness. But it wasn't the real reason. No, the real reason he didn't dally any longer was because he actually did like Russ who was a good-natured guy and didn't deserve to be in the presence of what lay on the other side of the door.

The thick drapes were pulled across the glass of the sliding door to the balcony, shading the room. There was a soft glow from the bedside lamp which nuzzled against the dimness and highlighted the warm autumn tones of the walls, carpet, and bedspread. It gave the room a semblance of comfort which is what the designer intended and what Declan would have felt had there not been someone occupying one of the dinette chairs near the balcony door. He closed the door behind him and tossed the key card onto the mahogany desk.

"They have telephones now, mate," Declan said. "Brilliant invention."

Panas Kovalenko stood up. He gave Declan a smile, slight but genuine enough to reach his light blue eyes.

"True," he replied, "but I like the old fashioned face-to-face better."

"They also invented Skype. You can be face-to-face without being so face-to-face."

Panas laughed, taking a couple steps closer to Declan and extending his hand out for a shake. Declan grinned, shook hands, and patted the man's back when he pulled the incubus into a brotherly hug.

"Then you would lose out, my friend," Panas said, stepping back.

"You were accompanied?"

"Of course," he replied. "As you should be."

Declan shook his head. "How long have we known each other?"

"Long enough to bring extra whenever we meet," Panas said with a knowing smile. "You should rethink your ways, comrade. These days are not as they once were and neither is the hunt."

"The hunt hasn't changed."

"Perhaps not, but the prey has, they've adapted. Their technology has advanced, you can't argue, can you?"

Declan thought about the cabin and the two bodies he'd left there. An argument with his old friend would have been ludicrous, so no argument there. If the human remains were left in the cabin a hundred years ago, even decades ago, they probably wouldn't have been discovered out in the middle of nowhere until they were decomposed to nothing but bones and dust, and even then who would have made anything of two nameless skeletons found there? The answer was no one. It would have been hushed up with the threat of some bit of bad luck for anyone to tell about it, like a curse or an urban legend. Now everyone was connected, even the homeless and downtrodden carried cell phones of some sort. It was what gave the hunt an even greater appeal but it was becoming riskier.

There were those who specialized in cleanups, of course. The Church of the Light Reclaimed was indeed one such organization with a long reach and countless resources. Why hadn't he contacted them to remove the bodies? He employed their services sparingly in the past, and they did a damn fine job. So why not this time for this little mess? Declan didn't know, not for certain anyway. Perhaps he'd just grown tired of it all. It was part of the problem with eternity, you were stuck with you eternally.

"No," Declan replied. "No argument there. So, what brings you here?"

Declan didn't inquire how Panas discovered he would be in town, in this hotel, or in this very room. The question would have been futile. They were of the same blood clan, hewn from the same maker, and transformed into the same species of demon by Asmodeus. True, there were members of the clan he didn't know and didn't care to know, but Panas wasn't one of them. Their connection was stronger, a bond sealed with shared feedings and many human lifetimes of walking on Earth.

"A shared business," Panas replied. His smile faded and a grave expression replaced the genial one. "And pleasure of course. How long has it been since we have supped with one another?"

Declan shrugged. "A decade maybe?"

"Far too long. I have taken rooms above you and invite you to partake in the delicacies. There are several choices, my friend."

Panas never traveled without an entourage of what humans would view as concubines, what those of their own species considered as sustenance. Declan felt himself harden, his breath caught in his throat as his heart quickened. Lust was a relentless bitch, no doubt about that. He couldn't help but sense the pulsing need to accept the invitation right then and there. One ride up the elevator followed by a walk down the hall and there he could plunge deep into each of the delicacies, sampling one and then another, consuming a bit of their life force with every thrust. With so many in Panas's harem, you could feed a little from several choices and be as saturated as if an entire life force was devoured from one.

The smile on his friend's face returned. "Ah, I can see you are interested, no?"

Declan stopped, swallowing hard. "The rule still applies?"

Panas nodded. "Yes, my friend. As always, you may take from one or all, but you must leave them intact."

Intact meant alive, and for this, he figured his fellow incubus to be a tad smarter. Panas refused to have any more dealings with the Church than necessary, and never for favors which might require compensation. If there were no bodies, there would be no demand to dispose of them, and no need to call on anyone for a cleanup favor. It was definitely convenient where feeding was concerned, but Declan was more of a lone wolf. He enjoyed the hunt, prowling for those who would be prey. Could he even think about resorting to keeping a harem? No. But he could share in Panas's bounty now and then, couldn't he? Declan shut his eyes.

Focus, damn you. Forget your hunger. Just focus on what is most important now. Think of Russ in the adjoining room. What about Alex? What would they think of this? Of you?

"Perhaps this isn't the best time," Declan said hoarsely.

There was a look of sympathy in his friend's eyes. "You fight hard against your nature. Be cautious, my friend, such things will take their toll on you."

Declan didn't reply.

"My invitation is an open one, should you decide differently."

Declan took a sharp breath, let it out slowly, and changed the subject.

"And your business here?"

Panas's smile faded again. "The business is ours, I'm afraid, not just my own. Although, I doubt you are familiar with her."

Declan narrowed his dark eyes. "Who?"

And Panas began telling him of the woman and his business here.

———

My beat-up computer with its super soul sat open on the table in my compact hotel room when the call came in. I was setting up my flight to leave, money pilfered from the Church of the Light Reclaimed used to fund my battle against all they stood for. The computer discovered the cheapest and soonest flight in a millisecond thanks to the upgraded guts Rob kindly installed.

When his name appeared on the screen of my cell phone, it took a moment for me to digest he wasn't peering over my shoulder to expound on my choice of airlines. No, this was something else, something new.

I tapped the button and answered the call.

"Samantha?" He sounded like he wasn't sure it was me.

"Rob," I replied patiently.

"Um, hi. I, well, I got a notification this morning. Your search terms pinged."

"In English, please."

"There has been another body, another murder. It's not in the system. I just captured the tale-end of a conversation online. But the sender clearly says the corpse is dried out, like dehydrated completely."

"Where?" I snapped, abruptly sitting upright and alert.

"Looks to be in the Smokies," Rob replied. "The address isn't specific as I'd like but…"

"Send me what you know," I exited the search for my flight home and quickly keyed in the alternate destination. If I could get there quickly enough, I might have a chance to catch the bastard. I was determined to get to the bottom of this, and if it meant trailing the monster all over the country, I was prepared.

"Ok, information sent," Rob answered.

I clicked out of the conversation and paused to look at the screen. I needed to tell someone I wasn't coming back to Kentucky. Alex was busy with the European law enforcement officer, and besides, she would ask too many questions.

I shot off a text to Abe and waited for the second it took him to respond, his phone probably already in his hand. Good. I gave him a brief rundown of my plans, explaining my flight didn't leave for a few hours yet. I was restless, but there was little I could do to speed things along. It would be nice if I owned a private plane I could catch at a whim, but those things were a limited commodity.

"Do you want us to meet you at the scene?" Abe asked, his voice pitched low. I wondered if Alex was in the room, listening in.

"It's your decision," I answered. I cast a brief glance outside, watching the sun bounce off the hoods of dated sedans, laser hot. Did I want Alex and Abe to be there? I wasn't sure.

"Ok," Abe replied. I could almost picture him pushing his dark-rimmed glasses up his nose. "I'll let you know. Keep in touch."

I agreed and tapped the button, my eyes drifting again toward the parking lot. There was something else out there in the sun. Something dark, something still, something which seemed to drain the heat out of the scene. I shoved the phone in my back pocket and headed for the door.

———

The banging on the adjoining door between the rooms came shortly after Panas left. Declan threw the deadbolt and opened it. Russ stood leaning against the door frame, grinning.

"Boss, you're in the same clothes."

Declan glanced down at his apparel and then back up at his driver's bearded face.

"So?"

"So, you can't go in the same clothes if you want to make a good impression on the girl."

"*You're* in the same clothes."

"And I am not the one trying to get a date," Russ answered. "You are."

"I'm not--"

Russ held up a finger. "I'm closing this door. Gotta do it, man. Somebody's gotta show you how to get the girl. And when I knock again, you best be in a new set of duds, got it? A shower wouldn't hurt either, for goodness sake."

The door slammed shut and Declan heard the lock click from the other side.

"Quirky bloke," Declan mumbled, closing the adjoining door.

He froze as the stink of burning brimstone filled his nose.

Not again, he thought. *And not now.*

Declan turned his head to the vacant dinette chair which Panas occupied just a few minutes ago. Tendrils of smoke wafted out of the upholstery and then thickened to the consistency of shadows which writhed within the dark folds like black snakes moving in and around the column until shadow became form.

Declan's jaw clenched as the figure became more detailed, more human.

Lucifer smiled. "Nice room. It's a pity you don't have the entire place to yourself."

"Leave him out of it," Declan replied. "He has no part in this."

The old devil's eyes gleamed with the tiniest trace of silver and there was nothing holy about it; a trapped soul gliding by the lens of his eye perhaps, or more than likely a warning to Declan to mind his bloody manners.

"You brought him in to play, Incubus, not I," he replied. "And if you're gonna play, you gotta pay. Isn't it the way?"

Declan moved his hand away from the doorknob to keep from crushing it in his palm. The last thing he needed was a bewildered hotel staff wondering what happened. Okay, so maybe it wasn't the last thing he needed. Declan turned and glared at the dark-haired clean-cut man in the designer suit. No, the last thing he needed was sitting right in front of him.

"He's an innocent," Declan said. "Only my driver. He knows nothing about any of this."

Lucifer's smirk widened as he stood up. "Well now, innocence can only make things more entertaining. I presume he doesn't recognize what you really are?"

When the incubus didn't answer, he continued unabated, approaching Declan as he spoke.

"No, he doesn't. Not one for truth, are you? Well, so be it. The young man will discover who you are in due time I suspect."

Lucifer stopped when he was toe to toe with Declan.

"Leave him alone. It's me you are after."

Declan winced as he felt the scorch of Satan's touch on his cheek. It was merely one finger but the pain was excruciating.

"You think highly of yourself, demon. Or maybe--"

He paused, running his finger down the side of Declan's face. Declan held his breath to keep from screaming as the touch scorched well beneath his skin, so hot he could smell his flesh burning over the brimstone stench.

"Maybe you don't," Lucifer answered, easing the fingertip down to Declan's chin and tapping it a couple of times before lowering his hand. "You despise what you are, don't you? Ah, you don't have to answer. I can see it now. Well, no matter, a psychiatrist I am not. Manage your self-hatred on your own time."

Declan hit his knees when the devil's human hand gave his already burning cheek a couple of taps. The fiery sensation exploded within him, wracking his whole body into spasms. Sweat poured from him, down his face, back, and drenching his shirt. He couldn't breathe at all for a few moments, but when he finally did the breaths came in sharp gasps. Lucifer glared down at him, the smile replaced with a sort of wicked sneer.

"Now, on to our present business," he said. "I am providing you with an incentive, something to help speed up the pace. Retrieve my artifact and return it to me or the young man dies. You have forty-eight hours. I suggest you use the time wisely."

Declan watched Lucifer fade away to shadow, then tendrils of smoke, and then nothing.

There was knocking at the adjoining door. When Declan couldn't answer, he saw the knob turn. Russ cracked the door and peered in at him.

"Dude, you're still wearing the same freaking clothes. And," he halted, inhaling the air, "good God you smell like Hell."

Declan looked up at Russ as he struggled to breathe.

"Aw, come on man. You're having dinner with her, not shagging her. There's no reason to have an anxiety attack over it."

Russ thrust a hand toward Declan in an attempt to help him to his feet.

"Don't touch me!" Declan gasped.

Russ drew his hand back as if it were slapped. "Aren't we touchy? Did someone wee wee in your Wheaties this morning? I do believe they did."

The incubus would have rolled his eyes at the comment but right now he was too busy struggling to restrain himself. Lucifer once again drained him dry with just a few touches and all he wanted was to grab Russ and absorb the life right out of him.

"Please," Declan mumbled. "Please just don't touch me."

Russ raised both of his hands up in a placating gesture. "Okay Boss, no touching. You get on up all on your own."

Declan managed a nod.

"Showering, right? Cause you smell, man. You smell--"

"Like hell," Declan mumbled, pushing himself up onto the bed. "Just give me fifteen minutes and I'll be ready to go."

Russ inched back into the doorway. "Better take twenty, Boss. There are demons that smell better than you."

Declan doubted it very much.

———

I wasn't a theological person; if God and the Devil existed then I'd seen only one of them. Of course, I'd been close enough to the Prince of Lies to know he was more than flesh and blood, but my brush with the supernatural went much deeper. Now I felt the sensation of someone walking over my grave as I opened the door and stepped onto the pavement. The air was still muggy and close. I stopped by the door, my fingers hovering by my hip. I was armed, but it didn't reassure me as much as it should. There was a stink out here, a stench caught in the air like a trail of filth.

"Who's out there?" My voice was firm. I wasn't afraid, but I held a healthy respect for my enemies, and by the smell of this one, it was someone I knew well.

The shadow glided into view, and I saw Paul's lapdog, Oliver, step forward. In the dying sun, his dark skin reflected the bloody red glow. He had abandoned the long coat but wore a long-sleeved shirt, something no doubt from a bygone era. The shirt was bordered by a vest made of some sumptuous material. He might have smelled bad, but in truth, he wasn't hard to look at.

"What do you want?" I deliberately loosened my stance, my hand by my side, close enough to the weapon to draw if I needed to. I knew a bullet wouldn't stop him. It might slow him, but I would need a blade to finish him off.

"I come with the invitation," he replied, his deep voice silky smooth.

"I don't think I'm up for a party."

He quirked an eyebrow, stepped forward, saw my expression, and froze. "This invitation is the one we spoke of earlier, to meet with my master. I understand you are interested in his opinion of the newly discovered," he paused, "victims."

My pulse was jumping yet I kept my movements tightly controlled. I leaned against the doorframe and measured my breathing to an easy inhalation. I didn't forget our conversation or Paul, but I would have much rather arranged the meeting myself than have this lap dog at my door.

"And what *does* he know?" I demanded in a long-shot hope Oliver would know something.

Oliver shrugged in an elegant gesture. "My master doesn't stoop to giving me details," he flashed a smile, his teeth very white against his skin. "But I do know he is disturbed by the recent events. These events should not be happening under his watch."

"So he's wanting some information," I snapped.

"Give and take," Oliver answered silkily.

"Where does Paul want to meet me?" I asked with an inward groan.

Face-to-face with one of the Infernal Lords, not a great place to be, but better it be someone I was familiar with. And besides, I suspected Paul was interested in me. At least enough so as he wouldn't try to cut me down at first sight.

"He left the arrangements up to you."

I let out a breath. The last time I saw Paul, it was at a horror house in Kentucky, and I didn't want to repeat another scene. My mind scrambled. I needed to be somewhere I could get away, somewhere with enough people to witness so Paul wouldn't cross me, but where no one would get hurt. There didn't seem to be a lot of choices.

"Tell him I'll be at the Beached Whale in thirty," I said.

Oliver cocked his head, eyebrows up, and then nodded. When he turned to leave, I felt as if a physical pressure lifted from my chest. I stayed on alert in the doorway until his back was nothing but a blur in the distance. Then I went inside to get ready for my meeting with the devil's favorite son.

CHAPTER SEVENTEEN

Alex answered the door after the first ding dong of the bell. She was all smiles and bright eyes. A white with red trim apron hit about thigh length on her and the phrase *Kiss The Cook* was printed in the same shade of red on the bib. It obscured her voluptuous figure but Declan knew how beautiful her curves showed in jeans and a shirt. His heart hammered in his chest as her scent wafted towards him.

So hungry, he thought. *So damned hungry*.

In his mind, he could see himself ripping the apron off of her and tearing at the clothes beneath to get to her, her skin, her scent, all of her. His body tensed at the thought of filling her, making her scream in ecstasy as she climaxed again and again, around him, on him, and with him as he moved in and out of her until the orgasm overtook him and the hungry beast within fed away until it was sated. He felt the front of his jeans tighten as he hardened and when she spoke, his breath snagged in his throat.

"Hey guys," Alex said brightly as she swung the front door wider. "Come on in. Dinner's almost ready."

Russ shot an elbow into his side, a quick jab which brought Declan back to himself. He glanced over at the young man with eyebrows raised in a what-was-that-for expression.

"This would be the greeting part, Boss. Here, watch me and follow."

Russ leaned over and gave Alex a peck on the cheek, causing her to giggle and put a delicate hand up over where he'd kissed.

"See? Directions are right there," Russ said with a grin, pointing at Alex's apron. "Now, you give it the old heave-ho, Boss."

Alex laughed.

Declan didn't. He wanted her so much. Right now. Right here. He glanced over at Russ to see him wave his hand in a go-on-now motion and Declan stepped forward and leaned in towards her. His mind was nowhere near anything as chaste as a peck on the cheek, but he managed the motion quickly and stepped back. The beast inside of him screamed in rage as the brief contact gave it nothing in return for its effort to siphon even the smallest bit from her.

"Thank you for your invitation," Declan said, managing a smile as the coldness he always held inside intensified. He held out a six-pack of bottled Corona. "This, uh, goes pretty well with burritos."

"Thanks," she replied. "I'll stick them back in the fridge until dinner."

Declan swallowed hard. His mouth was drier than the Mojave desert.

"The beer was Russ's idea," Declan's voice cracked at the stupidity of informing her about something she already knew, and he paused to clear his throat. "Sorry, Ohio Valley allergies."

Russ elbowed him again and the incubus shot him a severe

look. Russ shrugged and covered his mouth as he gave a little faux cough.

"Uh, yeah, allergies. But like the Boss said, thanks for the invite."

"You're welcome," Alex replied. "It really is our pleasure and I haven't cooked for anyone but me for quite a while. Now come on in. You can join Abe in the living room until dinner is ready. I thought I'd have to hogtie him to keep him from helping."

They followed her inside the foyer to the living room where Abe was stretched out on a LazyBoy recliner watching what appeared to be the local news report. Declan didn't get more than a cursory look at the guy before two huge black and tan Dobermans sprang up on either side of the recliner and charged them, stopping barely a foot away with hackles raised, teeth bared, and furious growls. Their brown eyes were filled with both rage and fear as they began barking ferociously.

"Whoa," Russ exclaimed. "Look at you two. You're like twins. What good doggies, protecting your home from the weird men coming to eat burritos."

He held out his hand and both dogs ceased barking, approaching Russ cautiously. They sniffed his hand and began wagging their nubby tails. The action really was more of a butt wagging than a tail wag. Declan watched as they allowed Russ to extend both hands out to scratch their heads.

"Good boys," he said, glancing over at the incubus. "Well, come on, greet the doggies."

Declan didn't want to come anywhere near the "doggies" but Russ urged him on and Declan reluctantly held a hand out, barely pulling it back in time to keep from getting bitten as both dogs lunged at him.

"Fluffy! Bart! That's enough!" Alex exclaimed. "Both of you, go lay down."

The dogs obeyed, undoubtedly well trained, and turned around with a sullen expression to move back to their spots on the floor alongside the recliner. Declan could still hear them growling low in their massive chests, their eyes locked onto him as if he were a fluffy bit of prey.

"Oh God," Alex said. "I am so sorry. This is the first time we've had visitors around since I took them in, but I've never seen them act so badly. I don't know what's come over them."

Declan knew. And he knew what came over the dogs was *him*. Animals were never terribly happy to see him in general, but when the hunger within him was raging, they despised him with a passion. Most of them were smart enough to either run in the opposite direction or at the very least keep their distance. Occasionally, he'd have one overzealous fuzzy bastard with a death wish, and he made sure to grant it.

"It's okay," Declan said, his voice hoarse. "No worries."

Abe leaned forward in the chair, lowering the footrest, and got up. His movements were restrained as though he was thinking three steps ahead. Whether it was because of the dogs' unpredictable behavior, or some feelings he was picking up from his guests, it was hard to tell.

"Some dogs just need a little time to get used to people. Come on Fluffy and Bart, you two can sit it out in the bedroom. Maybe a time out will help you mind your manners."

Declan saw Alex heave a sigh of relief as the dogs followed Abe out of the living room without protest. One of them, Bart or Fluffy or whatever, shot the incubus with a look of reproach over its shoulder. Declan cast his eyes downward in his best attempt at submission and did a little sighing himself as he took a seat on the couch next to Rus.

"Dogs smell fear, Boss," Russ told him when Alex left to go finish preparing dinner.

Declan nodded.

"You need to chill. You look all tensey like a jack-in-the-box, and you're sweating. Never let the women see you sweat, man. Not unless you're like working out and want 'em to see your manly glisten."

"What?"

"And you look paler than normal if it's even possible," Russ replied. "You'd probably do well to make a date with good ol' Mister Sunshine sometime soon."

"What *are* you going on about?" Declan mumbled.

"Deep breath, Boss, and relax. Just burritos and beer, man. You got this. Tomorrow morning you can call up the bone man and see if he can prescribe some Xanax or something for your woman phobia, cause dude, you got a problem."

Declan's head was starting to swim which was never a good thing and he was beginning to feel shaky like someone suffering from DTs. To Russ, he probably did look like some pitiful bloke in the early stages of some anxiety attack and Declan thought it was way better than the truth. If the guy really knew what was happening to him, he wouldn't dare sit this close.

Maybe just a bit, Declan thought. *Like the pilot. Maybe I could siphon a little from good ol' Russ. It's his fault I'm here in the first place, isn't it. Would he even notice if I did?*

And then he thought, *No. Not Russ. Not ever.*

Thankfully, Abe came back into the living room just as Alex appeared from the kitchen to announce dinner was ready. If they ate quickly enough, Declan and his driver could get the hell out of here, and then he could part ways with Russ at the hotel long enough to take Panas up on his offer. Maybe his old mate really was right. Maybe this harem thing was the way to go. Declan shook his head to try to clear out the useless thoughts and then glanced at Abe.

Russ was on his feet and trailing Alex to the kitchen as if someone lit his arse on fire. Declan didn't move. His eyes were drawn to a flicker of paranormal light. He frowned and looked down, his gaze now fixed on a greenish glow in the left front pocket of Abe's jeans. The man didn't seem to notice him staring. The realization of what the glow was washed over Declan. He couldn't believe he didn't sense it the moment he walked into the house. The ancient power of it appeared like webbing dancing in front of his eyes. The artifact.

If I could just get to it, the incubus thought, *I could take it back to the bloody devil and then this would all be over. I can head back to England and kiss this continent goodbye for a while.*

Abe finally noticed him staring.

"Are you all right?" Abe asked. "You don't look so great."

Declan stood, fighting back both a wave of dizziness and nausea. If he were human, he'd have thought he picked up a nice plague of something, but he wasn't and he knew what famished was when he felt it.

"I think I just need a breath of fresh air," Declan replied. "Do you mind if I step outside for a minute?"

"Not at all. Do you need me to come out with you?"

The greenish glow in Abe's pocket began to pulse in a soothing rhythm, and Declan wondered if the guy could see the light it emitted. But then again, he was showing no sign of alarm so he figured Abe didn't. It was too bright to ignore and surely Alex or Russ would have noticed it too. The hypnotic lines of power snaked across Declan's skin and he shuddered when Abe drew closer.

Let him come out with you, Declan heard in his head. It was definitely not Abe. *Let him come outside with you, and take the artifact from him. Kill him if need be, but take it.*

Declan pulled his eyes away from Abe, looking past him into the kitchen where Russ and Alex were already seated at the table waiting for them.

No. I'm not doing this now. I'll get your fucking artifact, but not now.

Declan winced as the sound of a hissing scream went through his head. The sound of a boiling tea kettle would have been an improvement. His demon side snarled inwardly at the sound while his outward flesh struggled to keep the misery off his face.

"On second thought, mate, I am a bit peckish. Low blood sugar is all it is." His face felt stiff when he forced an amiable grin.

Abe returned the smile. "Good then, after you."

Declan sat down on one side of Alex; Russ on her opposite side, too far to jab any more elbows in his ribs. In fact, the table was large enough to accommodate all four of them comfortably without any elbows touching, and Declan couldn't have been more grateful. The last thing he needed was brushing or bumping his super-sensitive flesh against anyone right now. He may not be able to feed off of either Alex or Abe, but he was pretty certain Russ wasn't included in whatever weird shit was going on with the two of them, and didn't desire to hurt the young man. Well, maybe the desire was there, but he would force himself to overcome it.

Alex passed the serving dish with the burritos to Declan first and he managed to take it without touching her. The bowls with beans and rice were too small to keep away from her skin without it either looking incredibly awkward or causing some dish-breaking mishap. He asked her to set them on the table next to him and she obliged without a remark. When everyone filled their plates and were shoveling food in their mouths, Abe set his fork down and spoke, directing his words toward Declan.

"Alex told me she briefed you on some of the recent events," his eyes were intense, studying the other man, daring him to say or do the wrong thing.

"She has."

"Then on her judgment, we have decided to trust you." Abe pushed his glasses up his nose in an uncomfortable gesture. "I won't lie. I have my reservations."

Alex grinned. "Trust issues, Abe. They call it trust issues now."

"Fair enough," he replied. "The point is, I'm not sold on bringing outsiders into this and I really don't think Samantha would be keen on it either. But I trust Alex and I respect her decision."

"Um, thanks?" Declan managed, not sure whether he was being insulted or not, and too distracted by the demon inside to give it more than a passing thought.

Abe grimaced. "But you are an investigator, so I guess this might work to our advantage. As for your friend Russ, no offense meant, but why are you in this?"

"None taken," Russ replied. "I'm his Uber driver, so I'm what you would call *essential*."

Abe's grimace deepened. "I don't see how that--"

"He stays," Declan said. "Whatever you tell me, you can share it with him."

Abe opened his mouth to protest but Declan held up a hand, stopping him cold.

"Alex asked me to help. Not you. And I mean no offense either but if Russ is asked to leave, I'll go with him. Understand?"

"It's true," Russ grinned. "He'll have to hoof it around town if I leave. I am the Uber man."

Abe shrugged, defeated, turning to Declan. "Okay then, you've seen the body so you know this isn't a murder committed by a normal human. In fact, none of this would be considered normal. How much do you know about the supernatural?"

Declan started to tell him a whole bloody lot more than he did but didn't. There was no sense in being an ass about it.

"I've several cases which don't follow what most would call normal," he replied, his mouth feeling more and more dry by the minute. He took a deep breath and forced himself to keep it together. "If it's worth anything, I do believe in ghosts."

Abe sat silent, pondering as he picked at his burrito with a fork for a moment.

"I think Sam would appreciate help," Alex said. "Maybe not right away, but when all is said and done. She would."

Declan watched Abe, waiting, hoping he would hurry the hell up so he could get out of here and feed before he went completely insane.

"I received a text from Samantha a little while ago," Abe finally said.

"Oh?" Alex asked. "You should have told me." Her face creased with something like concern. "Is she okay?"

"She's fine but she'll be making a detour to Tennessee."

Alex replied with raised brows, chewing the bite of food she took.

Abe said, "They discovered another mummified body in the Smoky Mountains near Gatlinburg, and she's leaving it up to us as to whether or not we join her."

Russ slapped the table causing everyone to jump. "Hot damn, road trip."

Alex and Abe exchanged glances.

"I don't know, Russ," Alex replied, looking at Russ with an expression close to horror. "It might be dangerous."

Russ grinned from ear to ear. "I love me some danger. Hand it on over and I'll whip up a pitcher of dangerous ass lemonade to wash it down. Besides, Uber driver, remember? Totally essential."

Abe cast Alex another look and gave an almost imperceptible shoulder shrug. Alex offered Russ a feeble smile. Declan sat silent, his thoughts muddled and meandering.

I've never been to Tennessee, let alone Gatlinburg. So who could have left a body? Panas? No, Panas thrives on his harem. It can't be him.

"We won't all fit in one car," Russ added, "not comfortably anyway. So we can take my van and I'll drive. That way, you guys can get some rest so you'll be fresh as daisies when we get there."

"Are you sure?" Alex asked. She was apparently up for the excursion, but still uncertain about this new development. "That's a lot of trouble."

"No trouble," Russ replied. "When do you want to leave?"

Abe spoke up. "Actually, I think having an extra hand in driving will be a good idea." He looked at Alex meaningfully. "If something goes awry, we can always change plans." He angled toward the overly enthusiastic Russ. "Is in the morning too soon?"

"Nope. I can gas up my big old beauty and be ready by six."

Alex frowned. "Ugh. Make it seven and you've got a deal." Her gaze went toward Abe, her eyes expressing something Declan couldn't quite read. "Abe and I will pay for the gas and food. You just drive the van."

Declan's eyes widened as the word finally hit him. "Van?"

"Yeah, man," Russ replied, grinning. "The *van*. I know you want to ride. Say it. It's okay. We're all friends here."

Declan groaned. "Bugger me."

"What was that, Boss?"

"Nothing," he replied.

————

Paul did not look like an angel or a demon. He didn't look like an Infernal Lord either. Paul looked like a middle-aged businessman who just stepped off the plane from Chicago. He wore a suit that was well cut but not exclusively made for him. His red hair was a fringe, dusting his head, a balding spot catching the light from the overhead fan fixture. He was seated at one of the tables in the dark interior of the restaurant, a bottle of bourbon in front of him.

I sighed and slid into the seat opposite him. It was ironic that if anyone glanced toward us, I would be the one who stood out. Paul was the epitome of normal if normal was Hell and all the demons wore suit jackets.

"Ms. Tyler," Paul greeted, his voice an ordinary baritone. His accent was easy, a flat twang placing him firmly in the northeast.

"Paul," I returned cordially.

A waitress wearing a tee shirt and blue jean shorts approached the table with her tablet of paper and pencil poised above it. "Happy hour," she began. "We have half-priced appetizers and well drinks."

I watched as her eyes went to the bottle sitting on the table. Clearly bringing in your own libations was frowned upon, but I suspected Paul would have quelled any complaints with a single look. When I dealt with him months ago, he was a mere servant of an Infernal Lord. By murdering his predecessor in front of me, he jumped ranks. Not that you could tell much outwardly. Maybe his suit was a shade more expensive, and I was positive the bourbon was a costly drink, but there was something beneath his eyes, a flickering which made my paranormal sense go on high alert. I became thoroughly disciplined in sensing the unnatural, courtesy of the nuns at the abbey, but I figured I probably could have predicted something was off by just passing by the man now. He had shed some of his humanity, and what was left, well, it stank.

"I'll take a coke," I answered the waitress.

"And bring me a glass of water, if you please." Paul leaned back in his chair, clasping his hands at his middle, the pearly buttons on his white shirt catching the light.

The waitress turned away, and I leaned over the table, careful to still maintain a distance. I didn't want to be too close to one of Satan's favored twelve, but I also didn't want the woman in the next booth with the floral top and walking shorts to hear much of our conversation.

"Your lap dog came to see me."

Paul nodded. "Yes, I sent him."

"Because?"

"We have much to talk about, you and I." He tilted his head. "I dared not wait until you took the time to work me into your busy schedule. I have been informed of the recent activities at the abbey."

"It wasn't you, was it? Maybe your lapdog?"

"I had nothing to do with it," he cut off my words. "I have no desire to get burned by the lovely servants of your God."

I frowned but didn't correct him. Was there a God? Was he mine? I didn't know.

"Okay then, not you, not your lackeys. So, what *do* you know about the situation?"

Paul was silent as the waitress put my drink in front of me, the carbonation tracing bubbles on the inside of the glass. She put his water glass topped with a wedge of lemon in front of him and stood back, waiting impatiently for our order.

"What is your special here?" Paul asked her, eyebrows raised.

"Our bar-b-cue is known all over the Island," she answered.

"Two of those, then," Paul replied with a gesture, and deliberately looked away from her.

The waitress gave an unintelligible grunt and strolled off toward the kitchen.

"Tell me what you know," I demanded, knowing full well I wasn't still alive by being coy. Granted, he wanted me to work as his partner on the side of Satan, but he wasn't likely to take me out anytime soon or so I could only hope. And hope is definitely a strange animal.

He drew in a breath and tapped the table with his fingertips. Like a magic trick, a shot glass appeared next to his hand. He took a moment to remove the cap on the bottle, poured himself a generous shot, and threw it back before answering me.

"I know one of the nuns from the abbey was taken," he began. "I know her body was found later, along with the remains of some other victim." His green eyes slid up to look at my expression. "The part I find problematic is the fact this is not the first set of remains we have stumbled upon. And I doubt it will be the last."

"We, as in the Church?"

He knew I meant the Satanic church he supported, the same one my father was an active member of for much of my life. The one my father then ruled.

Paul inclined his head. "The bodies we have found before were so apparently destroyed by some paranormal force, we felt it only benefitted us to dispose of them. Too many chances of discovery before they completely decomposed."

I shook my head and repeated my earlier question. "And you played absolutely no part in the deaths?"

"No." Paul poured himself a second shot and drank it hastily as though to wash something distasteful from his palette. "This is not an act committed or condoned by the Church." He was frowning now, and I felt his displeasure like a ripple of spiders along my skin. "We have simply been the cleanup crew for whoever is responsible."

"Why bother? The authorities could have saved you the trouble."

"Essentially, yes," Paul agreed. "Despite your belief to the contrary, there are rules to our world. Anything which puts us in danger of discovery is an equal threat to the Dark Lord and your God-loving community at the Abbey."

I sat in silence digesting the news. If the Church was not responsible for the killings, then whoever it was now showed up on a double hit list. The Catholic Church couldn't have a murderer running loose, and the Satanic Church didn't want their cover blown with some rogue killer.

"Does your boss happen to know what might be going on?" I asked the question delicately. I harbored no desire to meet his boss face-to-face.

"We have chosen to handle this at our level," Paul replied easily. I could see the question made him uncomfortable, though.

Did he just squirm like a snake in his expensive suit? I paused, thinking. *Surely the mention of his boss wasn't the reason, was it? Was there some sort of disturbance among the ranks?*

"Then you contacted me…"

Paul sat up a little straighter in his chair, almost like he was forcing self-composure. It fit him as well as a three-fingered glove on a five-fingered hand. The expression on his face though was unchanged and if I'd only seen his face, I would have never picked up on his ever-so-slight discomfort. He didn't hesitate to interrupt.

"We have a common enemy here, Ms. Taylor. I want this ended. To help you seems to be the most sensible option."

The waitress returned to the table with plastic baskets lined with paper. The smell of bar-b-que surrounded us, and my stomach growled. It seemed my body could be simultaneously hungry and on high alert for danger.

After she bustled away, I took a cautious sip of water and picked at my potato salad with my fork. Paul was silent for a long moment, and I watched him take a bite of the sandwich, chewing with obvious pleasure.

"What can you tell me?"

Paul glanced up from his meal. He wiped his fingers on his napkin, appearing to relish the delay. "Do you have an idea what you're up against?"

I frowned. To admit ignorance wasn't my bag. Instead, I chose to remain silent, waiting for him to go on.

"Are you familiar with either the term incubus or succubus?" He took another bite and chewed as I digested his question.

"Demons. Sex demons," I replied.

"Just so," he agreed.

I watched him take another bite and reluctantly tucked into my meal. I needed nutrients, and if my stomach wasn't turning from my dining companion, I figured I should take full advantage.

"The bodies are the result of one of these demons feeding," Paul continued. "They are not a common entity, so I have narrowed down the search for a few individuals."

"Are you going to clue me in on how they can best be stopped?" I wasn't sure where the conversation was going, but my mind was rushing through what I knew about incubi and succubi. I quickly realized my knowledge wasn't extensive.

Paul cocked his head. "They are demons, my dear," he said mildly, "and they can be relieved of their existence here by common means."

I squashed my irritation which was already brewing from his arrogance and took a drink from my coke. "Demons. Hmmm. That would be under your jurisdiction, wouldn't it? So tell me, why aren't you handling them? Why shove it on to me?"

Paul shook his head again. "They are not under my authority. My Dark Lord allows them more freedom. I have no doubt something has gone wrong, however. This behavior, sloppy and unprofessional, cannot be ignored."

I wiped my fingers on my napkin, my hand automatically straying to the blessed blade in the sheath by my side. It wasn't my only weapon, but it was a useful one. Just the mention of demons made my skin crawl.

"Why the mummies?" I asked, changing the direction of my thoughts.

Paul shrugged. "When these demons feed, they extract every drop of energy a body contains. Why the body is dehydrated has something to do with the extreme electrical and chemical exchange."

I took another bite of my sandwich. The fact I could eat while we discussed the condition of a corpse said something about my ability to compartmentalize my life. It was not reassuring. "Okay," I replied, drawing out the word with an exhale. "So these demons are like spiders, right? They just don't cocoon their victims in webbing or skidder around on eight legs."

I paused, eyeing Paul's face for any hint as to whether I was hot or cold to the answer. He gave nothing up with his expression.

"Or do they?" I asked, arching a brow.

Paul leaned back in his chair like a teacher ready to lecture on a favored topic. "All demons have their beginnings. Some are made, such as myself," he gave me a wolfish grin, "and some are born or called into being. One of our more experienced members of the family, Asmodeus, has a specialty." His eyes shifted around the room as though reassuring himself the devil in question wasn't lingering in the corner drinking beer and eating a fried fish sandwich.

I kept my eyes on Paul. I figured if something else wandered into the restaurant, I would feel it. "I take it his specialty is the succubus?"

"Um, yes, and incubus. They are lovely to look at. Beguiling in a way which can't be expressed."

I thought of the possessed painting I saw in the country house when I'd been invited for tea. The entity which slipped from the canvas was beautiful indeed. I couldn't imagine what he would have been like in real flesh and bone. A thought occurred to me. "If I were to meet one of his, um, offspring, would I know it wasn't a human?"

Paul's eyes flashed a deep red. "The creatures of Asmodeus are clever. They have been wandering the earth for much longer than you." He shrugged. "Could you discern what they are? I don't know."

I gave a grunt of dissatisfaction. I would have liked to know with more certainty I could detect these demon spawn just as I could other monsters.

"But you will find they are a worthy adversary," Paul continued. "They are not easily dispatched."

"Okay, so if we manage to take down this being," I began,

"then you would be in our debt, right?" The idea Paul owed me one was a little intoxicating. He might be a demon, but he still followed a code of ethics, as warped as it was.

"Naturally," he agreed. He raised his shot glass in a mock toast, and I nodded. Better the devil you know.

CHAPTER EIGHTEEN

I t took all Declan's composure to knock on the door of Panas's hotel room and not bang on it like some desperate lunatic. He could still sense his old friend, but it may be just residual energy, and he hoped for all he was worth Panas hadn't stepped out, or worse, checked out. Declan didn't trust himself to stop at the front desk to inquire, mostly because the beast inside was moved from simple hungered rage to a torturous screaming so intense he'd reached the point where any human would do, any human at all. He'd quickly parted ways with Russ at his room door with a curt goodnight, not waiting around for the young man to respond, and then retired into his room. He waited a few minutes until he was certain Russ would be out of the hall and then slipped back out to the elevator. His head throbbed and his vision was beyond blurry. He barely found Panas's room number.

Panas opened the door as Declan slumped forward, nearly hitting the floor, and would have if his old mate didn't catch him in his arms.

"You look like death," Panas said, easing Declan into the room and shutting the door.

"Death would likely be an improvement," he mumbled.

"You came to the right place then, my friend. Take a little from as many of them as you wish, just do not take to excess on any one of them."

Panas led him into the immense suite's master bedroom. Declan blinked a couple of times, struggling to clear his vision but failed. There were at least a dozen feminine forms in the room and half of those were lounging on the king-sized bed. The combined essence of them was intoxicating and he felt himself harden immediately as he began pulling at his clothes, trying to shed them and succeeding only in tangling the shirt around his neck.

"Allow me," Panas said.

Declan nodded and his friend undressed him, untangling and pulling his shirt over his head to reveal his chiseled chest and washboard abs. One of the women knelt down in front of him, unlaced his boots and removed them before easing back so her master could continue. Declan shivered as he felt Panas unfasten the button and zipper on his jeans, slipping them down so Declan could step out of them. The motion was too much and Declan almost toppled over, would have toppled over if Panas hadn't caught him again.

"Easy now," his mate said, steadying Declan.

Declan closed his eyes and nodded again. He felt his briefs slide over his hips and the bulge of his erection, down his legs, and then to the floor to pool over his feet. He managed to stay upright when he stepped out of them, thanks to his friend's steadying hand. At Panas's touch, a moan of want and absolute need escaped Declan's throat before he could even consider stopping it. Panas gave an amused but sympathetic laugh and lifted

Declan into his arms, carrying him to the bed and gently laying him on the mattress. When Declan felt someone straddle him he opened his eyes. It was one of the very blurry women of Panas's harem. She took his cock into her hand and guided it gently inside of her. When she settled all the way down onto him, he bit his lip to keep from screaming. Not from pain, no, but from sheer relief. She began rocking against him, slowly at first and then faster and faster and faster. The scream which caught in his throat couldn't be stifled and he let it out with his next breath.

"That's it," he barely heard Panas say to him, and then to the woman, "only a little and then switch with Gina."

And Gina gave and Declan took. And Gina switched with Camille who likewise gave and then switched with Amy. And on, and on, and on down the line, as Panas watched on with concern for his friend.

———

Waiting for my flight to be called at the airport, I sat stewing in the plastic chair and pulled out my cell phone. My meeting with Paul was uppermost in my mind, mostly for the fact I left the restaurant feeling like a member of the son-of-a-bitch's cleanup crew. Thankful for the information he could provide, but pissed he wasn't about to lift one cloven hoof to help sweep out whatever piece of murderous trash we were dealing with; one of his own, no matter what he claimed, who'd managed to escape Hell's garbage dump to terrorize and kill innocent people.

Plus, I still couldn't shake my concern for the nuns in the abbey. It wasn't above Sister Eva to hop a plane to come calling on us if she thought she wasn't getting the complete story and I hadn't done a suitable job communicating. I slipped from my seat and eased up close to the glass window providing a panoramic view of the pavement dotted with monstrous aircraft. They never looked so big when you saw them flying above you, tearing through clouds and leaving a dusty streak in their wake.

The phone rang three times before a slightly winded voice greeted me.

"Bonjour."

"Um, hi, bonjour," I returned, what little of the French language I knew flying from my brain.

"Oh, can I help you?" The accented English was charming, but the voice wasn't familiar. Maybe someone new to help in the office? Or perhaps, a novice who was thinking of entering the Abbey.

"I need to speak with Sister Evangeline."

There was a long pause. "She is not available just now. May I take a message?"

I puffed out a breath. Not available could mean she was in prayers, or it could mean she was thousands of feet in the air on her way to the USA. "This is Samantha. I need to talk to her. Can you just ask her to call me?"

"Naturellement," she replied. "Does she have your number?"

"Yes," I responded. "And let her know I won't be able to answer her call for a little while. I'm flying out to Gatlinburg, Tennessee. I have something I need to look into there." I hesitated. "She can leave me a message."

"I will let her know," the younger woman answered.

I thanked her and tapped the end call button. I could have asked for one of the other Sisters in the order. There were several I now considered friends. Many more I considered allies in our battle against Satan. But I felt like I needed to talk to the older woman since she visited me in the states and knew all the players on my side of the game.

I tucked the cell phone in my pocket and nodded. I'd finished what I could from here. Next stop, crime scene number two.

————

"Ah, man, ain't nothing better than this bitching beauty," Russ said, leaning back in the driver's seat of his van and stretching. He lowered his arms and picked up his paper cup from the holder in the oversized wood-paneled console. He blew lightly on the steaming brew inside and then took a sip. "Well, maybe coffee." He paused, taking another sip. "Okay, definitely coffee and probably tequila. Scratch that, definitely--"

Declan climbed into the front passenger seat and pulled the seatbelt on. "I think I've got the picture. No need to continue, mate."

He was feeling alive and refreshed, and so much better than yesterday. Every bit of vitality which Lucifer siphoned from him earlier was returned, and with a surplus. Panas really was the wiser one of the two of them, no argument there, and what he'd said about hunting seemed on the mark as well. It was becoming too risky in this day and age, not to mention unpredictable. You may catch and devour your prey one day with no one the wiser but the next day you may not be so lucky, and Declan definitely didn't want a rehash of yesterday. He made a mental note to address this solution whenever all of this business was finished and he got back to jolly old England. Maybe Panas would be generous enough to part with one of his harem long enough for Declan to start his own or perhaps he could give him some advice on how to start. The thought of being responsible for the welfare of someone other than himself was daunting at best and completely exhausting. But what was the alternative? Hunting? Starvation? Nope, he promised himself, never again would he allow his hunger to get so out of control. Never again. He glanced over at Russ, feeling incredibly guilty he'd even considered taking from his new friend.

No, he thought. *Never again.*

"Top of the mornin to ya," Russ bellowed. "You look a helluva lot more chipper today, almost like you just bathed in the beauty of a thousand virgins."

Definitely not virgins, Declan thought.

"Good night's rest," Declan said instead. He gave Russ a genuine smile. "That's all."

"That'll do it too. You ready for one fun-filled road trip party?"

"Uh yeah, but hang on a few moments. I've got a friend coming along with us."

Russ didn't pose an objection, but settled back and slid what looked like an eight-track cassette into possibly one of the oldest players Declan saw installed in a vehicle. There was static from the antiquated speakers for a second or two and then it was broken by the sound of Kiss. Russ leaned back with a satisfied grin as Paul Stanley wailed out Room Service which Declan knew was the first track in the Dressed to Kill album. Declan merely shook his head and laughed.

After a few minutes, he spotted Panas exiting the hotel door with two of his harem, Gina perhaps, and possibly Amy; he'd been a little fuzzy last night so he wasn't for certain. He glanced over his shoulder to ensure Russ's beast of a van could hold three more and then turned back around satisfied. This green monstrosity could probably carry five more people.

Russ turned the music down and nodded towards the oncoming group.

"Which one is your friend, and whoa baby, can you introduce me?"

"Down boy," Declan replied. "And for your information, my friend is the guy."

Russ pulled his eyes away from the windshield and looked at the incubus.

"Friend, or *friend*?" he asked with an arched brow. "Cause, dude, that would explain a lot about your woman phobia. No judgment here, of course. I believe to each his own. I'm just saying it would explain some things."

Panas crossed the lot to the van quickly and both women trailed a few steps behind, synchronized in fluid movements like one might encounter on a model's catwalk. He was at Declan's side of the van before he could even begin to answer Russ's question, which was a good thing because he was unsure how to even begin explaining what he was to the young man. And for some reason, he really wasn't looking forward to losing Russ's friendship so soon. It had been a long time since he even considered a human as a friend. Not since Abraham.

Declan cranked the handle around and around, reflecting all the while he'd been spoiled by the automatic kind. Slowly, and with a long squeaky pained sound, the window lowered. Panas gave him a broad grin. Clearly, he was taking in the close up of the four-wheeled green monster and struggling not to laugh.

"So, uh," Panas began, paused and cleared his throat, "Shaggy and Scooby in there by any chance?"

"No," Declan replied. "But if you hop on in, I'm certain we can give you a lift all the way to Woodstock."

"Hardy-har-har," Russ answered. "Only one rule to this trip, ladies and gents, and that is do not disrespect the van. Got it? Now, everybody aboard. This train is leaving the station."

Panas pulled on the handle of the bulky door and it slid on its tracks with a screeching sound as it yawned open. The women climbed in and took the very back seat, one of them brushing her fingers through Declan's hair before turning to join the others. He wasn't sure which one it was, but chills of desire ran through him at her light touch. Panas winked at Declan as he followed the women inside, pulling the door closed with another pained noise. He settled in between the women and smiled.

"I don't believe I've ever traveled in one of these before."

"You're in for a treat then," Russ said, starting the engine, "cause this baby can definitely glide. I'm Russ, by the way. I'll be your driver on this fine morning. Please keep all hands and various other body parts in the cabin. No smoking. And for all that is good and holy, no farting. We share the air in here, boys and girls."

Declan heard giggling behind him. "Just bloody drive."

Russ let out a whoo-whoo and put the green monster into motion. "Next stop, Abe and the lovely Alex." He glanced over at Declan. "Anybody else going, Boss?"

Declan shook his head. He introduced Panas, and Russ threw the man a nod in his rearview mirror. Panas took the pleasure of introducing both women himself, probably realizing Declan wouldn't have remembered who happened to be who last night. It was Gina, after all, he'd been right on that one, but instead of his guess at Amy, the other one was Camille. Win one, lose one. Oh well.

After a few minutes in the sparse traffic, Bertha, as Russ lovingly called the van, came to a halt in front of the house Abe and Alex were staying in. If Abe looked concerned last night at the dinner table, it was nothing compared to the expression on his face when he spotted Panas and the two women in the back-seat of Russ's green monstrosity. Declan pushed open the screeching passenger door and climbed out.

"Before you get in, I want to be on the up and up," Declan

said as he talked towards Abe and Alex. "Panas is a good friend of mine and is very knowledgeable in anything paranormal."

He paused, okay so maybe he was elaborating a bit but what the hell? When Panas finally managed to get a coherent sentence out of him last night, after his rather generous meal, he'd told him about the trip to Tennessee. Panas insisted on going with them and would go whether he rode with them or not. Declan didn't doubt his sincerity.

Abe stared at the back window. "And the women? Who are they? Oh, let me guess, clairvoyants?"

"Um, no. They are his assistants and he refuses to go anywhere without them. I know. I know. You're probably thinking it's a bit of a shit show, but hang on a bit don't get your knickers in a wad just yet."

Alex laughed. Abe didn't.

"We need this man," Declan said. "You have to trust me on this. He will be very useful."

"Fine," Abe growled. "Do we have anyone else coming? Maybe your housekeeper? Gardener?"

"No one else, mate."

Alex laid a hand on Abe's arm. "It's going to be fine."

"Samantha is going to lose her--"

"Sam will adapt. When things start to get crazy, if it gets crazy, she will appreciate more hands on deck. Okay?"

Abe nodded reluctantly.

Declan walked back to the van, opened the passenger door and got in, giving Abe and Alex a moment of privacy for more discussion if they needed it. They didn't. When they loaded up, Declan could smell Alex's intoxicating scent which became stronger when the door was shut. He kept his window down to allow the morning breeze to thin it out and keep the essences of himself and Panas from becoming overwhelming to the humans aboard. When they started moving, the smells would be less distracting. The small bulge in the front pocket of Abe's jeans, however, was a different story and Declan could see the artifact's greenish light through the denim material pulsing ever so slightly. When Abe took his seat, the glow faded some but not completely, and Declan forced himself to ignore its call for now.

Bertha took off like the immense green monstrosity she was, rumbling down the highway and onto the interstate bound for Tennessee. Declan leaned back in the seat and closed his eyes. Naps were needed for humans and other living creatures, but it couldn't hurt to allow himself one now and then. He gave a contented sigh at the first feeling of contentment in quite a long time.

Forget the artifact. Forget the lovely lady behind you. Let it all go.

And then Paul Stanley's voice ripped in an ear-splitting wail across the van's shared air.

———

It was well after midnight by the time the Uber dropped me off at the Mayfield Inn. I went cheap with this one, knowing all the hotels in Gatlinburg were pricey. If we were successful with finding the killer, I decided I would treat myself to nice lodging, courtesy of the stolen money from the Church of the Light Reclaimed. They took my father, turned him into a monster, and ruined not only his life but mine as well. They owed me a little privileged treatment.

The Mayfield Inn was situated toward the center of town; tiny rooms with tiny baths, and a tiny pool sunk in concrete outside. Parking was behind the building and limited, so the uber driver dropped me out front.

I checked in under an assumed name. I had at least a half of a dozen with the papers to match. Grabbing my bag, I went back outside and traversed the distance to my room. When I hit the light switch, I immediately locked the door behind me and made a thorough exploration of the room. Paul and his minions may not have known exactly where I was going, but I wouldn't have put it past him to put a tail on me.

I drew my phone from my pocket and texted the address to Abe. We were in for a fun-filled morning. Brother Joshua managed to contact someone he trusted within the police department to seal off the scene of the crime, keeping it as pristine as we could hope to see. It was being guarded with a twenty-four-hour watch, and they were expecting us early.

I pulled off my clothes and dropped them in my travel bag. I was down to my last clean pair of underwear, and it was getting on my nerves. I wasn't prepared for a long trip and I was running short on the basics. I couldn't travel with my katana, instead, I'd asked Alex to pack it for me. There were some things you just couldn't check in your luggage. By tomorrow, I would have it in my hands and feel better for it.

I finished my nightly routine, checking the locks again, and laying out my clothes for the next day. I was tired but my mind was filled with the information Paul provided. He was such a strange demon. After our meeting, he followed me out of the restaurant into the sun, and while I watched, he cut across the street and headed toward the pier looking like any other middle-aged businessman with some time on his hands.

I rolled over, dragging the sheets loose from where they were anchored at my feet. Deliberately, I focused my mind on some of the relaxation exercises I learned under the tutelage of the nuns. Breathing, easing, loosening, sleep rolled in like rushing tide and took me.

I was fortunate the hotel was noisy in the morning because I hadn't set any alarm and fatigue became my best friend. I was jolted awake by a door closing down the hall and sat up in bed. The sheets were rough but smelled of bleach, so at least they were clean. The same couldn't be said for the dubious carpeting which was threadbare with dark questionable stains in several placcs.

I climbed out of bed and eased on my clothes, my head pounding in time with my pulse. I showered the night before and my long hair still felt slightly damp. I combed it out and then absentmindedly braided it, my movements brisk and automatic. I loaded my bag with the necessities for the day. After sliding my cell phone in my pocket, I headed out the door. There was no free breakfast provided, so I stopped at one of the ice cream shops along the sidewalk and bought a large coffee and a muffin, grateful they planned on some morning patrons.

Unlike my modest lodging, the victim booked himself a room at The Cambury, one of the nicest hotels on the strip. I bypassed the lobby and the elevator, choosing to climb the stairs. The eighth-floor exit door sported a line of caution tape across it. I ducked under the tape and pushed open the door. The short hallway in front of me ended in a T with burnished brass plates indicating the numbers of the rooms to the right and the left. The sound here was deadened, muffled by the carpeting and the proper insulation that came with a price tag to match. It felt eerily quiet, and I knew the hotel staff cleared the floor of all occupants as soon as the murder was discovered. It took their substantial pull to cover up the crime from the general public or the press, but so far, it was a success.

I strolled down the hallway, my mind ticking off room numbers. There was a chair pulled up outside of room 813 and a man in a police uniform sprawled in the chair. The uniform appeared to be a ruse. I figured this guy was no more a cop than I was.

He scrutinized me as I approached, and offered me a salute when I reached the door.

"I have a reservation," I told him with a half-smile.

"Tyler, right?"

I nodded. He didn't get up, so I tried the door.

"It's locked," he said.

I breathed out a frustrated sigh as he stood and slowly pulled the plastic card from his pocket. No hurry there. He used the card to trigger the lock, and as soon as I heard the subtle click, I pressed at the latch and felt it give. I supposed law enforcement or the church finished their sleuthing here yesterday. Any fingerprints on the door should have been cataloged by now.

The rooms were assuredly more spacious than where I stayed. The Berber carpet led from the entry to the bathroom on the immediate right through to the small alcove with the requisite desk and chair. Beyond, the room was furnished with a single queen bed and matching overstuffed armchairs upholstered in tasteful plaid fabric.

The bedspread was probably a corresponding burgundy, but the stains spread across the fabric, obliterating most of the original color. It looked almost black now, and my stomach rolled when I realized it was blood. Dried blood and a lot of it. I frowned as my eyes scoured the surrounding carpet. More blood, spots and splatters.

"What the hell?"

My statement was lost in the emptiness of the room. This was not my first corpse, so I knew good and well, leaving it in situ for this long should have produced an odor, but what I smelled was not rot or the coppery tang of blood. It smelled of fire, of scorched flesh, and burnt entrails. Yet the body was the same husk of a human I saw at the earlier crime scene. The flesh was drawn and lined like tanned leather, the lips pulled back from the teeth in a grotesque caricature of a grin.

I stepped closer, studying the sad remains before me. The door closed softly behind me and I spun in place, my nerves jittering. The mock cop eased the door shut, but must have retreated back to his chair in the hall.

I blew out a breath and took another step forward. I wished Alex was here with me. She would be better at reading the remains. The victim was a man from the report I picked up, but I wouldn't have known it from what remained of the body. The man's arms and legs were stretched spread eagle, but whatever bound him was disposed of. There were marks on his wrists from the restraints, dark brown indentations in the leathery skin. What was more alarming was the neat line tracing from his collarbone to groin. A curl of fabric parted in his midsection and was rolled off to either side of his torso. I stepped a little closer, my eyes on his chest rather than his ravaged face. I leaned down over the prone form, my eyes riveted on the twist of material and the striations beneath. It took a second to register what I was really looking at. The seam down his torso wasn't in his clothing at all, it was his skin, and indeed the fold of material was flesh rather than fabric. What I thought was a flat expanse of skin beneath was the exposed muscles. I glanced again at the bed and the floor. So much blood. But skinning someone would not give you a neat death.

I stalked to the window and looked out blindly for a moment, trying to get the picture out of my mind. The reanimation of the corpse, stretching and screaming in agony as his skin was cut away with surgical precision. I eased around the bed toward the bathroom. The door was open a quarter of the way and the light was on. I pushed the door wider and eased through. There were more signs of crime scene investigators here. The tub was stained with rivulets of red-brown, a precise square of it cleaned down to the white porcelain where the investigators had gotten their samples. Any towels or floor mats were gone, taken no doubt, to some lab. I wrinkled my nose at the smell. Blood and bleach, and something underneath, something alluring, familiar.

I grimaced as a thought flitted through my head and then away. Something was prodding me, something I should have noticed but didn't. Something I knew on some level, but my conscious thought wouldn't bring it up.

I paced back into the bedroom. I heard the mutter of voices in the hallway and froze. Someone else had arrived. I eased back to the side of the door, my knife already in my hand. I pushed my back against the wall and waited. Friend or foe, I wasn't taking any chances.

I heard the click of the lock releasing a second before the door opened. I remained as I was, still and alert. The first person to enter was a tall man with black inky hair whose wide shoulders filled the doorway a second before he turned swiftly, a flash of surprise on his strikingly handsome face. I had the knife out and at his throat before he could take another step.

"Now that is a greeting," he murmured, his voice a mixture of brandy and heat. He gave me a quirk of a smile.

"Samantha, stand down," Abe's voice was predictably calm. He stepped in after the stranger, his long legs eating up the space between us.

I reluctantly drew the blade back and slid it into the sheath by my side. Alex slipped past Abe and moved to my side. Her eyes were on me, but I knew from the set of her jaw she had seen the massacre beyond. She pulled her gaze away from the carnage and focused on me.

"Sam, this is my friend, the law enforcement officer from

Scotland Yard I told you about. Declan Faulkner meet my friend Sam."

I peered from Alex to the handsome man. Hot. He was the very epitome of the word hot. He should have been adorning some magazine cover, most suitably in his undies. He could sell almost anything, I figured. As though he could read my mind, his smile widened.

I smothered my immediate hormonal response and gave a curt nod, lowering the blade. "Declan," I said, tipping my head. "Sorry."

"Apology accepted," he replied, still looking amused.

His smile died when he looked over my shoulder. I heard him exhale an oath, but it was in another language, so I wasn't sure what he was saying. He bypassed me in a few long steps, his face unreadable, and circled the bed. His head was down, his concentration so intense I figured he wouldn't notice if the ceiling fell in.

"Oh, no, no, no," he chanted under his breath, and then he was gone, out the door and into the hallway, moving almost too fast for an ordinary human. I frowned and shook my head. I was seeing spooks around every corner now.

"Declan!" Alex exclaimed, following him out into the hallway. I heard her call after him again. There wasn't a response and she came back in, shaking her head.

"I don't know what he saw," she said, "but I suppose he'll come back around."

A third man slouched into the room. He was average height and on the hefty side, with near-black, short, and extremely unruly hair. A dark, unkempt mustache and beard covered the lower portion of his face while a pair of thick black horned rimmed glasses occupied the upper part. He looked like a movie version of computer geek central. His eyes, however, seemed to tell a different story and with one glance I could tell there was kindness in them. The kind of kindness I didn't see a lot of the time in my line of work. The guy took one look around and slammed a hand over his mouth before whirling around and ducking out of the door into the hallway. I heard the distinct sound of someone getting sick.

"That's Declan's friend, Russ. I guess he hasn't been exposed to many crime scenes," Alex added. "And before you ask why he's here, he's the Uber driver. Declan wouldn't come without him and his other friend, Panas."

I frowned. "Other friend?"

Alex managed a slight smile. "And Panas's two assistants."

"Alex, this isn't a party. It's a crime scene."

"I know and these guys are familiar with the things bumping around in the night. Just trust me on this, okay?"

I could feel my aggravation rising, but tamped it down. Maybe she was right. If I could have a meeting to try and get aid from Paul, then why not bring in some people Alex trusted? My inner me, the paranoid part, was definitely not happy, but I gave her a nod of affirmation anyway for the sake of friendship.

"Let's just get to work," I said with a sigh.

Abe had come fully into the room and was standing next to the bed, silent and staring. I could tell his attention was split though, no doubt wondering where the enigmatic Declan had disappeared to. Alex joined him and I slid up next to her. We stood in silence for several long minutes, the horror of the room sucking away the words.

"We need to get as much information about the victim as we can," Abe declared, his tone clipped but his voice full of authority.

"Okay, what first?" I asked.

"I'll take a closer look at the body," Alex affirmed. "Maybe someone can go check for witnesses?"

I gave a short nod and left the room of death, happy to do anything other than stare at the remains of such an atrocity. The victim's brutal demise was causing a wave of anger to roll over me and I was ready to cause some uproar in this posh hotel.

CHAPTER NINETEEN

Declan leaned against the far lobby wall next to the front entrance of the hotel. It was becoming easier to breathe now and he could feel his heartbeat slow to the natural rhythm he'd felt for ages. Human bodies weren't meant for such shocks, and had he been human, he would have surely experienced something like a heart attack or a stroke. But since human he was not, a panic attack seemed to be the ailment, more of a bother than an actual problem honestly. He forced himself to cool down and consider what he'd just seen. And the woman, Sam, precisely what had she learned? Blood? Of course. The room was splattered in it. Human flesh dried like long-neglected old leather? Also obvious. So was the flaying of that very skin, a gaping slit a bloody blind man couldn't have missed. But did she notice what lay beneath the thin muscle membrane that had been scraped away to the bone in the very center of the sternum? If she had, she didn't seem phased by it, or perhaps she didn't realize what it was. But he did. He bloody well did.

Declan pushed off the wall with a slap of his hand which

caused a few eyes from the front desk to turn in his direction. He ignored them and slid through the front entrance automatic doors. Panas was waiting for him.

"And?"

Declan lowered his eyes and swore under his breath. "Just as you feared."

Panas grimaced. "I had hoped Asmodeus wouldn't have been so foolish to allow her--"

Declan stopped him with a grave look. "I don't think it was Asmodeus."

Panas lifted a questioning brow. "Who then?"

Looking across the lot, Declan could see big old green Bertha parked in one of the spots near an oak tree. Camille and Gina were still seated in the back, deep in conversation it appeared. Russ was standing at the front of the van, one hand on the driver's side door as if it were the only thing holding him upright. Even from this distance and the hair covering the guy's face, Declan could see he was pale enough to have seen a ghost.

Declan turned back to his Ukrainian friend. "My bet's on Lucifer."

"What? Why? He's never taken an interest before--"

"Before now? Yeah, I'm aware. But he's taking an interest now."

He thought about telling Panas about the artifact but ditched the idea again. Something was nudging at him to keep that bit of information to himself. Some *thing*? Maybe. And, then again, maybe some*one*.

"Let's just say the cloven foot gent has given a cameo appearance more than once in my presence." Declan frowned. "And a rave-up it was not."

Panas was silent for a moment, then he leaned closer to Declan, keeping his voice down.

"It was him, wasn't it? He drained you."

"How'd you know?"

Panas shrugged. "I've never known one of our kind so ravenous, my friend. And if I were to be honest, I'd have to say you were very near death's door, or as close to death as we can manage without suffering a beheading. In truth, I don't know so much as suspect. To drain an incubus without leaving a mark, that takes power."

"And your suspicion doesn't lead you to one of the righteous instead?"

Panas shook his head. "The righteous wouldn't have left you your head."

Declan couldn't argue with that. He leaned back, feeling the hardness of the wall behind him and the waft of a slight breeze against his face. There were so many smells carried along with it that the combination could make his head spin, but he detected just a hint of something he wouldn't have expected. An undertone of orchids maybe? He turned to Panas.

"Do you smell her?"

Panas looked off towards the foothills beyond the parking lot and a group of buildings set behind it.

"I've smelled her since I got out of the van. It's faint, but there. Residual. She made her presence known."

"On purpose?" Declan asked.

"I assume so. And if she is here by Lucifer's hand as you believe, then her agenda seems clearer to me."

"Care to share?"

Panas turned his eyes back to Declan who couldn't help but notice the sadness in them. Sadness and what? Disappointment? A touch of anger? He wasn't sure but the words his friend spoke next made him think it was maybe all of those things and more.

"Chaos," he replied. "She's not just feeding, she's mutilating.

Leaving a mark like the inverted cross you saw on her victim's sternum is a distraction, don't you think? And the only ones who could possibly be distracted by such an act are--"

"The righteous," Declan finished for him.

"The righteous," Panas repeated. "The question now is, what exactly are they being distracted from?"

Declan stared at Russ again, watching his friend pace the length of the van, turn, and then go the opposite way. It was probably the only thing the young man could do to calm himself.

Less than forty-eight hours, Declan thought. *I have less than that to keep you out of harm's way and I have absolutely no idea how to do it.*

———

The girl at the desk was the same one who had overlooked my arrival. She was joined by two other equally uninterested workers, a young guy in dark creased slacks that looked like he might have slept in them, and an older woman intent on sipping her coffee.

I stepped up to the desk with a swagger. A confident appearance could overcome a lot of bull in my business. I pulled out a thin wallet with a nondescript badge in it. It was totally fake, but it looked good, and Brother Joshua had made sure it would pass if someone decided to call in and ask questions. I was betting this girl wouldn't be interested in pursuing my story.

"Were you working last night?" My tone was challenging, and I flashed the badge. I saw the girl's eyes go wide.

"No, I'm only mornings. You can ask Mag." She cocked her head towards the older woman who had flipped the newspaper over to the back page and started a crossword.

I directed my gaze toward the new victim. She appeared to be unimpressed by my badge, but she seemed ready to talk anyway.

"I was here last night. I had to come by and pick up my check." She pulled the glasses down her nose and looked at me over the pink rimmed frames. "What do you want to know?"

"Who found the body?"

The older woman's lips thinned. "Eddie. He's our maintenance guy. Or at least he was. He opened that door, turned tail, and said not to call him anymore."

I nodded. It seemed like a perfectly sensible reaction.

"Does anyone know who checked into the room?"

Now the younger clerk was interested, and her fingers flew over the computer keys. "It was Andrew Weaver," she answered. "He checked in yesterday at 11:13 a.m.." Her eyes were alight with a new fascination. "Eddie said he'd never seen anything like it. He thought there were several people dead in there."

I shook my head. No sense in letting the story explode out of control. "No, just one victim. And it wasn't as bad as they made it out to be. Poor guy fell, hit his head, and it bled like a son of a bitch."

"Oh." The younger woman looked crestfallen with this piece of news.

"Did you check the guy in?"

She brightened. "Yes. It was just Max and me at the counter. I checked him in and gave him his key."

"Did he happen to say why he was in town?"

"Oh, sure. He said he was here for a business meeting. There's a few of them that took a block of rooms on the eighth floor." She hesitated. "The others have been moved to another floor. I don't know that they actually knew each other well. They weren't especially upset."

I nodded. It sounded like the same story we had heard. The

victim was a businessman who just happened to be at the wrong place at the wrong time. There didn't seem to be anything to connect him either to the abbey, the devil's church, or any other of the far-flung reaches in the battle between good and evil. He was an accident, a whim. Perhaps that was most frightening of all.

I decided my next destination would be checking on the group that was slated to meet with the victim. Even if they hadn't been close, they were my best bet in figuring out where the victim might have been the night before. I couldn't imagine the killer randomly broke into the hotel room and took him out in such a gruesome fashion. It left another possibility. If the man went out, even to grab a drink or a bite to eat, he might have met with his murderer.

"I need to talk to the people in his group," I told the older woman. "Can you give me a list of names and rooms?"

Ten minutes later I was stepping off the elevator and onto the ninth floor. I wondered if the hotel staff had even intended to use the rooms to house anyone that week. Of course, I didn't know the seasons in the hotel business, but the distinct smell of fresh paint made me think perhaps they were working on a renovation.

All the doors were closed but I could hear the normal shuffle of humans going about their business. It wasn't yet noon, and apparently at least some of the group were still in residence. I considered the list in my hand. Mag, in her wisdom, had printed the details out for me. There were four rooms now occupied with refugees from the floor below. I hammered briskly on the first door on the left.

The woman who answered was slim to the point of skinny with a sharp-pointed nose that dominated a drawn face. She looked tired. She was wearing khaki slacks and a bulky black sweater, but she had the peculiar air about her that indicated she would never feel warm again.

She opened the door only a crack at first, but when I flashed the badge, she let it swing wide. I felt a little guilty. She was easily fooled, and this soon after what appeared to be a murder of one of her companions.

"Nicky Sizemore?"

She gave a terse nod. "That's me. I've already talked to the police." She looked like she wanted to close the door in my face, but she didn't seem to have the energy to.

"I just wanted to ask a few questions. You were with the victim last night?"

"Like I informed the police, I only met Andy last night. We went out to dinner. All of us. Then some of us went on to a bar down the street. When I left Andy to walk back, he was drinking with a few other people. He was fine."

"Who was he drinking with?" I pinned her with my best investigator's eye. Whatever had gotten to old Andy last night hadn't been some run of the mill drunk.

"I don't know. There was a group. Connor would know. He was with him."

"Connor Bokaden?" I checked my list. He was in the room across the hall.

"Yeah, I think that's his last name. He was still going strong when I left, but I know he was with Andy."

I gave a brief bow. I pulled out my cell phone and was adding names to my notes on the glass screen. Nicky seemed to be flagging, so I asked her a few more questions and let her go back inside. As soon as her door closed, I took a few long strides across the hall and knocked at the next door.

Connor looked worse than Nicky. Whatever they did the night before had taken its toll on them. Connor was a short muscular guy wearing jeans and a polo shirt stretched too tight over his pecs. He was trying hard to look like a big man. A little too hard. When his eyes tilted up to meet mine, I felt an inward satisfied smile. I was enjoying being an inch taller than him.

"Connor Bokaden?" I demanded as soon as he opened the door.

He turned bloodshot eyes to me and nodded. "Yeah?"

"I'd like to ask you a few questions." I flashed the badge, gave him an outward smile full of teeth and a little menace, and watched with pleasure as he backed out of the doorway and gestured me in.

"I've already said all I'm gonna say to the cops. They rousted us out of our rooms at the butt crack of dawn," he grumbled.

"I understand that," I replied, "but there are some pieces from last night that aren't quite clear."

He rolled his eyes in my direction. "The same thing for me," he muttered. "Don't know exactly what I had, but there are definitely some foggy parts last night."

I waited for him to collapse on the bed before pulling up the desk chair and sitting across from him. Up close, he looked a little worse, his skin took on a sallow grey shade as the sunlight leaked through the blinds.

"You were out drinking with Andrew Weaver last night?"

"Yeah, a bunch of us were. We have some seminar later today. We decided to close down the town." He attempted a smile, but it fell flat.

"You all were out at a bar?"

He nodded and gave me the name of one of the local drinking establishments.

"How well did you know Andrew?"

"Andy?" He rubbed a hand over his jaw and I heard the scratching of whiskers against his palm. "I only met him last night. Nice guy. We had a few. Met this lady," he blew out a breath. "We kinda had a bet on who could get her to go to the room with us."

I didn't comment but looked at him with raised eyebrows. He had the grace to blush a little which made him at least look a little more alive.

"She knew what she was doing, don't worry about that," he snapped.

"A prostitute?"

He shook his head. "No, not like that. But she oozed sex." He ran his hand through his hair. "Sorry, but it's true," he added. "This lady was gorgeous and she knew it."

My mind was spinning. Interesting. I wondered if Andy was successful in getting the woman to go to his room. If so, what happened to her?

"So you had a few drinks, bought her a few drinks, then what?"

"She kissed me. Like, she kissed me, and I thought I might have a stroke. But then she told me I could go. And I was so damn tired, like the night caught up with me all at once, and I figured she was right. I felt so bad I thought someone might have slipped me a mickey."

I frowned. This didn't seem to be the kind of guy that would give up that easily on a woman he so plainly wanted. The fact that after she kissed him, he gave up and retreated to his room sounded downright unnatural. However, this wasn't an ordinary murder. The man one floor down had been creatively skinned, mutilated, and then killed in some fantastical way. I thought about Paul's explanation of a succubus. It sounded like a fairy tale just a few hours ago, but now?

"You said this woman was beautiful, what did she look like?"

Connor's expression clouded. "She was gorgeous, shapely,"

he made a gesture with his hands indicating approval for her curves.

"Yes, I got that. But what did she look like? Hair color? Eye color?"

"She was blond, or no, that's not right. Her hair was brown, maybe?" His eyes skated over my head as he tried to focus on the images in his mind. "Eyes were big, long eyelashes, dark," he crossed his arms in front of him in an almost protective motion.

"Was her hair long or short? Was she tall?"

"Her hair was," he stopped, his lips slightly pursed. "Damn, I don't know. I feel like I know exactly what she looked like, but I can't seem to bring it up."

"She spoke to you. What was her voice like?" I was getting irritated with this man and his mystery woman, but in the back of my mind, a greater concern was growing.

"Yeah, she talked. She had an accent. I don't know where it was from, but I know I remember thinking she wasn't from around here."

"What was she wearing?"

"A dress, or, I don't know, something tight. Dark." He put a hand to his head. "It's just, well I guess I had too much to drink."

I blew out a frustrated breath. Either the alcohol had gotten to him or something else had. Whatever was going on, he lost the chance to identify the woman.

I finally let him go and repeated my routine twice more. The other two witnesses were men as well, and of the two, only one stayed at the bar with Connor and Andrew. His memories of the conversation were about the same as what Connor claimed, minus the mind-blowing kiss.

I paused out in the hallway, listening to the muted shuffling noises coming from behind closed doors. It wasn't adding up. The hotel, despite its high fee, was not even close to being soundproof. So why hadn't any of the close neighbors heard a ruckus? Surely the victim wouldn't have remained mute. Not while having his chest flayed open. Or during his last moments before his flesh had become dried out like strips of bacon.

I headed back down the elevator still pondering the dilemma. If a man is brutalized in a hotel room, and nobody is there to hear him scream, does he make a sound?

I stepped out at lobby level and went directly to the desk. I didn't even have to flash my badge to gain access to the tiny room that served as the security office. The head of security, a round-bellied old man in a rent a cop uniform, followed me in.

"I just need to see if you have a video from last night. Any cameras in the lobby."

Bill Hastings nodded. I wasn't sure what skills he had as a security officer, but he was handy enough with the computer equipment and was able to pull up the feed from the night before.

"We saved a copy for the police as soon as we discovered the body," he added as he cued up the scene.

"Have you given it to anyone else yet?" I was wondering if someone from Church of the Light Reclaimed had gotten a jump on us.

"No." Bill raised a veined hand to his chin, scrubbing at his jaw before tugging on one earlobe in a nervous gesture. "Haven't had anyone ask."

"Okay," I kept it brief. "I'll take it with me."

I turned my attention back to the screen before me, a typical grainy showing of the sliding glass doors entering the lobby. The time stamp on the lower-left corner showed me it was just after 7:30 and showed the slender form of Nicky walking next to the bulky Connor. Stepping behind them was the other man I had talked to upstairs accompanied by a completely average looking guy in khakis and a button-down shirt. The unfortunate victim on his way out for his last dinner.

I paused the scene, backed up, and watched again as the small group exited the lobby through the glass doors and melted into the night. Someone would need to track down the rest of the journey. In a town as tight as Gatlinburg, I knew this could not be the only place to show up on film. But for the moment, I wanted to see the shots of them returning.

I was fortunate that my new companion knew exactly where the markers were for desired shots. He deftly navigated to the minutes when Nicky strolled into the lobby, walking in a straight line, apparently not too intoxicated.

The next to return were the three other companions, the men looking worse for a few too many drinks. None of them appeared to be able to maintain a facade of sobriety. It appeared as though they were mutually supporting one another on their weaving journey through the doors.

"Just watch 'em," Bill chimed in, and I observed the inebriated group disappear off camera. Not a minute later on the time-stamp, the glass doors opened again and a ripple of static sliced across the screen. I saw a half-second of the victim, Andrew, accompanied by the slender figure of what I could only assume was his last date. The static seemed to rip the picture in half, a flash of shapely legs, and the screen was obliterated.

I gave a grunt of frustration. "How long does this last?"

Bill glanced at me, almost nervous to give me the bad news. "There's nothing more for the rest of the segment. It takes over again about six in the morning. Can't see anything in between."

I stepped back. There was no doubt the data could be further examined. I was sure someone on Brother Joshua's team might have the expertise to get more from the damaged footage. But we didn't have the luxury of time. Whoever had done this to the victim upstairs was probably still in town, maybe resting, maybe even now hunting for a new victim. A new urgency prodded me to move along. There was something weighing heavily on my mind. I had rushed out to the scene of the crime, anxious to catch the monster. And I encouraged my friends, my closest companions to join me. Had I led us all into a trap?

———

Declan made his way back up to the eighth floor and into the room where Alex was studying the remains. Abe was taking pictures of the corpse with his cell phone when Declan first walked in, but moved on to the rest of the room, snapping the flash to capture whatever was there to look over later. Alex glanced up from her grim work.

"Glad you're back," she said with a forced smile. "I thought I'd have to send out the cavalry."

Abe turned and faced Declan, giving the incubus the full view of the artifact's greenish glow still tucked in the front pocket of Abe's jeans. It seemed brighter now, almost blinding, and definitely noticeable. What did it mean that he was the only one who seemed to see it? He didn't know, but somehow he needed to relieve Abe of the blasted thing and hand it over before Russ lost his life because of it. He was going to have to get Abe off by himself, and soon.

He pulled his eyes away from it and focused on Alex. She was pulling her exam gloves off of her lovely hands and tossing them in one of the red plastic bio bags set aside to go with the body when it was transported to the morgue.

"No cavalry needed," he said. "Just a breath of fresh air."

"You got that right," Alex said. "But it seemed like you picked up on something more than just the stink of it all."

"I did," he said, "but now's not the time to discuss it."

"Discuss what?"

Declan turned to see Samantha behind him in the doorway. Her expression appeared serious, her eyes grave. She wore some form of righteousness on her like light rose-scented perfume, it was mixed with an undertone he'd only detected on humans who have gone through more extremes than they were meant to, almost like a weathering of sorts. He inhaled, and what was that? Just a slight tickle of brimstone? Surely not. He met her eyes. There was nothing ominous there, only naturally colored and unclouded human eyes, void of taint. Perhaps, she had just gotten too close to someone not far from the hellfires of home. It wasn't unheard of, the stink was easy to pick up and hard to wash off, and if the being were evil enough you didn't have to even touch them.

He gave her a slight smile. "I think Alex believes I had an epiphany. Perhaps we can discuss theories once we're finished here?"

Sam looked suspiciously at him for a second, then shrugged.

"That's not a terrible idea. How much longer, Alex?"

"Actually, I'm finished. How about you, Abe?"

"Done everything I can. Let's pack up and let Brother Joshua's team handle the remains and the scene."

"You just chucked up on the asphalt," Declan said, standing next to the van. "How can you possibly be able to eat now?"

Russ gave him a sideways glance and smiled sheepishly. "One word. Pancakes."

Alex laughed as she walked alongside Sam. "To settle your stomach, huh?"

Russ nodded, pointing a finger at her and clicking his tongue like some seventies bachelor trying to pick a lady up at a bar.

Abe trailed at the rear of the group and Declan saw the man's faraway expression as he followed. It didn't take a rocket scientist to realize the guy was deep in thought and probably trying to figure out what could have possibly created the mutilated corpse they'd left behind. Declan was probably going to have to share information with him if this mess went on much longer and it was going to be tricky, trying to avoid the red-headed beauty Sam's intention to relieve both he and Panas of their heads. He shoved the unpleasant thought aside and turned his attention back to Russ.

"Pancakes? How silly of me. A billion-dollar industry does research for decades on medicinal aids for stomach upset and if they just fed their subjects pancakes, they could have saved nearly a billion dollars."

Russ laid a hand on Declan's shoulder. "Well, forget the bacon."

Declan winced when he felt the young man's finger brush the side of his neck and he focused hard on not drawing from him, not even taking a taste. It was difficult, and he could hear his inner beast screaming in protest when Russ lifted his hand away and passed the incubus up, making his way around the front of the van to the driver's side door. Sam gave him a skeptical look. Most likely she figured him to be a germaphobe who didn't appreciate being touched, but it was high-hoping. This wasn't just any normal human woman. She'd seen things. Done things. And most certainly dealt with things no normal human could even wrap their brain around. He wouldn't be able to shirk past her unquestioned for too much longer. Declan quickly turned and opened the front passenger door to climb in and avoid her suspicious gaze.

"What are you going on about?" Declan asked Russ, slamming the door shut.

There was the sound of the side door screeching along its track and the noise of three people loading up and getting settled. Panas was already between his two concubines and appeared rather comfy in the back seat, each arm stretched across the back of the seat like the loose protective embrace of a common street pimp.

"Bacon, boss. It ain't free," Russ said, peering at him over top of his horned rimmed glasses as Big Bertha roared to life. "And pancakes just really aren't the same without it. Those drug researchers would need to take a chunk out of their billions for it. And the price of sausage, well--"

Declan raised a brow, stopping Russ's rant. He was in complete awe at how the young man could pose such seriousness in the midst of what truly was a ridiculous conversation. The door screeched to a slamming close.

"Just drive to the nearest pancake house," Declan heard Sam say. "I'll pay."

The grin on Russ's face out shown his paleness.

"I like *her,* Boss. She's--"

"Just drive, mate."

Everyone was silent from the hotel to the Parkway and then to the Flapjack Pancake Cabin. Sam asked the hostess for the privacy of one of the rooms reserved for group events. The hostess accommodated her request with a friendly smile, leading the group through the crowded tables filled with hungry pancake eaters to a moderate-sized enclosed dining area. No one seemed ready to break the silence which hung in the air until after they were seated around the large wooden table sipping their glass tumblers of ice water.

"Can you give us a few minutes?" Sam asked the server.

The young woman gave a nod and gently pulled the door separating the room from the general dining area closed.

"Abe, I want you to forward the crime scene pics on to Father Joshua and the Abbey once we're finished going over them," Samantha said. "I want to see if they might be able to pick up on anything we may have missed."

"I figured you'd want me to so I sent them on already."

Sam merely nodded.

"Any idea what we're dealing with here?" Alex asked.

"My contact," Sam began, "has a concern with the murders and a theory I'm inclined to believe."

Declan took a sip from his iced water and then set it down in front of him, waiting for the inevitable.

"Your contact wouldn't by any chance be someone not bothered by the human condition, would it?"

Sam stared skeptically at him. "Is there something you want to share with the class?"

He smiled. "Let's just say I am familiar with a thing or two."

Her eyes narrowed and Declan could see her body tense. "Let's just say you tell me who you are, exactly. Or--"

Alex nudged an elbow into Sam's side. "We're all friends here, Sam, and I'm sure if we shoveled deep enough every one of us would have something the rest of us don't know about. I think we should go ahead and order first. Okay? We're all tired and hungry. And this kind of attitude accomplishes nothing."

Declan studied Abe from across the table.

I wonder if your friends know who you really are, he thought, *what you really are.*

Abe glanced up and caught his gaze. Declan merely nodded and then looked over at Sam to see how she would react to Alex's statement of the obvious.

"Sorry," Sam said with a sigh. "It's just been a very long

week and I'm edgy."

"All of us are on edge, Sam," Abe offered. "And I think it's safe to say we'll feel it until we figure out what's going on and what's to be done about it. But I agree with Alex. Let's order, eat, and then talk."

Russ was nodding his head vigorously. "Oh yeah. Preach it." He paused, picked up the cutlery set wrapped in a paper napkin, and began lightly drumming it on the table as he sang softly to the beat. "Gettin' me some pancakes. And bacon too. Know I'll be happy. Don't know about you."

Sam and Alex laughed. And then Panas's two women joined in. The laughter was light-hearted and warm. Even Abe and Panas stifled their grins and shook their heads at Russ's exuberance over pancakes. The tense atmosphere slowly began to unwind into a relaxing meal, but for some reason, Declan could only think about the last time he saw Abe alive.

———

Declan gazed over the alleyway at the two downed bodies, one of them very much dead, the other just hanging on by the last minutes of life left in it. The corpse lay alongside a row of cans for the inn's rubbish, which was completely dark at this time of night, and a tavern with its windows still glowing from the gas lamps. The few patrons left inside were perhaps either too drunk or too exhausted to care what was going on beyond their walls. Or, perhaps, they thought it would be wiser to keep their heads low and inside the safety of the tavern. Declan didn't know and didn't care.

He and his partner, Abraham, volunteered for the night's patrol in this downtrodden area as a favor to the overworked constabulary patroling this beat heavily for the past few months, thanks to bloody Jack the Ripper and his lust for fucking carnage.

"No good deed goes unpunished," Declan said under his breath, glaring at the mummified remains of the monster who'd caused such concern.

The knife the killer pulled out of his coat as his last hope for escape was held tight in one dried and withered hand, the muscles seized up in the serial killer's death grip around it and would hold it there until it fell to ash or someone with a strong enough stomach came in contact with the body to cut the fingers away and pull the weapon free. The blade from tip to the hilt was coated in the shadowy darkness of blood, for in the scant light of the alley it looked as black as pitch, and it was still glistening, still wet. A reddish glow caught his attention and he approached the mummified hand. Two of the fingers were spaced apart just enough for the red hue to be seen. Curious, Declan reached down and pried the fingers off the hilt to reveal an etching of a dragon just as the crimson glow faded. Thinking it was just a trick of lighting in this sodden alley, he pulled the weapon free and wiped the gore on the dead man's coat.

Would they have put such worry and effort into the search had they known good ol' Jack was just a man? A human? A bloody solicitor? He turned away in disgust as he slid the dagger in his trouser pocket and went over to kneel at Abraham's side. Declan removed his overcoat, rolled it up, and put it under his friend's head. His shirt he'd already stripped off and folded, covering the long and deep gash in Abraham's gut, then secured it as best as he could with the leather belt he'd taken off, trying to staunch the blood.

He'd blown the blasted whistle the constabulary gave him. Blown it several times in long whistling wails, and no help came. How long had it been? Five minutes? Ten? And nothing. Not out of the inn. Not out of the tavern. How could no one hear the stupid thing? The Ripper murders and the panic which ensued in this area were more than likely the cause of it. Everyone was terrified and everyone kept their head down so there would be no chance good ol' Jack, the solicitor from London, would attempt to sever it from the rest of their body.

"The girl?" Abraham gasped.

Declan laid a hand on his friend's forehead. His skin was wet with sweat, cold and clammy already.

"It's all right, mate. She's safe."

"Did--" Abraham coughed violently at first and then weaker. "Is he dead? Did you kill him?"

Declan nodded slowly. There was no reason to lie, not anymore. Help wasn't coming, not in time anyway. Abraham would die.

"I killed him."

Declan winced as a small bit of blood appeared at the corner of Abraham's mouth. The blade must have been angled up enough in the abdomen to at least nick a lung.

"How? You've no weapon."

The coughing began again and Declan held Abraham's hand, giving him something to squeeze as the coughs racked his body. There was so little life force left in him. When the coughing stopped, Declan placed his other hand onto his friend's, sandwiching it between his own.

"I have walked this world for a long time, my friend. I'm not human, have never been. I am an incubus. But I do not condone brutality such as the killer we sought and found tonight, and I will always try and help those who have no help and are mere prey for playing. If my confession is repulsive to you, I shall leave as soon as help arrives."

Abraham's eyes seemed unfocused and Declan watched as

the dying man tried to tilt his head. He blinked a couple of times and there were tears at the corner of those eyes. Declan hoped his confession wasn't the cause, for he'd never hurt Abraham on purpose, not for anything in this world or the next.

"An incubus?" Abraham managed a crooked smile. "You are not pretty enough. Banshee, maybe, but not--" The smile vanished and he coughed again.

A tear ran out of the corner of Declan's right eye. He didn't bother swiping it away, just let it fall. Abraham was his first human friend and he deserved that much.

"Rest, my friend. I have blown the whistle for help but am afraid to leave your side to alert those cowards in the tavern."

Abraham gave Declan's hand a weak squeeze.

"Too late," he wheezed. "I'm done for. Just stay with me until the end?"

Declan nodded. "Would you like me to pray with you? I'm not a Christian, far from it in fact, but perhaps it would provide some comfort to you."

Abraham managed to move his head slowly from side to side.

"No," he said, his voice strained. "No God would have allowed such a monster to live. Wouldn't have allowed such slaughter."

Declan frowned. He didn't know much about God, but he knew good and well now was not the time for his friend to burn a bridge and renounce his belief.

"Do not speak so, Abe. There is a God, I assure you. Take comfort."

There was a gurgling sound like Abraham was trying to laugh at what Declan said. There was no humor in the attempt and the tears which were at the corner of his friend's eyes let loose and trailed down the man's cheeks. Abraham took his last breath and died.

CHAPTER TWENTY

The sound of someone snapping their fingers in his face yanked Declan out of his thoughts and thrust him right back into the Flapjack Cabin.

"Earth to Declan. Come in, Boss. Can you read me?"

Declan startled in his chair and would have toppled back if Russ's knee wasn't right there to block it from moving. The young man's bearded face was less than an inch or two from his own and Declan could smell the smokey scent of bacon and maple syrup on his breath. Realizing he'd been walking through those memories deeper and for way longer than he should, he wasn't surprised to see all eyes were once again on him, especially Abe's. Declan gave an apologetic smile.

"Sorry," he said. "Long night."

He noticed Panas's arched eyebrow and ignored it.

"What did I miss?"

"Well, Boss, I was just saying, you need to eat up. You haven't even touched your food. You not a pancake man?"

Declan cleared his throat, picked up his fork, and began eating rather than answering.

The server brought in more coffee and refills of drinks on the house when Panas pulled out his card and insisted the woman ring up a grand for the wonderful service and the well-needed privacy of the room. When she returned the card, Declan couldn't help but notice the gleam in her eyes as she thanked Panas for his generosity. It was the look of pure and simple gratitude, not the dreamy eyes of a woman in the trance of lust Declan was so familiar with. Panas was looking at the woman casually, not averting his eyes as Declan was doing; a habit he started for fear of drawing anyone in at inopportune moments, but Panas made it look so easy. His Ukrainian comrade was indeed an example of how someone of his species might acclimate to the human world.

"It is my pleasure," Panas replied. "I hope you can make use of the tip."

When the server exited, closing the door behind her, they got down to business, and Declan managed to focus on something outside of himself which brought his own bit of thankful respite.

"My source confirms our suspicion of a nonhuman murderer," Sam said. "Which we all pretty much knew anyway. But there's a name for it. Incubus. Or Succubus if it's a female."

Declan tried not to react to being called an "it" but he felt the inward cringe all the same. The flaming haired woman wasn't wrong, brash maybe, but definitely not wrong. He would have to try and be more like Panas from now on, pull on the semblance of humanity like a new set of clothes. It was definitely something to strive for. More disconcerting was the source of her information and he started to ask who it might be but stopped himself before the question could come out of his mouth. He knew with all probability the source was someone from Hell; brimstone didn't lie, and she already seemed on edge about his presence in this mess so there was no real point in poking the sleeping bear. He let it alone.

He listened as Samantha defined what his species was, according to her source, and then proceeded to explain what she learned by questioning potential witnesses in the hotel.

"Everyone I spoke with says she was beautiful but could offer no other details."

"And the security cameras?" Abe inquired.

"From what I could see, I'd agree," Sam replied.

She began describing the woman as she passed around a couple of fuzzy still prints from the security system. They made their way around the table at opposite sides, passing from hand to hand until both Declan and Panas held a copy of the picture at the same time. He lifted his eyes up to see Panas nod ever so slightly. It was indeed the concern which brought his comrade to America.

———

I felt full and sleepy, the big meal weighing heavily in my gut, but my mind was racing. Alex's new friend, Declan, was an enigma, and he somehow picked up a second mystery man along the way. Panas and his female companions looked like they were just along for a fun ride, but appearances could be deceiving, and I wasn't going to drop my guard for anyone.

I was polishing the blade of my katana with a silk towel when a knock sounded at my door. I threw the coverlet from the bed over the weapon and strolled to the door. As far as I knew, the rest of our little party was now booked into rooms one floor up from me. Our agreement to meet after an hour of completing communications with our various sources still gave me almost thirty minutes of peace.

But not now. I checked the peephole and saw the elongated face of Abe reflected in the fisheye lens. I opened the door immediately. His face looked drawn, a shade paler and there was a glassy sheen to his eyes. If I didn't know better, I would have suspected he was drunk or high on something, but I was almost certain it wasn't the source of his distress. I caught his arm and pulled him inside.

"What are you doing?" I hissed, shutting the door behind him and applying all the locks.

"I needed, um, I was going…" he stopped and shook his head. "Can I sit down?"

I nodded and steered him to the bedside. I squatted in front of him, my eyes on his face. His eyes weren't tracking me, and I put my hands on either side of his face, focusing him.

"What happened?"

He was silent for a long moment, his eyes finally narrowing as his thoughts cleared. I dropped my hands to my knees still feeling the ripple of unease. "I was going to the lobby to pick out one of the tourist maps or brochures." He put his fingertips to his forehead. "I was stopped in the stairway. It was a woman." He shook his head, his hands falling to either side of him, bolstering him on the bed. "I am such an idiot. I should have been on alert. She caught me from behind. I barely saw her. But she touched me. It was just…"

He appeared so undone, and it caused a second flicker of apprehension. Abe might have looked like some kind of college professor, but I knew he was fully capable of taking down almost any foe. In my new world, the world of vampires and demons as next-door neighbors, I wasn't exactly sure where Abraham Shepherd fit in.

"Do you think she was after you specifically?"

Abe shrugged. "I don't know what to think. But I guess so, yeah."

"What did she look like?" I asked, thinking maybe this could be the woman with the magical kiss the guys I'd questioned spoke of.

Abe shook his head. "Sorry, it's a blank. I don't know why."

"So you're pretty sure she wasn't, um, human?"

"Whatever she was, it was bad, dark." He waited for a beat, his eyes skating to the closed door. "Do you believe the murderer would be so brazen to come here after us?"

I thought of Paul and how flippant he was about his minions. "Sure. If she wanted to see what she was up against, I can absolutely picture her coming here."

"Then this was some kind of reconnaissance mission." Abe looked up toward the ceiling, drawing in long breaths. His color was gradually returning to normal. He looked down at me where I was still crouched by the bed and his eyes flickered with something, a chasing shadow, a knowledge?

"Maybe," I stood and strolled to the window, attempting to clear my mind and escape from his gaze. There were two things at play here. We knew our murderer was some emissary sent by God knows what with their own agenda. But if we were on the tail of the right monster, and I was pretty sure we were, then this same creature was at the Abbey in France. The link between the two?

"The artifact," I blurted out. "Where is it?"

"Still in my pocket," Abe replied. I watched as he stood and shoved his hand in his pocket. When he brought out his fist holding the handkerchief and unfolded it, I breathed a sigh of relief. The unnamed item was there, an unimpressive bit of stone. Abe brought it out briefly at the restaurant to show it to me while the rest of our party were involved in conversation. It certainly didn't look like much, but it came from the abbey where the first kidnapping occurred, and there was a chance someone, perhaps the killer, was after it.

"I just don't understand it." I watched as Abe tucked the object away. His expression was clearing. "What was her plan, this woman who caught you? Why would she expose herself to you in this way?"

"To get my attention?"

I shrugged. "She made sure you didn't remember her," I answered. "But she wants us to know she's here. I'm sure of it."

Abe turned and walked toward the bathroom and I heard the water running. When he came out, he was drying his face on a hand towel.

"Feeling better?"

"Yeah," he answered. He straightened to his full height, stretching like he just awakened from a long nap. In the middle of the movement, he froze. His hand went to his chest, his fingers resting on the breast pocket of his starched shirt. He dipped his fingers into the pocket and pulled out a folded sheet of paper. I watched the emotions flicker across his face, surprise, curiosity, then he scowled. "Well, this might be the answer we were looking for."

"What is it?" I drew closer so I could see the spidery hand-writing on the hotel stationery.

"Seems I have been invited on a date," Abe replied.

"Where?"

Abe flipped the paper over so I could read it more easily.

"She says she knows something about the murders. Do you believe it?" My tone was sharp, my doubt very clear.

"I think she may know something, but she's no innocent bystander." Abe folded the note and tucked it back in his pocket.

"She said she wants to meet at midnight. It will give me a few hours to get ready."

"You're going to go? Alone?"

"It's what the note says, but I don't believe for a moment you will agree to it, so we need to plan."

"It's a trap, you know."

"I know," he agreed.

"Then we'll go in armed."

CHAPTER TWENTY-ONE

Samantha rang Declan up shortly after he went back to his room. They were supposed to meet again in an hour so he was a bit surprised to hear from her so soon until she told him about Abe's brief encounter. There was a knock on the door, and thinking it was just Russ coming in to be Russ, Declan opened it and turned to finish his phone conversation. He glanced over his shoulder to see it was Panas instead. Samantha was brief and kept him on for less than a minute. When he ended the call, the Ukrainian was helping himself to a bottle of water out of the mini-fridge. He plopped down on the foot of one of the full-size beds.

"Abe ran into Amelia Degas," Declan said, setting the phone on the small dinette table.

"Is he still alive?"

Declan nodded. "Sounded like a warning brush and a note in his pocket to rendezvous with her at midnight."

Panas rolled his eyes. "Ah, Amelia and her rendezvous notes.

Come into my web little fly, tangle yourself in the tendrils of quite a brutally unnecessary death. Is he going?"

Declan sat down on the bed beside him. "What do *you* think?"

Panas grimaced. "Are we going in with them?"

"The Samantha woman has a plan and asked for our assistance."

"And you have other ideas?"

Declan sighed. "I have other concerns."

"The young man?"

"Russ. His name is Russ. He is a complete innocent."

"What of the others?"

"The Samantha woman fights on the side of the righteous, but I have a feeling she's been dealing with some of our kind."

Panas tilted his head. "You believe she is corrupt?"

"No," Declan replied without hesitation. "Not corrupt. I think she's true but she's been close enough to appear tainted."

"A warrior walking the line then. And the other woman, the one you desire?" Panas smiled deviously. "Come now, we are both old hats to this existence. You cannot think I did not notice."

Declan shifted his eyes to study the thick blue carpet at his feet and was silent.

"I see." He laid a hand on Declan's shoulder. "You are not human, my friend and some desires shouldn't be followed."

"You think I'd end up killing her."

Panas nodded slowly, sadly. "We can walk, talk, fuck, and live like them. But we cannot love like them. In the end--"

He didn't finish the sentence. He didn't need to. Declan knew what the end would bring, even with the puzzling event of him not being able to draw from her, he knew. Hell hath no love, and in the end he would burn just like the rest of his kind. And Alex? Alex was much better off living her life away from him.

They sat quietly for a moment before Panas asked what he thought about Abe.

"Not human," Declan replied. "Was, but no longer."

Panas agreed. "I sensed it when I met him. No underlying human scent or of any other. I'd wager he's one of the rare ones."

Declan couldn't argue. It was the only thing that made sense. He'd heard rumors of the rare ones, those troubled souls who only wished to atone for their shortcomings in Purgatory, but he'd never actually come in contact with one until now.

"Do you know much about them?"

"Rumors, myths," Panas answered with a shrug. "Not anything concrete. They were in limbo, trying for atonement as you know. What could provoke one to leave such a state? I do not know."

"Can they be pulled out?"

"I guess anything is possible but then there begs the questions of who and why. Does he concern you?"

"I knew him once," Declan admitted. "He died in front of me, killed by a murderer we were pursuing in the 1800s. I don't think he has any recollection of me or his former life."

"Atonement requires you remember. Remember and then purify. If he is truly in the midst of limbo, he knows."

Declan thought for a moment. He hadn't detected any recollection in his old partner's eyes, but like Panas said, anything was possible. Glancing over at the clock, he saw a half-hour passed. He needed to focus on their next move and leave thoughts of Abe for another day.

"I don't want Russ caught up in the thick of it," Declan told Panas. "I need you to keep him back, safe. And if possible, keep him innocent."

"If I may ask, who is this young man to you?"

"My uber driver."

Panas raised a brow. "You're serious?"

"Just promise to do what I've asked of you."

Panas nodded. "I will. Can you do what needs to be done should Samantha and her friends' efforts fail? The repercussions will be immense."

Declan got up and went to the window, easing the drapes aside as he peered through, thinking.

"Damned if I do," he mumbled, "and damned if I don't. I will do what is required of me. Amelia will not see another sunrise regardless."

"You sound almost nostalgic. Surely you have no qualms about sending her back to Asmodeus in pieces."

"None," Declan replied, still gazing out of the window.

"Then what troubles you?"

"The deaths of those at my own hand. The nun. The village girl. I am the reason the righteous have taken notice and decided to take action. Amelia's fate could very well be my own, I'm afraid. And to be honest, I almost welcome it." Declan turned his eyes back to Panas. "Are we even capable of remorse?"

"Capable? Yes. Willing?" Panas shrugged again. "A harem, my friend, is what you need to calm your regrets."

Declan laughed. It felt good.

"We finish this business," Panas said, "and I will help you begin. I noticed Camille has taken a liking to you, which is good. I will give you Camille and teach you how to build your harem and not regret."

There was a knock on the door and Declan opened it to Russ who was standing there with a can of Pepsi in his hand. He looked like he'd just got out of the shower. His black hair was slicked back and wet, and he smelled of many different hygiene products. He'd also swapped out his jeans for a clean pair and was now sporting a black tee shirt with a Return of the Jedi logo on the front.

"Live long and prosper," he said with a grin as he strolled in the room like he'd not a care in the world. "So, are we ready to party or what?"

Panas got up and went to the door. There was a slight grin pulling at the corners of his mouth and Declan heard him mumble something about ubers and harems as he walked out. Declan closed the door.

"What was he talking about?" Russ asked.

"Just a bit of senseless blabber."

"Well, we've got a few minutes to kill before we have to meet the others. Mind if I hang out here?"

Declan didn't mind at all.

———

I called the abbey after Abe went back to his room and then spoke to Declan over the phone. Abe wasn't taking any detours and he even agreed to text me as soon as he locked himself in. I wanted Declan to know of the meeting, though, just in case. The phone rang only twice before the light accented voice of one of the novices answered in French.

I asked to speak to Sister Eva again. There was something I was missing and I hoped the older woman might have some pertinent advice before our meeting this evening.

Sister Eva, once again, was not available. I disconnected the call and stared at the blank screen. Sister Eva's absence from the abbey could be anything. She might have gone into town to comfort the family of Slyvie. She may be out doing errands. But I doubted it. Knowing the older warrior as I did, I suspected she was off trying to do her own investigation. I just hoped she stayed safe and on her side of the big pond.

I grabbed the bag Alex packed for me and dropped it on the bed. I opened it once, only to grab my favorite weapon. Now I decided I needed to complete a few other preparations.

The slacks were packed away in favor of a pair of dark jeans which hugged my figure, leaving less material to get in the way during hand-to-hand. The shirt was a close-fitting tee, black in color, and the leather jacket I wore over it was buttery smooth and supple. I was wearing practical flat shoes, but now I changed into a pair of low boots with a good tread. I was pleased with my friend's forethought. The boots would serve me well for my trek through the woods. Because there was one thing Abe was spot on about. There was no way I was going to let him go on this little meeting without backup. He might not know I was there, but I would be.

Weapons were my next choice. I strapped on my ankle holster with the blessed blade straight from the hands of the good sisters. Under their tutelage, I learned the fine art of blade throwing, and as a reward for all my hard work, they gave me a set of three knives. I didn't ask where they originally came from. They were old and well-wrought, but the balance was superb and I knew they must have been fashioned for someone important to the cause.

My katana fit in its own specially designed sheath, and I would add it to my arsenal soon enough. I selected a gun for my hip, a pretty little Derringer with enough firepower to make a long-distance shot. It made me more comfortable to feel the metal so close to my skin, my soul.

I headed up the stairs, two at a time. I didn't like taking elevators. A coffin was a coffin, whether it rode up and down on pulleys or stayed decently in the ground. Instead, I pushed through the fire doors to the next floor. I kept my guard up. The attacker might not still be in the building, but I was unwilling to bet my life on it.

Abe was booked in the largest room, and even with the slightly additional expense, he wasn't getting much for his money. The decor was still late 90's chic, stain-resistant carpeting, and all. I wasn't the first to the dance, but I also wasn't the last. Alex was seated at the small table by the window, and her new pal Declan was with her, knees almost touching, dark head bent next to her light curls.

I stifled the urge to grit my teeth. Protective, yes, I was. Overly protective, nope. Declan was just too perfect to be possible, and perfection made me antsy.

The Russ guy was leaned back on the small leather sofa next to the closed sliding doors with a soda can in his hand. His appearance shouted RPG.

He lifted his can up in a mock toast and grinned. "Ah, the beautiful lady returns."

I rolled my eyes but managed to smile back at him. The guy was just a goofball. Nice, but goofy all the same. How in the world he'd ended up attached to Declan was a mystery in itself. They couldn't have been more different.

The rest of Declan's friends were not in the room. I wasn't sure if they were off on their own mission or just laying low for the time being. Abe was at the third and last chair pulled up to the table, and I could see the shiny surface of a tourist map spread out in front of them.

"Sam," Alex greeted, her face tipping up to see me standing over them. She smiled with real pleasure, and I felt my muscles relax.

"Hey," I answered.

Abe, seeing me standing, hastily stood up and offered his

chair. In truth, he and Declan came to attention at the same time and I was given a choice of where I wanted to sit. Chivalry among the ranks? I looked from one man to the other, subconsciously noting, what? Were they alike in other ways? Other mannerisms? Or was my brain finding things, relations, which weren't really there.

"We think we have a better idea of the meeting place," Abe began as I eased into the chair. I shifted, repositioning my katana and getting a raised eyebrow from Declan who sat in the seat next to me. The man smelled so damn good like he'd just showered with some expensive designer soap mixed with enough pheromone power to draw in an entire Arabian harem. I made a conscious effort not to be distracted by it.

"I assume we've agreed we want her to think you're traveling alone," I added, speaking of the mystery woman. "Which of course, you won't be."

"I will go alone," Abe began.

"I disagree," Declan said, his voice all smoke and honey. "If what Samantha says about these creatures is to be believed, then no one needs to be caught alone with this woman."

I struggled not to glare at him just because he was that pretty, not because he said anything I disagreed with.

"No," I said to Abe, "you won't."

Abe lowered his eyes and sighed. Why he'd even think to approach this woman on his own after their first encounter was unsettling. I hoped it wasn't some kind of vampire thrall thing.

"We *are* going to split up. There is really no other way we can expect to draw this person out into the open." Alex supplied. "The meeting is at Big Head Rock so Abe will go in on the main trail. Alone. I know you're not comfortable with it, Sam, but it's the logical thing to do."

"And if she puts a whammy on him before we get there?"

Abe glanced up at me. "I'll be armed, Sam, and I'll keep my distance. One touch was enough."

I sighed and then consented, hoping his confidence was more bravery than stupidity.

Alex continued. "There are three paths leading to Big Head Rock, but only one is direct, and that's the one Abe will be taking."

"Then we can take the others on the other two or go off the beaten path altogether," I added.

Alex nodded. "Declan and I will follow over here," Alex added, pointing to a meandering trail drawn to cross over the pale blue line of a stream.

I looked at the map, the tracery of trails like spider webs across the expanse of green. Where did I need to be? I wanted to be with Alex, keeping her safe, making sure this Declan guy was what he appeared to be, what he claimed to be.

"I'll be following up," I stated, deliberately vague. It was going to be a challenge, keeping my little team in sight. But there wasn't one of them I could afford to lose.

Declan gave me a sharp look, but I didn't engage. He would do his job, I would do mine.

"Um, guys," Russ said from the couch. "Where do you want me? Cause I can pull some punches, you know. Maybe do a little jujitsu dance on the mummy making bi-atch. You know? Ninja style."

I raised a questioning brow at Declan, trying not to laugh. A knock on the door startled me and I barely realized how quick I'd reacted until I felt the cool hard surface of my hand on the handle of the katana.

"It's Panas," Declan said.

Abe was at the door before either Declan or I could get up to answer it. Panas strode in and stood by the door after it was closed again.

"Russ, you'll be with Panas on the third trail," Declan said. "Keep your progress on the path slow. We may need you as a backup if this turns bad."

I chanced another meeting with the beautiful man's eyes. There was concern there and I was willing to bet it was for Russ, so I didn't argue with his direction. So the beautiful man did have a heart? Interesting. I turned to Panas, studying him for a moment.

"Your *assistants* stay at the hotel," I said to him. "There are going to be enough people on the trails to worry about as it is."

Panas didn't offer a protest, just nodded.

We spent the remaining time checking weapons and taking measure of our troops. This was a complicated group, even without the two women Panas claimed were his assistants, and I didn't like all the moving parts. There were too many things to go wrong.

"I'm going to look at those maps again in the lobby," I said to the group in general and excused myself. I needed to make a few more plans and I wasn't sure I wanted everyone to know my business. I didn't see Declan watching my back as I slipped out of the room, but I felt his eyes on me until the door closed.

CHAPTER TWENTY-TWO

Declan watched Abe head off onto the main trail, the surrounding foliage obscuring the view as he progressed onward until seemingly vanishing into the night. The faint shine of the flashlight app on Abe's cell phone was the only proof he was still on the move and it bounced around like an energy orb with the man's stride. After a few moments, it too faded away along with the man, swallowed by the darkness. Declan gazed up at the full moon and clear dark skies above. At least there was natural light to guide their steps, not needed so much for him but for Alex and Russ. Allowing his inner beast to enhance his sight would probably be startling for the young woman, especially when his eyes turned their normal lavender hue and tended to glow when he pulled upon this nonhuman resource. Declan didn't want to frighten her, so he forewent the ability. His night vision without it was still much better than humans with twenty-twenty, so he could make do with virtual ease. He glanced over at Alex as she spoke in hushed tones with the Samantha woman on the far side of the small gravel-covered parking lot. The black ball cap on Alex's head made her look even younger than he estimated she was and even more innocent. He couldn't help wondering how on earth she'd teamed up with Samantha and Abe. Would her alliance with those two one day be the death of her? The old adage about playing with fire and getting burned came to mind. He swallowed hard, sick at the thought, and then hoped she knew what she was getting herself into. The world of the supernatural was dangerous at best, but it wasn't just your physical form endangered. At worst, the damage went deeper and many a human lost their souls in the process of touching those merciless flames of adventure.

Alex made her way over to him, leaving Samantha in her makeshift team huddle with Panas and Russ. Declan took a moment to appreciate Alex's form, her movement as she walked, and then lowered his eyes back to the gravel at his feet feeling as if he'd somehow committed some inappropriate offense.

"Are you ready?" Alex asked.

Declan nodded, resisting the urge to caution her about the dangers she'd be facing when dealing with one of his kind, especially one as sadistic as Amelia. What he wanted to tell her was to go back home and safely live her life without the terrible knowledge of anything supernatural, but it was too late. She knew and she seemed stubborn enough to not only ignore his advice but also add a few expletives about him minding his own business.

Amelia Degas, he so wanted to tell her, was likely as evil as one of his kind can get aside from Asmodeus himself. She was older than both he and Panas, having been the very first creation of Asmodeus sent down to this plane shortly after the celestial war and the fall of Lucifer and his angels. In her ancient wisdom, she likely knew Adam and Eve, Cain and Abel, and those which followed after. Declan believed whole-heartedly she crossed the line over to insanity long before he ever stepped a foot upon terra firma. Legend has it, her creation was for the pleasure of Asmodeus who, once again according to legend, raped her into submission to his will. An eternity of such treatment would very well likely drive anyone insane.

Declan wanted to tell Alex all these things and more, but instead he simply nodded dumbly and took off down the trail with her walking alongside him. The path grew darker the further they went but he could still see the lunar shine through breaks in the tree canopy, enough to reveal any rocks, branches, or roots lying in wait to trip them up. After a good ten minutes, she touched his arm and pointed ahead where Abe's orb of light came back into view. The touch of her fingertips on his skin sent a sudden and urgent desire to make love to her, not feed off of her. He jerked his arm away, feigning surprise to cover the awkward thoughts.

"Sorry," she whispered. "I didn't mean to startle you."

"No worries," he lied, wanting nothing more than to tell her what her skin against his own did to him.

He wondered briefly if she felt it too, if she could sense anything between them at all or if it was just some weird fixation of his own addled brain. The orb of light from Abe's cell phone became clearer and Declan could see bits of the man's shadowy form coming into view. Slowing his pace, Alex followed suit until the brush grew thinner and Big Head Rock loomed ahead in sighting distance. Declan swallowed hard and touched the sleeve of Alex's jacket to stop her from going further, hoping he wouldn't feel another rush of lust when he did so. She stopped and glanced over her shoulder at him and then nodded, sidling up beside him under the branches of a large tree.

Abe was just a short distance away now, pacing back and

forth in front of the huge rock shaped like the human head as was its namesake. His cell phone was in his hand and he seemed to be trying for a nonchalant approach, playing with the blasted thing as if this whole exercise were just a ho-hum part of his normal day. Declan watched the glowing flashes of the screen, waiting. He could smell the familiar scent of one of his own kind, the same one he'd smelled at the hotel, but the night breeze was mixing it up and pushing it around in the air so he really wasn't for certain which direction it was coming from. His body tensed and his hand reflexively went to the handle of the dagger he'd secured in a sheath at his side.

———

I watched Declan's broad back as he led the way into the woods, impressed by the silence and speed of his movements. Alex looked small next to him although I knew she wasn't without defenses herself. But I still felt the subconscious alarm of something, something not right. They melted into the darkened tree line and I increased my pace.

I took the high road. The trail I followed was more a footpath for animals than an actual hiking trail. It followed the curve of the land, keeping me just above and behind Alex and Declan as they moved swiftly down the path. I could see the dark shadow of a third shape in front of them, the flickering figure of Abe, lit by his cell phone. Dark was a frenemy for us. It might hide our movements, but it did the same for our opponents. I waited until my eyes adjusted before moving further into the woods.

My inner voice was picking at me, wearing at me to the point I was almost distracted by it. My hands skimmed my side, checking for my sheathed katana, my gun, and lastly the throwing knife, the twin to the one in my ankle sheath. There was no time to get any equipment for night surveillance, so our cell phones would have to provide the light. A flashlight app on my phone provided a thin beam, better to use when one wished to remain hidden. I knew from the maps the walk would take us only forty-five minutes into the woods. We were keeping a good pace, and I expected Abe would arrive at the meeting spot just on time.

And I was right with my estimate. Now, as I slipped into the shadows bordering the clearing, I could see the group of them all scattered below me like players on a chessboard. Abe was the first to arrive, or so it seemed from my vantage point.

No, Abe was the second. After precious minutes peering into the darkness, I realized we weren't alone. The first creature to arrive was a lithe figure who crouched on a low hanging limb on the far side of the ancient boulder. My eyes scanned the wood, noting the tall figure of Declan hovering above Alex's smaller frame. I felt adrenaline flood my system as the realization hit. From their viewpoint, neither would be able to spot the watcher, but after a second I could have sworn Declan's still form appeared to tense, his head angled to hear or smell something the rest of us remained unaware of, and his right hand dropped slightly to his side where I had noted a sheathed blade of some sort secured to him earlier.

And Abe? Abe looked like any slightly lost tourist, his head bent toward the lighted screen of his cell phone, the white-blue light reflected in his glasses. Either he was playing the ignorant rube well, or he wasn't what I thought he was. But the act was freaking me out. I opened my mouth to cry out, thinking revealing myself might be worth the risk, but my voice died in my throat.

The creature moved with incredible speed, launching herself into the air like some high wire act, landing with grace and inhuman accuracy, her arm reaching around Alex's unprotected side, grabbing a handful of Alex's shirt and yanking hard. Alex spun right into the beast's grasp, the move done so neatly, there was no time for Alex to recover, to fight back.

I watched Declan pivot in a blur of motion, arching toward Alex and her captor before stopping short.

———

The breeze stilled just long enough for Declan to pinpoint the direction of the scent. He turned his eyes upward and spotted the shadow crouched on the lower limb of the tree. It was already airborne, leaping off the branch and to the ground with all the agility of some crazed spider just as he released the leather strap holding the dagger in the sheath. He felt his eyes take on their demon part as he reflexively shifted to nonhuman sight.

Everything clearer now. Crystal clear.

Amelia. Dark brown hair cascaded down over her shoulders like waves of pure silk, her eyes the same lavender hue as his own. If he didn't know better, he would have sworn she was someone like Athena or Venus. She was truly beautiful, but it brought to mind the old saying beauty was only skin deep and the creatures of Asmodeus were of its truth. She lunged forward, grabbing Alex by the shirt and spinning her in before Declan could draw the dagger. Alex let out a short yelp of surprise and then a light grunt as her back was pulled hard into the front of Amelia's body, the ball cap fell to the ground. He stopped, hand still frozen on the handle as he saw Ameilia yank the young woman's head back with a handful of her hair, the silvery glint of a knife held at Alex's throat. Abe obviously heard Alex's distressed cry and was heading back towards them from the other side of the outcropping rock, rustling the leaves as his feet hit the ground and whipping the brush aside as he plowed through it. From Declan's periphery, he could see the flashlight beam confirming what he was hearing. Abe would be here in a few moments.

All of Declan's worries for Alex's safety slammed into him, and they were coming true right before him, and because of him. He'd hesitated one bloody second too long. Alex's eyes were wide with surprised fear at being taken until they found and locked onto his own. Her expression morphed to one of confusion and he knew she'd noticed the color change of his eyes. It was too late for it now. She knew something wasn't normal about him and in a short moment so would Abe, but he wasn't about to dumb down his sight and add any more risk to this situation. He'd deal with the consequences later, when she was safe and sound. Right now, she was nowhere near safe, and when the breeze shifted, he could smell the alarmed pheromones her body was giving off. Despite her fear, she kept her hands down at her sides, wisely keeping any panicked reflexes she may have felt at bay. He watched her exhale in one long steady flow as if she were self-calming. He couldn't help but admire her courage.

Declan lifted his hand off the handle of his weapon and showed Amelia empty palms, both hands half-way up in mock surrender, just as Abe broke the last bit of brush separating them.

"Let her go, Amelia. There's no need to add to your kill list."

Amelia smiled. It was genuine, reaching her lavender eyes which seemed to sparkle with delight.

"The famous Inspector Declan Faulkner," she purred. "Or should I say infamous? I've heard so much about you, naughty boy. It seems your reputation precedes you."

A chill raced up Declan's spine. The last thing on Earth he wanted was for this woman to know anything about him, but the amusement in her eyes told him she knew, and probably quite a bit at that. He was willing to bet she'd gained her knowledge from the top, or more accurately, the bottom of Hell's domain.

"I don't think Asmodeus qualifies as a reliable source," Declan said, taking a tentative step forward. "He tends to fib a lot."

Amelia laughed and yanked Alex back with her a few steps. "No closer, love. I have no problem with bleeding her out right here."

Declan glanced over at Abe to see he'd followed suit, his cell phone out of view and probably in his pocket, his hands open and raised slightly. Amelia looked over at him and gave a playful wink.

"Hey handsome," Amelia said to Abe. "I'm so sorry. It looks like I'll have to postpone our date for a little while, and I was really looking forward to it. Don't worry though. I'll save room for you too. Scout's honor."

She yanked Alex back through the surrounding brush with her and took off at a nonhuman speed through the darkness. If Abe noticed Declan's eyes changing color, he didn't let on. Instead, he took off running, matching stride for stride with Declan as they chased after Amelia and Alex.

CHAPTER TWENTY-THREE

I froze in my tracks, realizing with breathless fatality we fell for the trap. The slice of silver in the woman's hand betrayed the sharp edge of the blade as she held it just beneath Alex's chin. Alex, my best friend in the world, Alex the doctor, the healer, Alex, the innocent I dragged into this battle.

I could hear only sibilant whispers as the woman beast below spoke with Declan, but the effect was immediate. His hands came out on either side, the universal sign of surrender, and Alex was pulled further into the clearing.

When my eyes went to Abe, I saw he was stepping back, all the feigning of ignorance gone. But I could tell by his stance he was a moment too late. His hands came up, showing empty palms pale in the moonlight. He glanced from Alex to Declan, seemingly studying the man's face. Since Declan's back was to me, I couldn't see what caught Abe's attention, but it didn't matter once the woman took off running, dragging my friend along with a knife still at her throat. One slip up, one trip, one wrong move on this bitch's part and Alex could be dead or dying from a severed carotid artery or windpipe. There was no way in hell I was going to let it happen. I moved swiftly and quietly through the brush, following Abe and Declan along the higher ground as they took off after them.

Declan didn't hold back. Not this time. Not for Alex. He drew on every bit of demon inside of him, running full out to overtake Amelia who was somewhat burdened with her new hostage which was slowing her down just enough for it to count. She was headed down the trail straight towards Panas and Russ. He pushed himself even harder. No doubt Panas could hold his own, but not Russ. If she laid one hand on Russ...

Branches gave way, slapping back towards Abe, as Declan ran on with even more to lose. He saw Amelia drag Alex off the trail, bursting through a thick line of brush up ahead and to his right.

"Flank left, mate!" Declan yelled over his shoulder. "I'll take the right!"

Abe didn't answer but split off in the direction he was ordered to go, disappearing through the dark shadows of foliage. Out of the corner of his eye, Declan caught sight of Panas and Russ coming up the trail. He wanted to shout out orders for Russ to be kept back, away from Amelia, out of her reach, but time was running out on Alex's safety and since she was the one with the knife at her throat, then his focus needed to be on her. He would just have to trust Panas's word to keep Russ out of danger. And if he couldn't? Declan's heart sank at the thought.

One hand on Russ, you tiresome bitch, and all of hell won't stop me from ripping you apart!

He banked to the right and pulled the dagger from its sheath, a crimson glow broke the darkness and he didn't need to look at the blade to know it was coming from the dragon's eyes. Stealth wasn't a concern right now. Amelia knew he and Abe were after her, so the glow from the dagger would have no more effect on the situation than his own eyes did, speed and strength seemed to be what was needed. And he would meet the need, however much it took.

Declan leaped over the trunk of a large downed tree, never breaking stride as he moved over the uneven terrain. The women were about thirty feet away as he passed them up and tore through an almost solid line of thick undergrowth. The heavy scent of evergreen permeated his nose, so strong it nearly overpowered the smells of everything else around him, as he broke into a clearing. Abe came out nearly at the same time from the opposite side. Declan threw him a hand motion from their old partner days to ease back into the cover of the treeline and block Amelia's retreat should she try to take off again. It was a long shot, and all he could do was hope Abe remembered what it meant. When Abe ducked back into the brush, Declan breathed a quick sigh of relief and moved out in the open to take point.

Amelia's entrance into the clearing wasn't nearly as graceful as it would have been without Alex still held tightly in front of her, but she moved boldly in and set Alex's feet down on the ground, having carried her as she ran. The shiny metal of the knife still glinted against the front of Alex's neck. There was a smile on the succubus's face and she wore it like a cunning fox ready to spring whatever trap she planned.

"Inspector," she said by way of greeting.

Declan said nothing, his fingers tightening on the hilt of the dagger.

"You are spending a lot of effort on a void."

Declan tilted his head inquisitively and Amelia smirked.

"Surely Asmodeus explained the few and far between."

When Declan didn't voice a response, she continued.

"A void, Inspector. A blank. A nothing."

Declan's eyes narrowed. "What the fuck are you going on about?"

Amelia laughed, grabbing Alex's hair again and easing her head back. There was a small trickle of blood trailing its way beneath the blade and Alex's expression went from surprised terror to a hardened mask of fed-up determination. If he couldn't get her out of Amelia's clutches soon, Alex was sure to take it upon herself to do so, which just might get her killed a little faster. Abe stepped out of the treeline, the black metal of a handgun glinting in the scant beams of moonlight which cut their way through incoming clouds. His stance was one of a professional as he aimed the barrel directly at the back of Amelia's head. If he pulled the trigger, he may end her right here, but he could also hit Alex.

"Have you tried to feed from her?" Amelia asked.

Declan clenched his jaw.

"You have," she answered herself, then paused, studying his face for a moment. "Well, I'll be damned. You felt guilt. I scc it written all over your face."

Declan felt his cheeks burn at her words but didn't look up. He kept his sights on Amelia's hands, the one holding the knife especially, but this bloody bitch could just as easily snap her neck with the other hand. It was definitely better than having to look Alex in the eyes at the moment. He knew what he would probably see there; anger, disappointment, all of it pointing at him as a betrayer of her trust.

"Wait until Asmodeus hears about this," Amelia said. "He'll yank you back into the lake of fire and never let you out again. Oh well, it can be a pillow talk topic for later. As for the voids, my naive Inspector, somehow they are able to keep all of their yummy lifeforce protected from us."

She peered down at Alex. "Such a small and inconsequential human with the ability to deprive me of sustenance. Just one more trick of the righteous to try and keep us underfoot is what I think. You weren't aware of it though, were you, sweetie?"

Amelia yanked back on the handful of Alex's hair she held tight in her hands.

"God gave you a tongue," Amelia said. "Either use it or I'll cut it out for you."

"That's enough," Abe said.

There was a light click of the safety being released.

Abe, please don't fire, Declan thought. *It's too damned risky.*

The gun stayed silent but Abe didn't.

"Tell us what you want or kill her and be done with it. I'm already tired of the sound of your voice."

Bloody hell, Abe!

Declan reflexively glanced at Alex, their eyes meeting and holding still in one of those rare slow-motion moments which seemed to hold an entire lifetime in them; they held on regardless of what he wanted or what he was afraid he would see there. No accusation. No expression one would expect from a victim of betrayal. No hatred. What he did see was compassion, the confusion he'd noticed earlier seemingly turned to wonder. And then the moment was gone, shattered by Amelia's voice.

"Ah," Amelia said with a laugh. "The silent one bounced fresh out of Purgatory speaks. Didn't think I knew that little piece of information, did you? How'd repenting go?"

"What. Do. You. Want?" Abe growled.

"What? All business?" Amelia asked, lifting a brow. "I would have thought a tall, dark, and handsome man like you might have enjoyed a little more foreplay. I think I find it a little disappointing."

"This isn't a game, demon."

Amelia turned and glared at Abe over her shoulder. "It has always been a game, you ignorant bastard. But since you insist on keeping it all business, I'll tell you what I want. I want the little trinket in your pocket. You give it to me and the Inspector's little sweetheart void here gets to live another day in her own fucking game of life."

She sees the amulet's glow too, Declan thought. *There is no other way she'd have known it was there.*

Panas stepped into the clearing just a few feet away from Abe while Amelia droned on. His arms were crossed and there was a knowing expression on his face. Declan saw him nod once.

He saw the glow. It's what he was saying, right? Did he know what the artifact really was? Why Lucifer would want it? Why Amelia would have risked confrontation so openly for such a thing. What the bloody hell was going on? And where's Russ? Did Panas actually get him to go back to the van?

It was Abe with balls enough to ask. "Tell me what it is and I might consider your offer."

"You want to bargain?" Amelia asked. "Some friend you are."

"Just give her the sodding amulet," Declan said to Abe. "Whatever it is, it isn't worth Alex's life."

Abe ignored him. "I'll ask you one last time and then I pull the trigger. If it goes through you both, I'll apologize and move on with my night. What does it do, demon?"

Declan's stomach lurched. If Abe fired, it wasn't a matter of possibility Alex would be hit, it was a certainty. And from Declan's angle, the blow would be fatal. Was Abe insane or did he seriously just not give a damn about her? Purgatory wasn't supposed to be mind breaking from what little he knew about it, not like hell. If Abe spent five minutes there, Declan wouldn't hesitate to declare him certifiable, but the whole point of Purgatory was to build you up. Wasn't it? Ready you for Heaven, so to speak. And then it hit him, Abe was doing the old good cop bad cop routine they used so many times, so long ago.

You sly bastard, Declan thought. *I should have known you wouldn't have forgotten.*

"The amulet has the power to do many things," Amelia said. "Most of them you wouldn't understand."

"Try me," Abe said. "And you'd best keep your lying tongue at bay because I will know if you're speaking the truth or not."

"It can be used to open gateways between realms," she replied with a sneer as she turned her body and Alex's to where she could see both Abe and Declan. "Truth enough for you?"

Her eyes flicked to Panas and she smiled. "Well if it isn't the Ukrainian rogue himself. All this way for little old me?"

Panas said nothing, his expression stony.

"Why would I give you, a demon of hell, an amulet with so much power?" Abe asked Amelia.

Declan spoke up before she could answer. "Give her the damn amulet, Abe, or I'll take it from you myself and give it to her."

CHAPTER TWENTY-FOUR

C louds were rolling in from the north, bringing with them the threat of rain, and blocking out what little moonlight we could see by. Carefully as I could, I placed one foot in the loam of the forest floor, slipping closer to the little scene below me. As I shifted my weight, I felt a hand, hard like braided wire, wrap around my upper arm. I didn't cry out; I couldn't risk the noise, but I whipped around to face my assailant.

Sister Eva's pale face floated above a shrouded form like a specter from a B movie horror flick. It took a moment to register she was actually there. She raised one finger to her lips in a silencing gesture and I gave a short nod. No wonder I couldn't get hold of her at the abbey.

She let my arm go and eased up next to me. I glanced quickly to the clearing. I could see the argument continuing below, Alex still held tight against the monster's body, Declan speaking in a low, barely audible tone.

"She wants the amulet," Sister Eva hissed.

I blinked in surprise. So much happened, so much death, I almost forgot about the amulet Abe had found at the abbey, the one he carried in his pocket.

"*That's* what this is about?" I mouthed the words, incredulous.

Sister Eva drew close. "I found records in the vault at the abbey. There was a collection uncatalogued and I didn't remember it until after you left the country."

I nodded, listening to her words but keeping my eyes on the events below.

"The scrolls were in poor shape, but as soon as I recognized the name of the artifact, I knew what happened." She paused. "The piece holds tremendous power, and in the wrong hands, it could allow for the creation of an undead army, a page out of armageddon. The text hinted at other powers, but did not specify as to what they were. I'm afraid I have greatly underestimated its importance. These creatures were sent to retrieve the amulet, sent by something so ancient and evil," her words died and I shivered at the tone in her voice.

"So she's the succubus?" I didn't look toward Sister Eva, but I could see her sharp nod. "Do you know a quick way to kill her?"

"As any other serpent, you must separate the head from the body," the older woman replied.

My mind caught a turn of phrase, and I glanced at my friend. "You said creatures were sent? There are others?"

Sister Eva's gaze went down to the tableau before us, and she shook her head slowly. "Surely you must know who I mean. You have felt it."

I looked back to where my best friend was gripped by the woman. A gust of wind cleared the mist from the moon's face, and I could see the succubus more clearly. She was tall and willowy, even restraining her captive, she held an inner grace. And her face, when she tipped it up to see Declan standing near, was breathtakingly beautiful. Full pouty lips, a long slant of eyes, and hair so dark it looked like an inky cloud on her shoulders. And who else was fairly glowing with beauty in the moonlight? Declan looked like a fallen angel, all carved lines and beguiling grace. The color of his cycs seemed to match those of the Succubus, an unnatural lavender hue.

"Declan," I breathed.

"He must not get the amulet," Sister Eva agreed.

Rage and betrayal swept over me like a sucking tide, and I felt the power of it. I suspected of course, but I fought it, the knowing, the energy. And why? For what? I read the affection in Alex's expression, saw the softness there, and my oversight which was meant for friendship might well be her death.

"This is not a time for regret," Sister Eva hissed in my ear. "It is time for action." She stepped forward, the toes of her practical black leather sneakers at the edge of the shallow cliff. I joined her, and we crouched, ready to join the fray.

———

Abe's face hardened and Declan couldn't help but think what a contrast it was to the usual unreadable expression he seemed to be wearing these days. He watched his old friend thrust his hand into his pocket and pull out the amulet. The greenish glow radiated all around the small cylinder-shaped piece of petrified wood, the radiance so intense it was nearly blinding.

"Is this what you're after, demon?"

Amelia's eyes were locked onto the piece and Declan could see the reflection of the artifact's glow in them.

"Place it at my feet, Purg, and then back up," Amelia ordered.

Abe turned it around in his fingers, holding it up to the moonlight. "Nah, I think I'll hold on to it."

"No." Declan exclaimed. "Please, mate. Don't--"

Abe narrowed his eyes at Declan, silencing him.

"I know what you are," Abe said. "And I think you're a part of this charade. If you want your demon bitch to have the amulet, you *will* have to take it from me."

Chaos, Declan thought. *It is all about chaos.*

Abe turned to Alex, readjusting the gun barrel to aim straight at the center of her forehead. It would definitely penetrate her skull and then go on to relieve Amelia of everything from the neck up.

Chaos.

"I'm sorry," Abe said to Alex. "There's just no way I can let anyone from Hell take away something this powerful. Not happening. I hope you understand."

Declan saw tears filling Alex's widened eyes and he couldn't help but feel for her. Never in his entire existence had he felt emotions like this, and now anger at Abe was entering the equation. He glanced from Alex to Amelia and suddenly understood.

Amelia appeared completely confused at this weird turn of events. She started to take a couple of steps backward, possibly considering a way out of the growing chaos, and then froze as Declan launched himself towards Abe just as his old partner pulled the trigger on the gun. The bullet exploded out of the barrel, whizzing through the air, and colliding with Declan's shoulder as his body blocked the projectile's path to Alex and Amelia. Pain ripped through him, burning as the bullet tore through one side and straight out of the other, the speed of Declan's movement was just enough to change its trajectory. He hit Abe head-on, tackling him to the ground and pinning the man's gun hand to the ground. Declan raised the dagger and rammed the blade into the ground next to Abe's head. Alex screamed.

Out of the corner of his eye, Declan could see her struggling in Amelia's grasp, the knife no longer at Alex's throat but still in Amelia's hand with the tip of the blade held skyward as if she were holding a sword instead of a knife. Declan turned back to Abe, the dagger standing straight in the ground by the man's head, the dragon on the weapon's hilt seemed alive with power, its eyes pulsed the same urgent shade of crimson, its reptilian body writhed and tail flailed, almost demanding its own sustenance or raging at its missed opportunity.

"Be ready," Abe said, sliding the amulet into Declan's empty hand.

As soon as the piece touched Declan's skin the greenish glow faded to nothing. He closed his fingers around it, feeling a growing warmth and a strange sensation of calm. It wasn't what he expected, not in the least and especially not for an artifact supposed to open gateways to places which would aid the fallen to bring on Armageddon. He met Abe's eyes and anything which might have hinted at the man's normally stoic expression since Declan met him the second time around was gone. In its place was the same expression he was familiar with, his partner, his friend from a couple of centuries ago.

"Do you remember?" Declan asked, not being able to stop himself.

"I should have listened to you," Abe replied in a low voice. "Death is not the time to turn away from God."

"Were I you," Declan said shoving the artifact into his pocket, "I should think there never would be a time."

Abe merely nodded and thrust his hand into the wound on

Declan's shoulder with enough force to send the incubus back, reeling in pain, and on his ass several feet away.

———

The shot from Abe's gun rang out simultaneously as a loud clap of thunder sounded in the night sky, shuddering the ground beneath it like a beast shaking off its confusion. Declan threw himself in front of Alex, taking the bullet. He hit the ground and was back on his feet again with inhuman speed. Alex's scream cut through me as clean as the lightning slicing through the thick growing clouds above when Declan tackled Abe and jammed a knife at his head. I pulled the katana free and leaped to the ground below, landing just a few feet shy of the men and easing the sword back to slice through the neck of the incubus, the traitorous Declan. I froze when I saw the blade Declan was wielding. It wasn't embedded in Abe's skull but buried to the hilt in the ground next to his head.

What the hell? No one would have missed a target at so close a range. It can't be an accident.

Looking over at the succubus, her beautiful face painted in complete confusion, I saw her wicked knife was no longer at Alex's throat. Her grip loosened, barely holding my friend by the upper arm. I put two and two together, came up with the proverbial four, and took off with my katana still raised to put Declan and Abe's distraction to good use. A racing shadow caught my attention, bolting from the left-hand side, and I heard Declan yell.

"Russ, no!"

I glanced over my shoulder to see Declan on his butt several feet from Abe. His face was a mixed brew of emotion, but intense pain and terror seemed to be the two main ingredients.

Russ sprinted past me, grabbed Alex by her freed arm, and yanked her away from the grasp of the hissing succubus. His momentum was sufficient to pull off the move, but he wasn't fast enough to get out of the swiping range of the knife. I saw the blade move in blurred motion, a beautiful strike, running straight across his gut as he pushed Alex away and down to the ground, covering her with his own body. I took one moment to glance over at Declan and Abe who were now on their feet and heading my way before I leaped toward the creature, crossing steel with the succubus bitch, she with her knife and me with my katana.

The color of the monster's eyes seemed to glow an intense lavender shade as the metal clanged together, ringing through the katana and sending the buzzing sensation, a paranormal vibration, up to my arm, icing my muscles and freezing my bones as it rose. She was strong, this unholy thing, her defense refusing to give an inch.

"The righteous ride again," she said, rotating the knife's blade so it slid down the katana's sharp tip and circled out of the hold. "I see you have no problem with taking demons on the ride with you these days."

I swung in with another strike and she met it with her blade, then angled her body back a step before reaching behind her and pulling out a twin of the knife she already held. This time I circled away, pulling the sword back toward me.

"What? No retort?"

"Shut up and fight," I said.

"Should I tell you what it was like to take them?" Her voice was a melody sung one note off, a sound discordant in the dark. "To pull out their soul, to rip it to shreds, to tear into their skin and carve the insult to your religion onto their bones." She grinned.

I thrust the katana again, following it with a roundhouse kick.

The sole of my boot was planted into the center of her chest and the force of it sent her back several feet. I could see movement from the corner of my eye, Abe and Declan gathering themselves, ready for the kill.

"Oh, but the game isn't over," she hissed. She made a quick slicing gesture with her free hand, and her smile widened, almost splitting her beautiful visage in two. The wind whipped up behind her, and I heard a new sound, a click and clatter of armor, of something alien.

"Filii ortum," she screamed. "Occidere!"

From between the trees, a rush and rustle of sound rose as indescribable mounds of flattened fabric and fur, trash and debris filled out with knobs and hollows of bones. Soon, a small army of skeletons, bones of beasts and man thrown together, rose and staggered into the clearing. These things held no weapons, nor did they need them, using their very own limbs and remnants of sharp teeth to strike out at my frozen comrades.

A creature with the skull of a wolf tore from the underbrush, striking Abe and knocking him to the ground. A second, similar beast circled behind Alex where she struggled to slide out from beneath the weight of Russ, her protector. Soon, the ground was littered with cast-off bones, the only sound over the wind carrying grunts and curses.

I saw the robed figure of Sister Evangeline battling two abominations of bestial bones topped with human skulls. A bastard sword with a cross-shaped hilt I'd seen her wield many times angled one way and struck one, and then gracefully angled the opposite way hitting the other with such intricate precision I was awed. Each blow shattered old bone when it landed, turning out rifts of dust immediately whipped away in the wind.

With a roar, Abe used a fallen limb to bash into the bony globe of the attacking wolf-like creature, sending it flying like a prehistoric baseball straight at me. I ducked down and the skull smashed into the face of the succubus, breaking into countless serrated shards and cutting some of her flawless skin as it hit. Shadows of crimson-colored blood oozed from the cuts.

I stood up straight with a grim smile.

If you can bleed, bitch, you can die.

CHAPTER TWENTY-FIVE

Declan got to his feet just as Panas blurred by, thrusting the wolf creature away with one mighty shove and passing through what little space there was between him and Abe. The skeleton hit the trunk of a nearby tree, breaking the spine of the unnatural beast. It hit the ground with enough force to weaken whatever bond held it together, allowing physics to do the rest and scattering the bones all over the packed earth at the tree's base. Panas made it to where Russ lay over Alex. Rolling the young man over onto his back freed Alex and she climbed to her feet as Panas assessed the man. One of the bone beasts drew closer, head tipped back as though scenting weakness in the downed man. Declan's breath caught in his throat as the weakness mercilessly presented itself. Blood pooled on Russ's stomach and the front of Alex's jacket was soaked in it. Although Declan doubted these cursed things feasted on blood, he didn't doubt their opportunistic nature.

"Panas!" he yelled.

The Ukrainian nodded, pulling a machete out of the sheath

attached to his back. "Already on it." He glanced over at Alex as Declan moved on past them. "You care for the young man. I'll give you the cover you need."

Pure fury fueled Declan's movement now and before realization set in, he was already crossing the clearing where Amelia and Samantha were fighting. He bare handedly struck the rotting animated carcass of a bear charging from the right. The creature clattered as it turned, fur shredding and flying as it sent a powerful paw in his direction, claws exposed like lethal black blades. Declan dodged away from the swipe, avoiding more shedding of his own blood as he pulled the dagger from his sheath. There was no flesh on the beast to speak of, none which a weapon could do any more damage to anyway, but the blade was indeed sharp enough to cut through something hard as bone. Declan glanced down to see the etched dragon now held its head aloft and outward, it's dangerous mouth open and spewing an inferno redder than the color of its eyes. The hilt was warm, but not unbearably so, and Declan tightened his grip to move in for the kill of something long since dead. The bear swiped out another long-nailed foot which the incubus effortlessly avoided when he leaped up onto the back of the beast and rammed the dagger's point straight into the center of the thing's cervical spine. The blade moved through as smooth as butter, separating the skull from everything which followed and then he jumped off to flank Amelia as the body of bones crumpled to the ground.

Amelia caught sight of him out of her periphery as she blocked a swipe from Samantha's katana with one of the knives she held. The other she pointed at him.

"Did you enjoy your gift?" Amelia asked. "I made it special for you. It took me only an hour or so, and I think it turned out perfectly. Of course, it's not as romantic as leaving a red rose as you do, but I'm sure it made an impression. Did it not, righteous bitch?"

Samantha didn't reply but Declan saw a hardened look in her eyes and he knew he would be on the opposite end of her sword soon enough. He'd go out as fate would have it and not complain. He committed his share of killing, never on Amelia's level of course, but a victim was just as dead carved up as it was, left whole, with a rose in hand.

"Who sent you?" Declan asked. If he was going out, he could at least leave with some answers. "Asmodeus or Lucifer?"

Amelia pulled the knife she pointed at Declan back into play, blocking another of Samantha's swipes. The metal rang out against the sound of the growing gusts as she pivoted away, putting a little space between her and the katana.

"Asmodeus writhes under Lucifer's thumb at the moment, so who do you think?"

Declan didn't need to ask why. He knew. The more chaos in the world, the more Lucifer enjoyed it. As far as the artifact was concerned, the head demon didn't give two shits who handed it to him while chaos reigned, just as long as one of the players in his sick and twisted game did. Well, Declan was tired of playing the sodding game and he'd hand the piece over to the righteous before he'd let Lucifer touch it. As for Russ, he'd make his last plea for the young man's safety before Samantha's sword ended his earthly walk. Somehow he knew she would do everything in her power to protect him, no doubt there.

Let's end this, he thought, *and let it be the end of me.*

The katana struck out again in a powerful jab straight at Amelia's chest. She brought both knives up, crossing them to block, just as Declan moved in quickly from his position off to the side. He thrust the dagger deep into the center of Amelia's back, feeling the etching of the dragon writhing with pleasure in his hand, almost as if the awful thing were feeding. Amelia let out a grunt of pain, her block weakening as her arms started to lower. Declan ducked down when he heard metal sliding off metal.

Samantha reeled the sword back and sliced it forward through the air, the sharp edge of the katana cutting smoothly through Amelia's neck, parting sinew and bone, flesh and muscle. Declan backed away as the head of the succubus toppled from the still standing corpse and landed with a muffled thud right where he'd been standing. Her body followed it, crumpling to the ground as the knives fell away from her dead hands. As though a switch was thrown, the animalistic travesties she called to her dropped in the same way, their frames tumbling into untidy heaps on the ground.

Declan turned and ran to where Russ lay dying.

———

Time stood still while a breath of wind blew in from the east. I stood over the body of the succubus, my eyes trying to register what I was seeing. Her head rolled a few feet away, but her eyes were open and knowing. I feared she was still smiling.

I held my katana extended, waiting for a movement, waiting to see if she would rise again. The body trembled, the skin paling quickly until it glowed a pearly white in the blackness of the grass. The eyes glazed over, white marbles in a chiseled alabaster face. This was not like one of the infernal lords with their fiery demise of ash and heat. The body stiffened, firmed, then stone, only the clothes she wore still holding their color. There was a high creaking noise, and the body shifted, a perfect statue of a woman, still terrible in her beauty.

"It is done." I felt Sister Eva put her hand on my wrist and I let the katana drop.

———

Declan knelt down next to Russ's head, opposite of Panas, as Alex held pressure on the wound with her jacket. He couldn't help feeling the sensation of deja vu waft over him, but when he looked over at Abe standing next to Samantha, he doubted it would end the same. If Russ died, Declan knew in his heart he would stay dead. Extending a hand onto Russ's sweaty forehead, the incubus suddenly felt very tired, very old, and very, very worn. A hand covered his. Alex.

"The wound is shallow. He's going to be okay. Sam is calling in an ambulance to meet us at the entrance lot." Alex's voice grew firm. "Look at me. I'm a doctor, and I know what I'm talking about. We just need to continue the pressure, and he'll recover. It won't be quick, but he's going to be fine."

Russ's voice broke Declan's daze.

"Good thing I packed on the padding, Boss. Told you pancakes were a good thing."

Declan nodded. He could feel his eyes, now faded back to their human chocolate brown color, filling with tears. Crying was a human reaction to a human emotion. It wasn't supposed to be something a demon would normally do, but nothing seemed normal these days. He blinked the tears back, but Russ noticed them spot on.

"Don't cry. 'Tis only a flesh wound."

Declan choked on a laugh and shook his head. "You're a hot mess."

Russ grinned and then winced with pain. "Yeah, but you'd be lost without me. Admit it. You love the Russ."

"Without a doubt, mate."

Sam came up behind Alex, pocketing her cell phone. "The ambulance is on its way. Can he be moved?"

Alex nodded. "I think I can secure a makeshift bandage to hold while we transport him."

"Good," Sam replied, kneeling next to her on the opposite side of Russ's head. "Thanks for saving my friend. You're a brave man."

Russ's grin grew wider. "Why thank you, beautiful lady." His voice was weak, but damn if he wasn't still flirting with her.

"Panas," Sam said, "you and Declan are to carry Russ once Alex has him ready to move. Abe and I can switch you guys out if you need a rest."

"Can I use your jacket?" Alex asked Declan.

He stood up, pulled it off, and handed it to her without a word. Declan heard someone clear their throat and turned to see it was Sister Eva.

"While Alex secures the young man's bandage, I believe there is a small matter we need to discuss."

"The artifact," Declan breathed. He'd almost forgotten shoving it in his pants pocket just before he'd plucked the dagger from the ground and joined in the fight to help Samantha.

The older woman nodded, her bright blue eyes on his face. She was calm, so serene in the face of blood and death.

I watched as Declan pulled the amulet from his pocket and was startled to see an unnatural glow. It wasn't green, the color of life and earth, the color I noticed before in so many things such as this, but a deep amethyst. Whatever Declan was, and I suspected now I knew how he was created, at least the general gist of it anyway, he had power and the amulet was responding to him.

Sister Eva's words were low, but I was keenly aware my new teammate was equipped with unnaturally acute hearing. Their conversation was not for me to hear. But there were a lot of questions I would need to have answered later.

I watched with astonishment as the incubus dropped to his knees, tipping his chin back, his face awash with watery moonlight. His features were each so perfect, eerily so, as he remained frozen like the statue the succubus became as she died in this realm. His hand was still outstretched with the stone nestled in his palm.

Sister Eva held her blade. It rested in her hand, the shiny surface dulled from where the bone beasts fell to its strike. And Declan was giving her his throat, his life.

———

Declan gazed at the righteous woman in the habit for a moment before approaching her, stopping only when he'd reached arm's distance away. The others were occupied caring for Russ, preparing him for the move to where they'd meet the ambulance and take him on to the hospital. He was going to live according to Alex. Ah, Alex, with her fierce anger, she would save his friend and Declan couldn't have been more grateful if he tried. Russ would live on to be Russ, hopefully it would be a happy long time. Glancing over his shoulder, he could see Samantha several feet away, watching, waiting to be his executioner most likely. It would be a fate he rightly deserved.

The nun studied him silently, a wordless action which provided its own discomfort, and then spoke softly.

"You may begin."

Declan swallowed hard, ready to not only confess but take whatever medicine she dealt out.

"I am the one who took the lives of the village girl and your fellow nun," he said, looking her in the eyes. "I have walked this plane for many decades and I have taken my fair share, probably more so. My guilt is great, as is my burden which is everlasting."

The nun gave a slight nod. "The rose you left as payment for your theft of life?"

"Yes," Declan replied, feeling his face flush with shame.

"You feel remorse."

It wasn't a question, more like a vocalized observation as if he were a bloody lab rat being studied by blokes with pointy needles. Poke. Do you feel that? *Squeak.* Poke. Poke. Did you feel those? *Squeak. Squeak.*

Let her do her worst, he thought as she pulled her blade into view.

"I am tired, sister. Bone tired. I have been for centuries and what I do to survive sickens me. What I am sickens me. If it is remorse, then so be it."

He pulled the amulet out of his pocket, wondering at the warmth he felt and the strange new amethyst hue it was now emitting, as he held it out to her.

"You may take back what is yours," he said, "and I have only one request before I am put to the blade."

"What is your request?"

"Lucifer gave me forty-eight hours to hand over the artifact to him or he would kill my friend Russ. My time is nearly out. I ask that you take him under your protection."

Declan fell to his knees, his outstretched hand still holding the purplish glowing object.

"Please, sister. I beg this of you. He is an innocent."

The nun's face was stern, but Declan thought he detected a bit of understanding wash over her countenance.

"You beg for the life of another when yours is about to end?"

"I do," he said with certainty.

She was silent for a moment, pondering. Her gaze fell to his hand where the glowing artifact lay and then up to his shoulder where the bullet tore through the material of his shirt, leaving a good-sized gaping and bleeding hole in the flesh beneath. Her eyes traveled back up to meet his, locked onto them, and then she began to chant. It was an ancient language, one he'd not heard anyone speak out loud for several thousand years, and it was a song spoken first by a man named Soloman. There was no melody as the nun voiced the words, but Declan could hear the notes in the air, a singing plea for wisdom and understanding, for a light in the darkness. Indeed, it was the most wise and true song a king could sing.

He lifted his chin up, revealing his neck, offering it to her blade.

———

I heard her words but knew she slipped into an ancient language, a tongue forgotten to all but the scholars and the church. Declan angled his face in her direction, clearly surprised not to feel the bite of steel. His features were sharpened by the night, but the expression of astonishment was all too human.

Sister Evangeline reached beneath her robes into one of the hidden pockets which held all kinds of mysteries. I could clearly see the cross as she drew it forth. It looked as though a long ago blacksmith hammered it out with vengeance, crude and dull. It hung on a heavy chain. Sister Eva held it out to the demon, and I waited in breathless anticipation. If he accepted this, then I would let Sister Eva proceed with whatever madness she chose. But if he lashed out, if he so much as made a twitch in her direction, I would take off his pretty head with my katana without a breath of regret.

Declan took the cross into his hand and placed the glowing amulet into hers, the violet color now bright enough to cast a shine on his face, to reflect in his already glowing eyes. She could swear she saw tears in them just before the incubus lowered his head.

————

The nun closed her hand around the amulet and shut her eyes, finishing the last words of one of Solomon's songs and closing with a soft prayer. Normally, he would have been repulsed by such things as this, and holding a crucifix would have buzzed through him with all of the annoyance of a bee circling on his insides stinging with a vengeance. Now, he wasn't certain how he felt exactly, but the cross lay in his hand, as warm as the artifact was and didn't seem ready to set him on fire or devour him in any way. The song and prayer seemed oddly comforting. He lifted his eyes back up to her as she took the last step towards him.

"I will not grant your request, Declan, because it will be you who provides protection for the young man."

She extended the closed hand with the amulet nestled snugly within towards the wound in his shoulder. The glow of amethyst brightened and pulsed between her fingers the closer it got to him and he closed his eyes, readying himself for the pain he suspected would come. The warmth of her human hand radiated against him, but he refused to pull on it. He'd taken enough of what was not freely given. There was a quick sharp stab into the bullet hole and then a numbness which began to warm, tingling as it spiderwebbed from the wound throughout his entire body. He opened his eyes to see the nun smiling down at him.

"I do not know your exact purpose," she said, "but be sure God has one for you."

He glanced down at his shoulder to see it was whole. The wound healed over and there was just the faintest purplish glow coming from the new skin. He watched in wonder as it faded to the color of his normal complexion.

"Sister," Declan said, handing her the cross. She took it, tucking it within her billowy robe, before setting a hand upon his shoulder.

"I'll not tell you how hard the road from here on in will be to travel. I'm certain you are already aware. But I will tell you to be true to your purpose. For it is God, not I, who has been merciful to you." She gave him a slow bow. "The Lord works in mysterious ways."

Declan nodded and the nun lifted her hand away so he could stand. And then it began to rain.

CHAPTER TWENTY-SIX

Russ looked like a king ruling over his minions from the hospital bed. He wouldn't be held much longer, but for the moment, he appeared utterly content with the attention he was receiving. Declan's friend Panas and his little harem of women were getting prepared to leave, but the excess of female companionship made Russ look flush and happy. I smirked as they ooohed and ahhed over him, laughing at his jokes and goodhearted mannerisms. It was hard not to like the guy. He was just a good ol' country boy with a quirky sense of humor.

Declan walked Panas out of the room, and I eyed them from my station at the foot of the bed. Something changed in their relationship. Gone was the easy camaraderie. I wondered if it was something to do with the exchange between the nun and the incubus. Whatever the shift, they seemed to be at an uneasy truce.

I didn't follow as the group left the hallway toward the elevators. I'd taken my little jaunt out already with a quick stopover at the airport. Sister Eva was now ensconced in her seat on the transoceanic flight, her bag packed with valuable religious artifacts such as a dagger which dated back to the twelfth century, recently used in battle, and a number of stones and ornamentation to go into the church's archives. I saw the amulet in her hand at the clearing and then it was gone, so I could only assume she tucked it back into one of the pockets of her robe, destined to return to France along with her.

Abe was looking a little worse for wear himself. While I never got the story about the exchange in the clearing with Declan, I did have the distinct impression their story was a long and complicated one. I didn't have time for it now, but someday, I would demand it. If Abe was going to be a partner in our little group, he was going to have to come clean someday soon. And right now, he and Declan were circling each other warily.

Alex bustled into the room, her curls finally tamed and her hands and face newly washed. It was a long night, and I knew we were all running on fumes.

"Is Sister Eva settled?"

"On her way to France," I confirmed.

"Where is Declan?"

I felt a surge of irritation and tamped it down. Alex liked the man for some reason, and even if I didn't trust him, I was going to have to tolerate his presence a little longer. She seemed able to swallow his true identity as a lesser demon, an incubus, for God's sake, with shocking ease.

"He and Panas' group were going to the parking lot. Panas said he called an Uber. I'm not sure where they're headed to now, but they seemed anxious to get out of town."

Alex frowned. "I didn't get to say goodbye."

I shrugged. The vibes I got from Panas were a little paranormal, and the fewer demons buzzing around me, the better in my estimation. The fact these particular supernatural beings helped us bring down one of their own wasn't going to win me over easily.

"Declan said he'd be back," Russ interrupted.

I nodded, well aware there were things we could not discuss with the curious Uber driver in our midst. Whatever Russ knew about Declan, well, I didn't know, but it wasn't my place to tell him his buddy wasn't human.

As though the thought of the man was enough to conjure him from thin air, Declan swept into the room. He was smiling, his eyes warming when he saw Alex. I frowned at him and shook my head.

"Samantha," Alex turned toward me, her eyes full of meaning. "Will you be staying with Russ for a while?"

Would I be babysitting him, was what she meant. I drew in a breath and released it, nodding. "I'll stay."

"Don't need a babysitter," Russ complained, "but the beautiful lady can stay and comfort me. Maybe hold my hand?"

I ignored him and watched as Alex gestured to Declan. "Can we talk?"

He nodded, his expression growing serious. His chocolate brown eyes scanned her face, looking for clues to her thoughts.

"I'll be here," I said, keeping my tone low and ominous, "waiting. Babysitting."

Russ grinned mischievously. "Baby might want a sponge bath, beautiful lady."

I rolled my eyes, plopped down in the visitor's chair next to him and watched my friend and the incubus leave the room.

———

Declan walked side by side with Alex out into the early morning sunshine. It was going to be a gorgeous day according to the weather guys on the waiting room television, the thunderstorms moved on to leave a cloudless sky and gentle breeze. For the second time, Declan strolled outside to see the goofy chap pointing at the regional map on the screen may be right for a change. When he'd walked out with Panas and his harem earlier, he could sense the uneasiness of his old friend just as he could feel the warm breath of air against his skin. Panas was never a creature to mince words, but he was always cordial even when put into situations that didn't require it. They stopped at a bench nestled against a large oak tree and sat side by side as the women strolled along one of the paths into the hospital courtyard.

"I worry for you, my friend," Panas said. "All hell will consider what you have done as treason."

Declan nodded. "Do *you*?"

"No. I consider it survival, but my opinion will not matter much I'm afraid."

Declan watched as the women chatted and laughed, taking their own seats on top of the low rock wall surrounding one of the wildflower beds.

"I will send Camille to you once we return."

"You don't have to--"

Panas held up his hand to stop his protestation.

"Yes, I do. You will have enough to deal with as it is and Camille will keep you from having to add the hunt to your concerns. I am not giving you an option."

Declan grimaced, knowing any other protest would be futile against his friend's stubbornness, and mumbled, "Thank you."

"What are your plans now?" Panas asked with a sigh, leaning back on the bench.

"I think I've let the Yard run its course for this century, so I'll hand in my resignation and stay here for a while I guess. Maybe do what all the other American ex-cop blokes do and start private detecting."

Panas nodded approvingly. "Give me your address when you have one. I will send Camille but do not tarry. You are in no good position to put this off."

Declan couldn't have agreed more. He didn't know what nasty business waited around the corner or lurked within the shadows, but he knew good and well Panas was right. There would be hell to pay. The weight of choosing sides hung heavy, but his choice was made.

He approached Panas's harem and nodded humbly at them. One of the women, a brunette with light-colored skin, stood up and walked towards him.

"Camille?"

The woman smiled. It was the same woman who brushed her fingers through his hair when she'd climbed into the van. She extended her hand and Declan took it, feeling the gentlest pull of her life force. He forced himself to stop, clearing his throat and meeting her gaze.

"You do not have to do this," he said.

"I want to. You are noble inside, I feel it."

"But you are a young woman. You've your whole life to live."

Camille gently stroked his hand with her delicate thumb. "Declan, this is my life and I will choose my lifestyle. So, don't feel guilty, okay? What Panas could do for me, what you did for me the other night, it's all I need, you know?"

Declan gave a slight nod. "I will not hold you against your will. You are free to leave whenever you want."

Camille laughed lightly, leaned towards him and brushed her lips against his. Declan closed his eyes, breathing in her scent as she gently pulled away.

"As soon as you're ready, Declan."

He watched them leave, feeling a little nostalgic as if he were saying goodbye to part of his family. He would see them again. Camille for certain.

Declan's thoughts turned back to Alex who stood beside him. A sad smile on her face and a large band-aid covering the cut Amelia's knife made on her neck. Alex was lucky this time. He shuddered to think of what might happen to her in the future when she wouldn't be so lucky. Offering his hand, she took it and they strolled out into the courtyard, taking a seat on the same rock wall where Panas's women were seated earlier.

"Alex, I know my advice will probably fall on deaf ears, but you need to distance yourself from Samantha and Abe. What they're doing is dangerous and if you're in the thick of it with them, then it will eventually get you killed. You were lucky today but tomorrow, maybe not so much."

Alex gave his hand a gentle squeeze. "And what about you? Should I keep my distance there too?"

He sighed, hating the unspoken words already, and nodded.

"Think of me as a lightning rod. Evil things are going to be standing in line to take a shot from now on. I want you far away from me."

She smiled. "I know last night makes it look like I'm a poor damsel in distress, but trust me, I can hold my own."

Declan laughed and gently stroked the top of her hand with his thumb. His mind swirled with thoughts and possibilities on how a relationship with her could work, all of them ended gruesomely. His smile faded.

"It wouldn't work," he said, "you and I, a relationship I mean. I'm sorry."

Alex lifted her hand and ran a finger down the side of his

face. Her touch made his skin tingle with desire. He leaned in and kissed her tenderly on the lips, then deepened the kiss as she responded to him. When he pulled away, breathing hard, he could see tears in her eyes. One of them broke free and started to trail down her cheek. He gently wiped it away.

"If you ever change your mind--" she started.

He ran his fingers through her soft curls and rested his forehead against hers.

"Then all of Hell wouldn't keep me from you," Declan said, pulling her into his arms.

They sat, holding one another for a while, watching the passersby before breaking apart and going back into Russ's hospital room. Alex, Samantha, and Abe left together shortly after and Declan felt as if the beautiful woman carried his heart out the door right along with her. He heaved a deep exhale and plopped in the chair next to Russ, ready to wait out the end of Lucifer's forty-eight-hour deadline. It came and went without any threat to his new friend's safety, but it was little comfort. Declan knew this wasn't something the old devil would let go, he would bide his time and attack or send another demon to do it in his stead. Either way, Russ would probably always be in harm's way.

"So, you're an incubus," Russ said after Declan told him of his true identity. "*Seriously?* I don't mean to insult you, but dude, you're terrible with women."

"I get by," Declan replied.

Russ shook his head and laughed. "If you say so. Are you going to go back to jolly old England now, maybe sip tea with the queen?"

"Uh, no. I think I'll stay here and keep an eye on things. Besides, I don't think the queen would enjoy my company very much."

"Why? Did you forget to hold up your pinky finger when you were taking a sip?"

This time Declan laughed, long and hard.

"No, mate. I just don't think I'd be her cup of tea."

Russ pointed at him and grinned. "Ha. Ha. That's a good one, Boss. Cheesy but good." His grin faded and his expression became more serious. "So, since you've decided to stay, I guess you won't need an Uber driver anymore."

"On the contrary, I think Ernestine would very much enjoy having you behind the wheel. Besides, you Americans seem to enjoy driving on the wrong side of the road and it's going to take me a while to get used to that lunacy."

Russ smiled broad and nodded. "So, you *need* the Russ?"

Declan rolled his eyes. "Yes mate, I need the Russ."

I peered over the rim of my glass, slightly surprised to see it empty.

"More?" Alex held up the blender. It was our first foray into mixed drinks, and the margaritas were surprisingly good. Of course, it would be hard to mess up something which came prepackaged.

"Um, yes," I agreed, and I held up the glass.

"To victory," Alex toasted.

I tapped the glass to hers, letting the ringing sing out for a note. She was putting on a brave face. It was a win, at least it was from the church's point of view, but for her, perhaps not. I wasn't sure if she was ready to let go of the feelings she held for Declan, but I respected the hell out of him for breaking it off to protect her.

"What will you do now?" Alex asked. She pushed back a

blond curl and took a drink. Her eyes were a little glassy, tipsy but not drunk.

I shrugged. My life had been a roller coaster for so long I didn't know how to live without a crisis.

"What about you?" I returned. "Have you thought about going back to Georgia? Picking up where you left off with your practice?" I watched her eyes flicker away and felt my heart drop a bit. "Alex, I would understand. You've been through so much. You could go back to a normal life, a natural life, no more vampires and monsters. And what you were doing at the clinic, you were making a difference." Her desire to take her sharp brain and medical skills and treat those who couldn't afford treatment was an enviable quality. Alex was a good person, through and through, and I didn't know for certain if she belonged in my world where Satan held meetings with demons like business luncheons from Hell.

"Are you trying to get rid of me?" she teased. She took another sip of her drink and Fluffy appeared next to her, a tennis ball between his teeth. The Doberman looked like the guard dog he was, but we both knew his heart was more of a lapdog's. Alex pried the ball from his jaws and tossed it, causing Fluffy's twin, Bart, to swing into action. They took off across the floor, their nails clattering against the wood.

"I don't want you to feel like this is it for you," I replied, watching the dogs' antics.

"Maybe I want this to be it for me," Alex answered, one blond eyebrow cocked.

"Here there be monsters," I quoted darkly.

"I get it. But I think it is also a calling. This is something I was meant to do."

Fluffy let out a sharp demanding bark, his request to go outside.

"I still think you need to take some time," I stood to head for the door. "You don't have to make a decision now."

"Yeah, I know," Alex answered as I opened the back door.

The dogs stood alert at my side. Neither was moving. I glanced down at them, my muscles tensing. Something attracted their attention, and while it might be a wandering squirrel, it could just as well be something more dangerous.

"Sam?" Alex's voice came from behind me.

"Hang on," I said, my voice sharp.

"Sam. Look down."

I glanced toward my feet and saw the glittering paper on a wrapped present, complete with an oversized bow.

I bent and examined the box, squatting down next to it while the dogs went around me to escape into the yard. Whatever made them nervous was gone now. I finally picked up the package and carried it inside.

"Who is it from?" Alex's voice was low.

I gently eased the attached card from under the sumptuous royal blue ribbon. My last name was scrawled across the front of the envelope in bold script. I quickly tore open the flap and slipped the card out.

"In eternal admiration for a remarkable woman. We shall meet one another very soon." I looked at Alex's face after I finished reading aloud. I knew who the package was from as soon as I saw the handwriting.

"It's from Paul." It wasn't a question she was asking. She knew.

I dropped the card on the table and tugged at the ribbon which fell free in my hand. The box was cleverly wrapped, the kind which needed only to lift the lid. Inside, nestled amid gold tissue paper was a pair of shoes. They were high heels, silver and sleek, with tiny seed pearls decorating the toe and the base of the long sharp heel. As I lifted out the shoes, a tinny sound emerged from within the wrapping, a music box tune I recognized from musicals watched on television with my father when I was a child.

"Shall we dance," I whispered softly.

"What is that?" Alex was pointing to a loosely wrapped bundled where the toe of the shoes had lain. I put the shoes on the table and pulled out the papers. I parted the thin layers of paper until the object was uncovered in my hand.

"It's a skull," Alex said, "from an infant."

I started at the remains, the fragile bones knit together to make a miniature grinning mask, somehow more horrible for its size.

"Well, I guess I do know what I'll be doing tomorrow," I muttered, carefully looking at the object in my hands before allowing Alex to take it from me.

"And I'll be with you," she added, her eyes glittering with something new. "No one should get away with hurting a child."

I nodded slowly. "I agree. And I'm glad you're staying on."

Alex flashed me a smile despite the gruesome thing in her hands. "What are friends for?"

ABOUT THE AUTHOR: TONY ACREE

Tony Acree is an award winning author, screenwriter and publisher. Tony lives near Goshen Kentucky with his wife, twin girls, two female dogs, a female cat, and the way the goldfish looks at him, he believes she's female too.

ABOUT THE AUTHOR: RACHAEL RAWLINGS

Bio information

Rachael Rawlings is a full-time mother, writer, pet owner, and Speech Language Pathologist. She likes the unusual and quirky.

She lives in her hometown of Crestwood, Kentucky with her three children, Faith, Nicholas, and Chase. She has three dogs, a couple geckos, and five loudmouthed birds she is pretty sure are talking about her behind her back.

She thrives on good coffee, chocolate, and great friends and family. To learn more about Rachael's work and her upcoming releases, visit her on her website:

https://www.rachaelrawlingsauthor.com/

ABOUT THE AUTHOR: MARY ELLEN QUIRE

Born and raised in Kentucky, Mary Ellen Quire has been dabbling in the craft for nearly three decades. As a child, she found a love for reading and a fascination for anyone with the ability to tell a good story. Wanting to be just like the grownups who would sit around the kitchen table to swap all kinds of tales, she began creating her own to read in front of family and friends just for fun. When she took Mrs. Wallace's creative writing class at Henry County High School, the childhood interest kindled a tiny spark. However, it would be another four years after graduating from Kentucky State University with a degree in psychology that this slight fancy could morph into a passion.

After Mary's fourth and last daughter was born, she started writing short stories and bits of poetry which she kept to herself until the secret hobby was discovered by a family member who urged her to pursue it further. In 2005 her first novel, Link Detonator, was published under the name Mary E. Rose, with the sequel Detonator Time's Up following a year later. Her vampire novel, Dark Deliverance, was released under the name Mary Ellen Quire in 2010 and in 2014 Sheldon's Diary was published with tales of two knighted felines that are members of a secret animal society known as The Paws for the Imminent Cause. Back Home Magazine printed her article Choosing Your Veterinarian in their July/August 2014 issue and in 2016, her compilation of short stories entitled Fairview was published in electronic book format through Amazon. Her most recent work, a light-hearted contemporary crime fiction thriller entitled Defined, was released in January 2018. It is the first book in the Assassin Series and tells the tale of Price MacCann, a female assassin, who is struggling to find herself after the death of someone close to her.

At the present time, Mary Ellen resides in the quiet town of Crestwood with various animal squatters who have somehow managed to hitch a ride to the Quire abode. You can find out more about her at www.maryellenquire.net.